MW01138049

Bakery Detectives Cozy Mystery Boxed Set

Books 1 - 3

By

Stacey Alabaster

Table of Contents

Introduction

Thank you so much for buying my book. I am excited to share my stories with you and hope that you are just as thrilled to read them.

If you would like to know about all my new releases and have the opportunity to get free books, make sure you sign up for our Cozy Mystery Newsletter.

FairfieldPublishing.com/cozy-newsletter

Stacey Alabaster

A Pie to Die For

Chapter 1

I let out a little squeal as I brushed the foul, winged creature aside. "Not today buddy, not today!" I watched it intently as it flew away, a tiny black dot disappearing into the fall sky, and was glad that I hadn't needed to swat the poor thing. I heaved a sigh of relief as I took the lids off my desserts and a sweet cloud of vanilla, chocolate, and coffee bean, all mixed together, hit my nostrils.

That was the danger of serving food outdoors: flies. I was hoping that I'd seen the last of them for the day. Normally, I had my cakes and pastries sequestered safely away in my bakery, Rachael's Boutique Cakes. But today, being outside was a necessary evil. It was the annual Belldale Street Fair and it was my last chance to show the town that my cakes were worth stopping for, my last chance to save my failing bakery and keep the bank from serving me an eviction notice.

My fingers trembled as I removed the last of the lids and rearranged the decorations on my stall. I'd chosen a pink and white theme for the day and I piled cupcakes and macaroons high on a cute little pink cake stand, trying not to drop them with my shaking hands. Meanwhile, I watched the numerous employees of the Bakermatic food tent set up their factory made cakes with soldier-like intensity. My stomach dropped as I saw a sign go up with "Free Samples" written on it.

I glanced at my own price tags. How was I ever going to compete with free samples? Slowly, I reached over and, with a black marker, slashed my prices in half.

It was going to be a long day.

***

Midday. Three hours into the fair and I'd had a total of four customers. Meanwhile, the Bakermatic tent a hundred feet away was bursting at the seams with people trying to claim their free samples, which never seemed to run out.

Maybe I should just pack up and take the cakes back to the store.

I saw a figure out of the corner of my eye waddling towards the stall.

Oh no, not this woman, I thought. The lady, middle-aged with cat-eyed spectacles and a streak of pink in the front of her otherwise brown hair, only ever seemed to come into my bakery for the sole purpose of tutting and telling me that my cakes were twice the price of the cakes and pastries that Bakermatic sold.

"But that's because mine are twice as good." I would try to reason with her, only to be met with a sharp lift of her eyebrows.

"I use quality ingredients. And I pay my staff a proper wage." After I would tell her that, I'd lean back with my arms crossed over my chest. She could hardly argue with paying people—students, single mothers—a living wage, right? Wrong. She always tutted and stuck up her nose before informing me, loudly, that she was going to take her business to Bakermatic instead. "I can get a coffee AND a cupcake there for the price of just a cupcake here!"

And it seemed like half the town followed her. Every day, more and more customers chose their low prices over my painfully handcrafted selection of cookies, cupcakes, and pastries. Thus the ever growing pile of bills on my kitchen table. And I thought going into business for myself at age twenty-five was going to be glamorous.

Now she was here. I bristled as she approached with bull-like intensity, her eyes focused on my table, waiting for her to cast more disparaging comments. She pointed to a fresh baked pie on my table. "I'll have a slice of that."

My face stretched into a wide smile. "Really?"

Her coin purse paused in midair. "Are you trying to turn away a customer?"

"No, of course not! Just surprised that you would want a piece of my pie. What with Bakermatic giving away free samples down the road."

She screwed her face up. "Don't worry! I'll be sampling theirs as well!" She threw my pie a look of disdain. "It's for my food blog. I've got to try something from every stall. So don't go getting a big head, thinking that I'd choose you over them!"

Of course not. "Your blog?" I watched eagerly as she sampled my pie. "Well, surely you'll have to give my pie a better review than Bakermatic's, despite the price. Mine are fresh, made from all local ingredients, all hand-made every day."

She cut me off and slammed the plate down on the table before scribbling something in her notebook. "I will be taking cost into account as well, don't you worry about that, young lady. I still don't know how you can get away with charging an arm and a leg for this!"

She picked up her piece of pie with disdain and walked away—heading straight for the Bakermatic stand. I stood there with my mouth hanging open before I remembered I was supposed to be attracting customers, not repelling them. I tightened my apron and put on my brightest smile as a man with ginger hair and a portly waist line hurried past.

"Hey!" I said, throwing him my best flirtatious smile as I tried to usher him back to my stand. "You gotta try one of these."

He screwed his nose up. "I think I'll try one from Bakermatic instead." He patted his oversized tummy before adding, "Gotta watch the calories, you know. I can't have too many."

"But mine are made from all natural ingredients." Ahhh, it was too late. He was already waddling towards the Bakermatic stand, like they needed one more customer to add to the overflowing mob already crowding their tent.

I sighed. What was the use? How could I compete with thousands of free samples? This street fair was supposed to be my way to attract more customers, to get the word out that I had the best baked goods in town, and I couldn't even get anyone to stop and try them.

"Hey there," a kind voice called out. "Why are you looking so sad for?"

I glanced up. There he was. Tall, dark floppy hair. I guessed he was about five years older than me, which was just about perfect. Five years older and five inches taller.

A grin swept over my face in spite of myself. "Nothing," I said hurriedly, scurrying to tidy all the rows of unsold cakes and pies. Must look professional. Must look successful.

"Aww come on," he said, with a smile that brightened the damp day. "A gorgeous girl like you, with cakes that look so good. What's got you down so bad?"

I sighed. "That's very kind of you to say. But even though my cakes might look good," I brushed over his compliment about my own appearance. "it doesn't mean they're selling." I pointed down the road to the line that snaked out of the Bakermatic tent. "I think they've got the monopoly on baked goods."

"Ah, I've heard about them." He nodded slowly and pursed his lips. "They're supposed to be evil, right?"

"Pure evil." I raised my eyebrows and let out a little laugh.

"Well, I'd rather try one of yours."

He cast me a lingering look that made the butterflies in my stomach take flight. I perused the table, trying to find the best piece for him. I settled on my delicate carrot cake with cream cheese frosting and little red heart-shaped dots sprinkled on top. *Too much?* I told myself I'd explain that I hadn't noticed the hearts if he pointed them out.

He took the cake and—was it my imagination?—smiled a little when he saw the heart-shaped sprinkles. "Very nice," he said before opening his mouth wide.

It was a nervous few seconds before he gave his verdict.

"Perfect." He dusted off his hands and nodded. "If all your cakes are this good, I think I'll be seeing you again very soon. Rachael, wasn't it?" He nodded at the shop sign name.

"That's me." I grinned. "And you are?"

"Jackson. I'll be seeing you again soon, Rachael."

As I watched him walk away, I grinned to myself, my stomach warm and gooey as a cupcake fresh from the oven. Maybe today wasn't such a disaster after all.

***

I kicked off my heels. As soon as I sat down there was a knock on the door. Great timing.

But I grinned when I saw Pippa's shock of red curls peaking through the windows. After the day I'd had, I'd forgotten what day it was. Time for Criminal Point.

Pippa had her hair tucked under a baseball cap wearing the logo of a company I didn't recognize. She threw it off and it rolled under one of my designer chairs. "How did it go today?"

I held my hands up. "I don't even want to talk about it." Not even the cute stranger, although that was the kind of thing I usually shared with Pippa. But talking about Mr. Handsome was going to mean dredging up all the other junk: the unsold cakes, the bills piling up at the door, the imminent eviction notice. I slumped back onto the sofa.

"All I want to do is lie here, tune out, and watch some TV."

"What's on the box tonight?"

I grinned at her. "Pippa, you know very well what night it is."

She stuck her tongue out. "Shall I order the pizza?"

I nodded gratefully. "Pepperoni thin crust! You know the deal. We always order the same thing."

***

Five minutes of Criminal Point left to go. The on screen detectives had just reached that point where the light bulb goes off and they were about to burst through the door of the final suspect, the one who had committed the murder.

Pippa and I leaned over, breaths held, pizza cheese dripping onto our plate below. Just as they were about to reveal the killer, the broadcast was interrupted for an "Important Local News Update."

"Nooo!" I squealed, reaching for the remote, stabbing at it randomly as though I could bring the program back to life. "What happened!"

"Shh," Pippa said. I felt her nails dig into my bicep. "Listen!" Pippa hissed for me to be quiet.

"What?"

"Shh!"

I dropped my pizza as a shot of the street fair flashed onto the screen. My mouth dropped as the anchor, a woman with a helmet of blonde hair and a stern face, delivered the news. "A woman has died following the Belldale Annual Street Fair, and police suspect that foul play may have been at work. They are investigating suspects now, and are urging anyone with details to come forward." An image of the victim flashed onto the box. Middle-aged, brown hair with a pink streak down the front. Her name was Colleen Batters.

Pippa and I stared to look at each other. "I know that woman!"

Pippa gulped. "How? Rachael, please tell me you just know her from your book club or something?"

I shook my head. "I served her today. Oh, Pippa! She was one of the few people to actually eat at my stand!" My heart started thumping and my head felt like it was pumped full of helium. Had I killed Colleen? My mind started fumbling back through the day's events, to all the other people who'd eaten my food. What about that cute guy? Jackson. Was he okay?

There was a knock on the door. I was too stunned to

even stand up so Pippa bounced over and pulled it open. A voice on the other side cleared his throat. "I'm looking for a Miss Robison."

Pippa turned slowly to look at me. "It's a cop," she mouthed in an exaggerated way with her eyes popped.

I walked over to the door like a zombie.

There he was. "Jackson?"

He cleared his throat again. "Officer Whitaker actually, under these circumstances. Miss Robinson, I'm afraid I need you to come in and answer a few questions. You're under suspicion for the murder of Mrs. Colleen Batters."

Chapter 2

"But you don't understand, I use only the finest, organic ingredients." My voice was high-pitched as I pleaded my case to the policeman. Oh, this was just like an episode of Criminal Point. Hey, I wondered who the killer turned out to be. I shook my head. That's not important, Rachael, I scolded myself. *What's important is getting yourself off this murder charge.* Still, I hoped Pippa had recorded the ending of the episode.

I tried to steady my breathing as Jackson—Detective Whitaker—entered the room and threw a folder on the table, before studying the contents as though he was cramming for a test he had to take the next day. He rubbed his temples and frowned.

Is he even going to make eye contact with me? Is he just going to completely ignore the interaction we had at the fair? Pretend it never even happened.

"Jackson..." I started, before I was met with a steely glare. "Detective. Surely you can't think I had anything to do with this?"

Jackson looked up at me slowly. "Had you ever had

any contact with Mrs. Batters before today?"

I shifted in my seat. "Yes," I had to admit. "I knew her a little from the store. She was always quite antagonistic towards me, but I'd never try to kill her!"

"Witnesses near the scene said that you two had an argument." He gave me that same steely glare. Where was the charming, flirty, sweet guy I'd meet earlier? He was now buried beneath a suit and a huge attitude.

"Well...it wasn't an argument...she was just...winding me up, like she always does."

Jackson shot me a sharp look. "So, she was annoying you? Was she making you angry?"

"Well... Well..." I tripped over my words. He was now making me nervous for an entirely different reason than he had earlier. Those butterflies were back, but now they felt like daggers.

Come on, Rach. Everyone knows that the first suspect in Criminal Point is not the one that actually did it.

But how many people had Jackson already interviewed? Maybe he was saving me for last. Gosh, maybe my cherry pie had actually killed the woman!

"Answer the question please, Miss Robinson."

"Not angry, no. I was just frustrated."

15

"Frustrated?" A smile curled at his lips before he pounced. "Frustrated with Mrs. Batters?"

"No! The situation. Come on—you were there!" I tried to appeal to his sympathies, but he remained a brick wall.

"It doesn't matter whether I was there or not. That is entirely besides the point." He said the words a little too forcefully.

I swallowed. "I couldn't get any customers to try my cakes, and Bakermatic was luring everyone away with their free samples." I stopped as my brows shot up involuntarily. "Jackson! Sorry, Detective. Mrs. Batters ate at Bakermatic as well!"

My words came out in a stream of breathless blabber as I raced to get them out. "Bakermatic must be to blame! They cut corners, they use cheap ingredients. Oh, and I know how much Mrs. Batters loved their food! She was always eating there. Believe me, she made that very clear to me."

Jackson sat back and folded his arms across his chest. "Don't try to solve this case for us."

I sealed my lips. *Looks like I might have to at this rate.*

"We are investigating every place Mrs. Batters ate today. You don't need to worry about that."

I leaned forward and banged my palm on the table. "But I do need to worry about it! This is my job, my livelihood...my life on the line. If people think I am to blame, that will be the final nail in my bakery's coffin!" Oh, what a day. And I'd thought it was bad enough that I hadn't gotten any customers at my stand. Now I was being accused of killing a woman!

I could have sworn I saw a flicker of sympathy finally crawl across Jackson's face. He stood up and readjusted his tie, but he still refused to make full eye contact. "You're free to go, Miss Robinson," he said gently. There was that tone from earlier, finally. He seemed recognizable as a human at long last.

"Really?"

He nodded. "For the moment. But we might have some more questions for you later, so don't leave town."

I tried to make eye contact with him as I left, squirreling out from underneath his arm as he held the door open for me, but he just kept staring at the floor.

Did that mean he wasn't coming back to my bakery after all?

***

Pippa was still waiting for me when I returned home later that evening. There was a chill in the air, which meant that I headed straight for a blanket and the fireplace when I finally crawled in through the door. Pippa shot me a sympathetic look as I curled up and crumbled in front of the flames. *How had today gone so wrong, so quickly?*

"I recorded the last part of the show," Pippa said softly. "If you're up for watching it."

I groaned and lay on the carpet, my back straight against the floor like I was a little kid. "I don't think I can stomach it after what I just went through. Can you believe it? Accusing ME of killing Mrs. Batters? When I *know* that Bakermatic is to blame. I mean, Pippa, they must be! But this detective wouldn't even listen to me when I was trying to explain Bakermatic's dodgy practices to him."

Pippa leaned forward and took the lid off a pot, the smell of the brew hitting my nose. "Pippa, what is that?"

She grinned and stirred it, which only made the

smell worse. I leaned back and covered my nose. "Thought it might be a bit heavy for you. I basically took every herb, tea, and spice that you had in your cabinet and came up with this! I call it 'Pippa's Delight'!"

"Yeah well, it doesn't sound too delightful." I sat up and scrunched up my nose. "Oh, what the heck—pour me a cup."

"Are you sure?" Pippa asked with a cheeky grin.

"Go on. I'll be brave."

I braced myself as the brown liquid hit the white mug.

It was as disgusting as I had imagined, but at least it made me laugh when the pungent concoction hit my tongue. Pippa always had a way of cheering me up. If it wasn't her unusual concoctions, or her ever changing hair color—red this week but pink the last, and purple a week before that—then it was her never-ending array of careers and job changes that entertained me and kept me on my toes. When you're trying to run your own business, forced to be responsible day in and day out, you have to live vicariously through some of your more free-spirited friends. And Pippa was definitely that: free-spirited.

"Hey!" I said suddenly, as an idea began to brew in

my brain. I didn't know if it was the tea that suddenly brought all my senses to life or what it was, but I found myself slamming my mug on the table with new found enthusiasm. "Pippa, have you got a job at the moment?" I could never keep up with Pippa's present state of employment.

She shrugged as she kicked her feet up and lay back on the sofa. "Not really! I mean, I've got a couple of things in the works. Why's that?"

I pondered for a moment. "Pippa, if you could get a job at Bakermatic, you could see first hand what they're up to!" My voice was a rush of excitement as I clapped my hands together. "You would get to find out the ways they cut corners, the bad ingredients they use, and, if you were really lucky, you might even overhear someone say something about Mrs. Batters!"

A gleam appeared in Pippa's green eyes. "Well, I do need a job, especially after today."

I raced on. "Yes! And you've got plenty of experience working in cafes."

"Yeah. I've worked in hundreds of places." She took a sip of the tea and managed to swallow it. She actually seemed to enjoy it.

"I know you've got a lot of experience. You're sure to

get the job. They're always looking for part-timers." Unfortunately, Bakermatic was planning on expanding the storefront even further, and that meant they were looking for even more employees to fill their big yellow store. "Pippa, this is the perfect plan! We'll get you an application first thing in the morning. Then you can start investigating!"

Pippa raised her eyebrows. "Investigating?"

I nodded and lay my head back down on the carpet. "Criminal Point—Belldale Style! Bakery Investigation Unit! I will investigate and do what I can from my end as well! Perhaps I could talk to people from all the other food stalls! Oh, Pippa, we're going to make a crack team of detectives!"

"The Bakery Detectives!"

We both started giggling but, as the full weight of the day's events started to pile up on me, I felt my stomach tighten. It might seem fun to send Pippa in to spy on Bakermatic, but this was serious. My bakery, my livelihood, and even my own freedom depended on it.

Chapter 3

"You look amazing, don't worry," I said, covering my mouth to hide my laughter as I tried to swallow it.

Pippa looked herself up and down in the full-length mirror in my hallway. "This is the ugliest uniform I've ever been made to wear, and believe me, I've worn a few."

On any other day, I would have been the first to admit that the scratchy yellow polyester shirts Bakermatic forced their employees to wear was the worst thing my eyes had ever seen (except for their week old, pre-packaged cakes), but I was trying to convince Pippa that her new job was a good idea, and I couldn't let this yellow monstrosity get in the way.

"It's fine." I assured her, though I could still feel the tears prickling my eyes. "It goes with your hair."

Pippa turned, hands on her hips. "Bright red hair with bright yellow? I look like a clown."

I spun her back around. "It's only for a few days Pippa, maybe a week. Two weeks at the most."

She sighed and attached the neon yellow visor to her

head. "I still don't know if this is a good idea, Rach. What if I can't find anything? What if I get caught snooping around? You know how ruthless the Bakermatic Company is. What if they find out I'm there to spy on them?"

"Well, don't let them find out."

Pippa turned back and gave me a reluctant smile. "I want to do this for you, Rach, I really do."

"So then, what's the problem?" Cripes, I could tell that Pippa was losing her nerve. And she had a pretty strong nerve. Was she really that scared of Bakermatic's lawyers?

"You know me, Rach!" She sighed heavily and her shoulders slumped. "I'm always screwing everything up. I'll probably put salt in someone's coffee on my very first shift and get fired right away. Then I'll be no good to you at all! I'm going to let you down, Rach."

"Hey." I put my hands on Pippa's shoulders. "You're not going to let me down. I have faith in you, Pips. All you gotta do is go in there, keep your head down, try not to put any salt in anyone's coffee, and we'll be good." I felt my stomach clench. It all sounded simple enough, but I knew Pippa, and nothing was ever simple with her. Still, I tried to keep my face positive.

Pippa nodded. "You're forgetting one very important thing, though."

"Am I?"

"Find out what Bakermatic did to Colleen, and find the evidence to put them away."

I nodded. "Right," I said with determination. "We're going to prove that they poisoned Colleen Batters, and maybe—just maybe—my little bakery will survive."

***

10 AM. The perfect time to relax; take a little time and have some coffee and a cupcake.

At least, so you would think. The customers—or rather, the lack of them—at my store told a different story.

I sighed and sat down on my stool, untying my apron and throwing it on the bench. There was only so many times I could rearrange the cake stands and wipe the benches before I went out of my mind. I glanced around. The bakery was so clean it glistened, the baby pink and white surfaces so clean you could eat off them. And behind the glass cases, there was row after row of designer donuts, exotically flavored macaroons, gourmet cakes, and homemade pies. A sign advertising the ten o'clock coffee and cake special was flying in vain.

There wasn't a single customer in the shop.

I shook my head and muttered to myself for a second. "I bet that cop, Detective Whitaker, leaked the details of the case. Does everyone know I was taken in for questioning?"

Clearly. My reputation had been dashed.

I leaned forward and tried to peer down the street. I snapped back once my fears were confirmed. There was a line out of Bakermatic ten feet long. They'd clearly mopped up all my ten o'clock customers.

I sprung out of my seat when I heard the bell above the door jingle. "Hello there! Oh." My face dropped when I saw that it was just the mailman. He had a stack of little white envelopes for me, and I felt that clenching in my stomach again.

The mailman scrunched up his bald head and surveyed my empty store. "I wasn't sure you were even open by the looks of it from the outside."

"Well, we are open," I said, trying to remain bright as I ripped the top envelope open. "I couldn't interest you in one of my homemade selections, could I? How about..." I stopped and sized him up, coming up with just the perfect desert for him. "A slice of cherry pie?"

For just a moment, a look of temptation crossed his face and I could tell he was considering it. But then his face fell and he looked at the tiled floors before muttering an awkward, "Uh, no... I, uh, better not."

He hurried to the door.

"Hey, wait!" I called out after him.

He stopped, the door half pulled open. The bell above gave a sick little cough of a jingle. His back tensed and I knew he just wanted to escape before I asked him any more questions, or tried to force any more of my baked goods down his throat.

He turned back slowly and I read the name tag on his grey shirt. Gavin.

"Gavin," I said, still trying to remain upbeat and nonchalant, as though I was just innocently wondering the following question. "Is there any particular reason you don't want to try my cherry pie?"

He fidgeted for a second as he pretended to look at the price list. "It's just a little too expensive for me, miss."

Like I hadn't heard that one a hundred times before. I plastered on my brightest smile. "Oh, don't worry about the price," I said, swooping my arm around my mouth-watering selection of glossy pastries. "For you, Gavin, today, a slice is on the house. As a reward for all your hard work." And all the bills you delivered to me.

His mouth dropped open slightly and he handled the doorknob with an increasingly slippery palm. He patted his stomach. "That's generous of you, miss, but I'm real full right now. I had a big breakfast: eggs, sausages, and two pieces of toast."

I folded my arms. "You can take it with you and eat it later."

"Well, er, if I can eat it later," Gavin said, a look of relief flooding his face. "Then that should be fine."

"You can eat it later, as long as you have one little bite now," I cut him off. "Will that also be fine?"

I could see the beads of sweat forming on his brow. "Oh...ah...erm..."

I let out a short exhale. "I thought as much. Gavin, just tell me. Just give it to me straight. Why won't you eat any of my baked goods?"

He swallowed and I could see all the veins in his

neck pop out like they were trying to escape through his skin. "No...no reason, miss. I already told you, I'm real stuffed full right now..."

"Come on, Gavin. Cut it out."

He let the door fall shut. "Well, it's just... I'm afraid if I eat one of your cakes..." He glanced around the tins and cabinets. "Or pies, or pastries, or donuts. Well, I'm afraid..."

"You're afraid you might die?" I asked boldly, looking him straight in the eye.

He sighed. "I didn't want to say anything, miss. Didn't want to hurt your feelings. I see how hard you try in this store, and I got a daughter about your age, you kinda remind me of her. So I don't like to make things harder on you than they already are."

I felt bad all of a sudden that I hadn't even known Gavin's name 'til a few minutes earlier. I'd just always thought of him as "that man who brings me my bills" or, today, "that man who is trying to escape my clutches without telling me the truth."

"I didn't know you had a daughter, Gavin. What does she do?"

His face softened. "She's just finishing her medical

degree. I'm real proud of her. She'll be starting her first year residency soon."

I sighed internally. Being a doctor sounded a lot better than being a baker right now. "My father always wanted me to study medicine," I said wistfully. "Perhaps I should have taken his advice."

I slumped against the counter.

"Hey there," Gavin said, taking a step towards me, though still eyeing the cakes as though they were venomous creatures that might leap out and bite him. "Don't look so sad. I'm sure things will turn around."

I raised my eyebrows. "You're too scared to even take a bite of my pie. Gavin, what are people saying about me?"

He scratched the back of his neck. "Aw, it ain't so bad."

"Please. Tell me."

He looked at the floor and shrugged. "You know how people gossip. There are rumors flying around that you got taken in to the station, that they think your pie killed Colleen Batters."

"But everyone who took part in the street fair got taken in for questioning! The cops only talked to me as a precaution. To rule me out. They said anyone could be to blame." I pointed down the road at the overflowing line out the front of Bakermatic. "Even Bakermatic got brought in for questioning. Yet people aren't scared to eat there."

Gavin shook his head. "That's not what I heard, miss."

I spun around to look at him. "What do you mean?"

He shook his head. "I ain't heard that Bakermatic got brought in for questioning. In fact, their employees are telling every one that the only suspect is you. That you've been told not to leave town, and that it's only a matter of time before you're arrested for the murder of Colleen Batters."

My jaw dropped to the floor. Well, that explained the wasteland that my bakery had become. As if Bakermatic didn't have any problems soaking up my customer base on the best of days, undercutting my prices and stealing my ideas, now they were telling people my cake had killed Colleen?

"Thank you for being honest with me, Gavin," I said, ushering him out the door. "If you don't mind, I have some business to attend to."

He tried to protest for a moment. "It doesn't look

like you've got much business to attend to," he said, clutching his mailbag to his chest.

"Thanks for pointing that out." I waited until he was out the door before I turned the sign over to closed. "But it's not bakery business I've got to attend to."

It was detective business. I dusted my hands off and locked the door as Gavin tried to peer in through the windows, confusion clouding his face. If Bakermatic was going to try and pin the blame on me, then I was going to have to dedicate all my time to proving they were really the ones who killed Colleen Batters. I leaned against the cold glass door. *The nerve of them. They steal all my customers, and now they try and pin a murder charge on me!*

I pulled out my phone. Time to text Pippa.

***

It seemed like it took forever for Pippa to get back to me. *Don't tell me she's actually being responsible and not taking her phone out at work for once.*

Finally, just after 11:30, she texted me back. I grabbed my phone and glanced out the window while I read it.

Sorry Rach, so busy! First there was training and then we got slammed with a bunch of new customers. Wonder where they all came from?

My hands sped across my phone screen in a blur.

They came from my store Pips! There are practically tumbleweeds blowing through here. Have you heard anything yet? Is anyone talking about me or my store?

It took ages for her reply to come through, and as I waited, a sinking feeling entered my gut, like when I was trying to ferret the information from Gavin. Her silence spoke volumes.

Finally her reply came back.

Not much. Just a few rumors.

I stuck my phone back in my apron pocket. She didn't have to elaborate. Gavin was right, then. Bakermatic was telling everyone that I'd killed Colleen. I wondered if Pippa was even out there defending my honor.

Well, it was time to stop standing around waiting. I had Pippa in there as my eyes and ears, but I needed to do more. I needed to take advantage of her new position.

I pulled my phone back out. **Pippa I need you to sneak me into the store. I need to look in their kitchen. Maybe go through their paperwork.**

What? I can't do that! I could lose my job.

I held back from telling her that was only a matter of time, regardless of whether she did this for me or not.

We'll be careful. I need to see the place for myself Pips. Please. The store is dying. I need to do something.

OK. Once my shift is finished. I'm closing the store with another girl. I'll make up an excuse for why I need to hang back. I'll see you here after six. Don't come until it's dark.

Got it Pips. See ya at six.

***

Belldale looked particularly pretty as the light began to disappear from the sky and the stars started to make their first appearance. I shivered in my red peacoat as a sudden bolt of hope radiated through me. *Maybe it's going to be all right. Maybe I can sneak in, find some evidence, clear my name, and my bakery will thrive while Bakermatic goes under.*

"Psst!" I heard Pippa call. I squinted, trying to make her out in the dim light. She gestured for me to join her.

"A bright red coat, Rach? Really?"

I pouted a little. She was right, though. All the detectives on Criminal Point wore black or navy overcoats. You didn't see them gallivanting about, solving crimes in bright red. Still, it was dark so I didn't think it would matter too much.

"Stay here. We have to wait for Simona to clear out." Simona was Pippa's shift manager. Pippa had been telling me via text message that Simona was distracted due to a breakup with her boyfriend. Perfect, I'd thought. She might just let her guard down.

"What are you going to tell her?" I whispered. It was only Pippa's first day at Bakermatic, and it was going to take a lot of trust from the company to allow her to lock up on her own on her first day, even with a heartbroken shift manager in charge.

"I'm gonna wait till we're both done. Then, just as we're leaving, I'm gonna tell her I left my jacket inside, and ask to borrow the key." Pippa winked at me. "I've been buttering her up all day, being really sympathetic about the breakup with her boyfriend Charles, who seems like a real jerk, by the way."

Pippa suddenly pushed me out of the way and commanded me to be quiet. Behind her, a sniffling woman in her mid-twenties with a long dark ponytail walked out. "He hasn't returned any of my messages all day!" she wailed, shoving her phone in Pippa's face.

I pushed my back up against the wall and tried to remain flat, feeling the rough edges of the brick through my peacoat, which had been designed for fashion and not for practicality.

Pippa murmured her sympathy as she stared at the message-less screen. "Simona, honestly, you're too good for him. You're so pretty, and smart, and a manager already at your young age!" Pippa shot me a covert wink as she grabbed Simona by the shoulders so that she was facing away from me. "You don't need him, girl."

Simona sniffled and laughed a little. "You're right. You're so sweet, Pippa. I'm so glad you came to work here!"

I smiled to myself in the dark. It looked like Pippa had done a good job of worming her way in. Simona turned the key in the lock and they both walked towards the parking lot opposite me, until I saw Pippa stop suddenly and begin her charade. "I'll give the key back to you in the morning, Simona," she said, voice dripping with sweetness as she patted the other woman on the back. "You don't need to wait for me."

"I'm not sure, Pippa."

"Come on, Simona, it looks like you really need some rest."

"Eek!" Simona let out a squeal and jumped up and down excitedly. "He just texted me! He texted me!" Her eyes ran across the screen hungrily. "Oh, Pippa, if you don't mind just letting yourself back in, I really need to go. He wants to see me!"

Pippa's mouth spread into a wide grin, which was matched only by my own. "No, that's fine. You go!"

Pippa hurried back to me as Simona ran in the opposite direction.

She jangled the keys in front of me with a wild grin. "That worked out even better than I'd planned."

"You're a genius Pips. You always seem to shmooze up to the right people, no matter what job you get."

"It's a gift." She let out a short sigh. "Just too bad that I don't have a gift for actually keeping jobs."

I shot her a sympathetic look as she pushed the door open, and finally, we were inside, and alone.

"So this is what an evil lair looks like." I spun around the pristine looking kitchen with its stainless steel pantries and countertops. "It's a little disappointing."

Pippa flicked another light on. "I'm still not sure what you're hoping to find in here, Rach."

I shot her a look. "Anything." I hurried past her.

"Where's the office?"

Pippa was hot on my heels. "It's 'round the corner, to the right, but it's for managers only."

I spun around. "So what?"

Pippa stopped. "Well, it's locked."

I glanced down at the keys in Pippa's hand. "Isn't Simona a manager?"

She slowly lifted up the jangling bunch of keys. "She's only a shift manager. I'm not sure these will work."

I grabbed her by the arm. "Come on, we have to try."

"Okay, but quickly." Pippa looked over her shoulder. "Who knows how long we've got before someone calls security. You've already been to the police station once in the past twenty-four hours, you don't really want to make a second trip, do you?"

I kept a lookout while Pippa tried every key on the key chain with no luck. "Last one," she said, raising an eyebrow as she showed me our last hope of breaking into the office. "Wish me luck."

I took my eyes away from the hallway while I watched the key inch its way into the lock, and finally, after an eternity of waiting, click as it slotted in just the right way and allowed the door handle to turn.

"Phew," I said. "Thought we were going to have to break in for a second there."

Pippa raised an eyebrow. "Isn't that what we're already doing?"

"No, this is still legitimate," I rationalized. "You forgot your jacket, and we're just looking for it. You think it might be in this office." When Pippa still didn't look convinced, I added, "Breaking in—real breaking in—would have been if you'd had to pick the lock."

"Hey," Pippa said in mock offense. "What makes you assume I know how to pick locks?"

I gave her a look. "You don't?"

"Well, I do, but that's not the point!"

I laughed as I gently pushed her into the room. "Come on, let's go!"

I began to sift through the piles of papers on the desk. It was mostly mundane stuff—staff rosters, lists of stock to order for the following day, health and safety memos—while Pippa kept an eye out at the door. "Rachael, what are you looking for exactly? Do you really think there's going to be a piece of paper with 'We Killed Colleen Batters' written on it in bold text?"

"No, of course not." I continued to shuffle through the piles, not caring too much if I messed them up. "I'm just looking for something that shows how dodgy Bakermatic is, something that I can take to the police and show them."

"Rachael, careful! They're going to know someone was in here if you keep flinging the papers around like that! And they'll know I was in here because I had the key!"

"Oh, you're right," I said, hurrying to pick up the papers I'd knocked on the floor. It wasn't going to help my case if Pippa lost her job on day one.

"Here, let me help." Pippa raced over and knelt down on the floor, helping me put the stacks back in order. She frowned. "Does this look right? Is this what they looked like when we walked in?"

"I'm not--" I stopped speaking and brought my finger up to my lips.

"What is it?" Pippa whispered.

"Shh." I kept my finger pressed against my lips. Just as I was about to relax a little, I heard them again: footsteps.

"Oh cripes, someone's called security!" Pippa tried to

crawl under the desk. "We need to hide!"

I frantically looked around the room. There was only one cabinet along with the desk, and any attempt to spring out the door would only take us straight to the owner of those footsteps, which were drawing closer and closer. Pippa was right, the best option was under the desk. But was there enough room for the both of us?

Pippa pulled me in after her, not allowing me to make the decision or second-guess myself.

I heard her swearing under her breath as the steps drew closer. A pair of small feet in black boots appeared in the crack underneath the desk.

"Pippa?" a voice called out.

Not security after all. It was Simona. Pippa could barely conceal the groan that escaped and I shut my eyes, hoping that Simona hadn't heard it.

"Pippa," Simona said in a stern, booming voice. "Where are you? If you've broken into this office..."

So maybe Pippa had been right. Maybe it was technically breaking in. I felt her nails dig into my forearm again and I could hear her mutter, "Oh no, not again."

The footsteps drew closer and I sucked in my breath

and held it tight as a long brown ponytail appeared in front of the desk, swinging in front of us. Within seconds, Simona was down on her knees, her eyes glowing as she captured her prey.

"Simona, I can explain." Pippa said, clambering out of the desk. "I was... I was just looking for my jacket."

"Underneath the desk?" Simona already had her phone out and I could see her fingers taping 911.

Oh no!

"Please," I said, scrambling out after Pippa. "You don't need to call the cops. I can explain what we're doing here."

Simona's finger froze above the phone and her jaw dropped open. "Are you the girl from the bakery down the road? The one who has been killing people?"

"Yes...I mean, no! Not killing people!"

Her fingers jabbed frantically at the screen. "Police, please! We've had a break in at the Belldale Bakermatic Company, and the suspects are extremely dangerous."

I rolled my eyes while beside me, I noticed Pippa drop her head to the floor, all her usual enthusiasm drained from her. "Simona, does this mean?"

"Yes, Pippa. You are definitely fired."

***

Pippa was still grumbling when we finally got to the station. "She doesn't even have the power to fire me. She's only the shift manager, for crying out loud." The heat was off in the station and I shivered inside my red peacoat. It really was not built for sleuthing, or getting caught sleuthing. I made a mental note to buy a more practical coat in the future if we were going to keep up this detective work.

"Pippa, that isn't the most important issue right now," I started to say, before a tall man wearing an expensive navy suit strolled in with an arrogant swagger.

I groaned inwardly. *Nooo, not him.* This was exactly the last thing I had wanted to happen.

He shot me a sly grin. "Fancy seeing you in here again, Miss Robinson. Will you follow me please?"

"Good luck," Pippa whispered, shivering besides me. "He looks terrifying."

I braced myself for Jackson—Detective Whitaker— to give me another dressing down. I knew what he was going to say.

This doesn't look good for you, Rachael. Caught breaking and entering while you are suspected of killing a woman.

He was going to turn the screws, try to get me to confess while I was under stress. Not that I had anything to confess. But he didn't know that. I knew how guilty I looked.

Jackson kicked back in his seat and a wry smiled danced on his lips as he dangled a pen from them. "Not exactly keeping yourself inconspicuous, are you?"

Was this casual, friendly banter a way to unnerve me, a tactic to make me feel as though I could confide in him, open up?

"No," I had to admit. "I didn't exactly intend on ending up in the police station two nights in a row."

"What were you doing in the Bakermatic premises, Rachael?"

So, it was 'Rachael' now, rather than 'Miss Robinson.'

I decided to go with the truth. "I was trying to find evidence."

"Evidence of what?"

"Evidence that they did it. That they killed Colleen."

The wry grin was still on his lips but an edge of surprise had crept into his expression. "What did I tell you about not doing my job for me, Rachael?"

"I know. But you wouldn't listen to me last night when I tried to tell you that Bakermatic must be to blame."

"Rachael, you sound kind of obsessed with Bakermatic."

I leaned back in my seat. "I'm not obsessed with them. I just can't stand them. They've put me out of business, Jackson." I didn't stop and correct myself by calling him Detective. "And now they're telling people that I killed Colleen. My bakery was dead today. I didn't make a single sale."

"Well, I'm sorry to hear that." He sounded genuine. "But that doesn't give you the right to break into private property."

"But we had a key," I tried to protest.

"You're being charged with breaking and entering," Jackson said matter-of-factly as he scribbled something across a piece of paper. "And I'm sorry to say, this doesn't look good for you regarding the other matter,

Miss Robinson."

Back to Miss Robinson. I tried to take a few calm deep breaths. "But, when you think about it, it does actually look good for me."

Jackson looked up sharply. "How so, exactly?"

"Well, why would I be breaking into Bakermatic if I was guilty?" I masked my voice with a thick layer of boldness. "If I knew that I was guilty, why would I be so intent on trying to prove that Bakermatic did it? Why would I need to break in?"

Jackson shrugged. "To plant fake evidence? There are a hundred reasons why you could have broken in, Rachael, and not one of them makes you look less guilty."

I felt the ice run down my back. "I wasn't planting evidence."

Jackson stood up and placed his pen back in his breast pocket. "We'll see what the investigation turns up, Miss Robinson. I've got a detective down there sweeping the scene."

I gulped and subconsciously ran my hand along the front of my coat, where, nestled in behind the interior pocket, I had the paperwork I'd snatched just before

Simona walked in and caught us.

I hadn't planted any evidence, but I might have stolen some. Would the detective down on the scene know?

I shook my head to try to clear it and stood up. "So am I free to go?"

Jackson gave me a slow look up and down. "I can't hold you any longer. For now. But you'll have to go to court for those breaking and entering charges."

"Right."

"And Rachael," he said, showing me out the door, "I strongly advise that you stay out of trouble from this point forward. Or next time, I won't be able to let you go quite so easily."

Chapter 4

"Pippa!" I shook her shoulders as she woke, startled from a deep sleep. My sofa had become her new apartment following the recent eviction from her own.

"What? What is it?" As soon as Pippa opened her eyes, she groaned and slapped her head. "Rach, I just remembered what happened yesterday."

I jumped onto the sofa next to her, excitedly waving around a pile of papers. "Yeah, we got arrested. It was a real bummer."

"No, not that. I mean, I just remembered I got fired again."

"Pippa look at these. Hang on, what are you talking about, Pippa? You think the worst thing about yesterday was the fact that you got fired?"

She motioned to the sofa as she buried her face in a cushion. "Look at this, Rach! I'm sleeping on your sofa."

"And you can stay here for as long as you like," I pointed out. "Pips, did you think your job at Bakermatic was a serious thing?"

She rolled over, revealing her Teenage Mutant Ninja

turtles t-shirt she wore as a pajama top. "I mean, maybe it was stupid of me, but I thought I could actually stick it out there. The conditions were good, and I liked my manager—well, at least until she caught us breaking in."

My face fell. "Oh, Pips, I'm sorry. I never thought you were taking that job seriously." I swallowed. "But I'm sure the conditions weren't that good there. I mean, they take advantage of their employees, don't they? They are famous for giving out low pay and making their staff work overtime." At least, that's what I'd heard. That's what I'd assumed.

Pippa shrugged. "They paid a decent, livable wage..." She caught the look on my face. "It's okay, though, Rach, I know the only reason I took the job was to help you out. Like I said, I was just being silly, getting ahead of myself. Imagine me, actually able to hold down a job!" She let out a hollow laugh. "It was never going to happen."

I patted the sofa. "I mean it, Pips. You can stay here, free of charge, for as long as you like."

Pippa's face finally broke into a smile and she sat up. "So, what have you got there?"

I gulped, wondering now if it was such a good idea to tell her. She was clearly a little sensitive over the

Bakermatic issue. And I was still reeling from the news that it might actually be a halfway decent place to work. I tried to tell myself that Pippa just hadn't been there long enough to realize how terrible it really was. She only worked there a day! Any job can seem all right after only one day.

"Well, come on," Pippa begged, grabbing the papers out of my hands. "Oh," she said, her face falling when she saw the Bakermatic logo on top of the letterhead. "Where did you get these?"

I grimaced. "I swiped them before Simona caught us last night."

Pippa's mouth fell open and at first I thought she was going to give me a lecture, maybe throw the papers back in my face. But instead, her eyes began to twinkle with what looked like admiration.

"Good work, Rach."

"Phew, I thought you might be mad that I got you into even worse trouble."

Pippa laughed. "I've already been fired, how much worse can it be for me?"

"I guess that's true." I pointed to one of the documents. "Look at this, Pippa. It shows the kitchen cleaning log. It's where Bakermatic fills in all the health and safety details of the kitchen. For example, every night before closing, they need to check the temperature of the refrigerator, and they record everything in that log."

She frowned and read over the chart as she clutched it tightly in her small hands. "Yeah?" she said, confused. "This is what you were so excited about?"

"Look at the dates on it." I jabbed my finger.

"It's for the second week of October," Pippa said. "So?"

"So? What week is it now?"

Pippa screwed her face up in deep concentration. "I dunno? The second week of October? The first?"

I snatched the papers back from her. "It's the first week of October, Pips."

"I still don't see the big deal."

"Look at this log! They've already filled it in, in advance, for next week! How can they know the temperature of the refrigerators the week before? It's impossible."

Pippa slowly began to nod as she finally understood what I was saying. "So someone was clearly trying to save time."

"Cutting corners." I shook my head. "Typical of that place." I waved the papers in front of her. "If they don't even bother to make sure all the food is stored at safe temperatures, who knows what kind of stuff they are serving to customers!"

Pippa leaned back against the sofa and gave me a careful look. "I agree, it's a little dodgy that they did that. It's not right, but, Rach, it certainly doesn't prove anything."

"It proves that they don't take proper safety precautions. It proves they don't care about their customers. Pippa, I take a careful log every single day. I would never do my safety checks a week in advance like this."

Pippa looked away and didn't say anything for a long moment. "I know you wouldn't, Rach. But this is just one piece of paper. All it proves is that they cut corners on their paperwork this one week. It doesn't prove they don't care about their customers."

I could see the look in her eye. It was the same one Jackson had at the police station. She thought I was obsessed as well; I could tell.

I shuffled the papers in my lap. "I think I should take

these to the police."

"And where will you say you got them from, exactly?"

"They already know we broke in. What does it matter?"

"It matters because you were only charged with breaking and entering. You want a burglary charge as well?"

A smile threatened to take over my lips. It was very strange for Pippa to be the one giving me sensible advice. Was she right? Would handing this over to Jackson only get me in further trouble? After all, it wasn't the only thing I'd swiped.

But maybe it would finally make them investigate Bakermatic seriously.

"Come on," Pippa said, jumping up. "Don't you have a bakery to run?"

My mouth was agape. "Right now? No, I don't actually. I've got no customers. Hence, no business to run."

Pippa pulled a sweater on over her Turtles t-shirt. "Come on, you never know what today is going to bring! You don't know what you're going to find when you get to work."

I nodded. "You're right. I should at least go in. Are you coming with me?"

"I've got nothing else to do."

I wrapped my arm around her shoulders. "I'll have to pay you in cakes though, at least I've got plenty of those."

***

Pippa was right. I didn't know what I was going to find when I got to the bakery. What I didn't expect to find was the word "Killer" painted in bright red letters on the front window.

"Who did this?" Pippa asked as she took off her sweater and began to frantically mop up the paint. I noticed too late that it was actually my sweater she was wearing.

"Yuck." Pippa shook the sweater, the white of it now streaked with red, blood-looking paint. "This is kind of turning my stomach."

Even though she had managed to blur the word

"Killer" a little, it was still clearly legible.

"I think too much of the paint has already dried. Maybe we should have come in sooner."

I turned my key in the lock and shoved the door open. "Come inside, Pippa." On any other day, I would have been at the bakery at the break of dawn, getting the pastry rolled and mixing the muffin mixtures for the day. But the shelves were still brimming with the previous day's bake and I didn't feel particularly inspired to flush even more money down the toilet. But if I'd just come in, maybe I would have seen the person who'd sprayed that on my window.

Once the inside of the store, I didn't even bother to turn on the lights. If my bad reputation hadn't already been keeping the customers away, that word across my windows would have done the trick nicely.

I looked down at my hands and noticed that they were shaking.

"Rach," Pippa said, placing a hand on my shoulder. "Hey, it's not that bad. We can call a window washer to come get rid of the blood...I mean, paint." She pulled her hand away and gasped an apology when she realized she'd left a red hand print there.

"Don't worry about it," I said, shrugging it off. "And

don't worry about calling a window cleaner." I could hear the shake in my voice.

"It'll be okay."

I shook my head. "How? All I ever wanted to do was run this little bakery, make my own cakes and sell them to people. And I thought—just for a little while—that it was actually going to happen. But now, what's the point?"

Suddenly the door pushed open and a touristy looking woman with a large sun hat and sunglasses bustled in and began peering at the selection of cakes on offer. She nodded to herself with a look of appreciation on her face.

I straightened up. Perhaps she hadn't seen the paint on the windows. Racing behind the counter to tie my apron on, I asked her, "What can I do for you today, ma'am?"

She stood up straight. "I read online that this is the best boutique bakery in Belldale."

I nodded. At least the online reviews were still untarnished. I had the highest rated bakery in the area, with an average of 4.8 from over fifty reviewers. The kinds of tourists who check those sites always mentioned it when they came in.

"That's right," I said, gesturing to the still-full shelves of cakes and slices. "The best in town."

"Far better than that mass produced place down the road," the woman murmured.

"Bakermatic," I said, nodding. "Yes, of course, far better than them! They get most of their cakes pre-packaged from a factory. They are so chock-full of preservatives that they can last in their plastic packaging for months—maybe even years."

"Not these, though," the woman said, nodding at a row of Vanilla Slice. "You bake everything right here every day, don't you?"

"Well." I swallowed and looked over her shoulder at Pippa. "Yes, ma'am, everything is baked right here, on the premises."

"Fresh today?"

"Well...I...er. No, not today," I had to admit finally, seeing the woman's face fall into a pit of disgust.

"What do you mean, not today? Are these cakes fresh or not?"

"They are! They are only from yesterday, ma'am. They've all been refrigerated..."

She screwed her nose up. "And why haven't you

been baking today then? Why do you still have yesterday's cakes out for people to buy?"

I wanted to explain that, although not 100% ideal, that cakes baked only the day before were still fresh, and still a hundred times fresher than Bakermatic's atrocities. And more than that, I wanted to explain that I could hardly justify using hundreds of dollars of ingredients on cakes that were only going to end up in the trash. I hadn't even intended to open the bakery that day! But to explain all of that, I would have to explain why the store had been completely empty the day before.

Pippa stepped forward. "Rachael's just been a little sick, that's all."

I shook my head at her. I knew she was only trying to help, but that was the worst thing she could have said. Well, maybe the second worst.

The woman recoiled. "Well. I hardly wish to purchase cakes made by a sick woman, when those cakes aren't even fresh!" She cast an eye up towards the price list. "And at those prices! Why, miss, you have some nerve!" The woman turned on her heels and stormed out of the shop. She stopped as she saw the blurry blood red paint on the widows before hurrying away as though she'd seen a ghost.

I turned away. "There goes my good online rating."

"Come on," Pippa said, walking over to the door. "We're going to do something about this."

"Where are we going?"

She yanked the door open and stopped to stare at me. "Bakermatic."

***

The best thing we could come up with for disguises was the baseball visors and sunglasses that Pippa had in her bag.

"Pippa, if we get caught, there's gonna be big problems!"

"What are they gonna do? Call the cops again?"

I thought about Jackson's warning to me. "Yeah. They might."

"We better keep our heads down then," Pippa said as she pushed open the door into Bakermatic.

I cleared my throat. "Excuse me," I said to a young

wisp of a woman with blonde hair who was stacking muffins onto a stand.

"Yes?" she said nervously. Her name tag told me her name was Anna and that she was a trainee.

"Can you tell me, dear, are these muffins fresh?"

She shifted nervously. "I'll have to check with my manager."

"I'll take that as a no then. And can you tell me anything about your kitchen practices? Do you throw food out when it past its used by date? Do you keep a good temperature log? Or do you pretty much make it up as you go?"

"Rachael!" Pippa hissed as she pulled me away, leaving the tiny blonde girl wide-eyed on the other side of the counter. "You're going to give us away. She clearly doesn't know anything! She only started yesterday with me, she was one of the new recruits."

"Well, we can't leave yet. I need to catch them in the act." I looked over my shoulder covertly, hoping to see one of the new young employees drop a muffin and put it back on the shelf or something.

I walked back to the counter and, while Anna wasn't looking, I gently nudged one of the muffins onto the bench, cursing to myself when it teetered on the end of the counter without falling.

Anna spun around and cried out "Oh no!" before picking the muffin up.

"Oh, that's all right, just put it back on the stand," I said casually. "That's what you usually do, right?"

Anna shook her head. "No, they were very strict about this in training. If a cake falls off its stand, it goes straight in the trash. No risks get taken here, not when the health of our customers is at stake!"

"Right." My mouth was a thin line as Pippa pulled me away.

"I think we've stretched our luck far enough," she said. "Let's get out of here."

"Hey!" a loud voice bellowed. I recognized that one. "Not you two again! I'm calling the cops...again!"

There were murmurs and gasps from the full store as Pippa and I raced out the door before Simona could pull her phone out. She chased us and, just as I thought we were going to make it clear out the door, Simona reached out and slammed the door shut. "Uh-uh. You two aren't going anywhere."

Her hand still pressed the door shut above my head.

That's when I saw it. The palm of her hand, streaked with blood-red paint, faded in a clear attempt to get rid of it.

I turned slowly to Pippa. She'd seen it too.

"Go ahead, call the cops," I said, reaching up to pull Simona's hand away from the door. "But you're going to have to explain how this paint got on your hand."

Simona's cheeks turned as red as her hands. "I burned my palms on the oven," she muttered, pulling her sleeves down.

"Really? You want to tell the cops that when they arrest you for defacing property?"

Simona glared at us as Pippa yanked the door back, now that Simona had dropped her guard. "Come on, Rach, let's go!"

We sprinted the entire way back to the bakery, doubling over when we finally got through the doors. "I can't believe Simona did that to the window," Pippa said, breathless. "Why is she so hell bent on making sure you take the blame for Colleen's death?"

"Because, Pippa," I said, turning to look at her slowly. "I think Simona did it. That's why she doesn't want us snooping around, and that's why she is doing every thing she can to frame me. Now, all we've got to do is prove it."

Chapter 5

I told Pippa to go home and get some rest while I chucked all of yesterday's baked goods into the trash. It was a depressing enough task without a witness to add to my indignity.

Still, there was a little ray of hope beginning to dance in my stomach. Now I had a strong suspect. I was certain Simona had done it—the way her face had turned so red, the fact that she hadn't chased us, and the fact that the cops hadn't shown up at my door. Now, all I had to do was prove she was to blame and I could finally restore my reputation. I looked down at the rapidly filling bags of trash. *This is the last time I will ever throw out a day's work,* I vowed, dusting off my hands. Things were about to turn around; I could just feel it.

After filling four entire trash bags with cakes, slices of pie, donuts and pastries, I pulled the bags out into the alley, passing my stack of unopened mail from the day before. I'd been so distracted by Gavin that I hadn't actually finished opening the envelopes he'd passed me.

I dropped the trash bags and rummaged through the pile. My heart did a little flip when I saw that one of them was from the real estate compnay I leased the shop from.

I knew I was a little behind on the rent, but surely it couldn't be that bad. I ripped the envelope open and digested the contents of the letter.

My heart sunk to the bottom of my stomach and the room began to spin.

"EVICTION NOTICE."

"No... No..." I said, frantically reading the rest of the letter. I had one week to come up with the back rent or I was out of there.

"But I'm only a few weeks behind!" I wailed, throwing the letter down on the counter as I pulled my apron off, the straps suddenly so tight they felt as though they were blocking my air flow. But I knew the real estate company wouldn't care that I was only a few weeks behind. This was a high traffic street, prime real estate, and they'd have no problem finding a new business owner to take over the lease.

"I just hope they're not planning on opening a bakery here," I said bitterly, trying to fight back the tears. So much for things turning around. How was I going to find the back rent in just one week? Even if I could get Simona convicted before that and restore my reputation, it seemed totally impossible.

I glanced out the window. The lights at Bakermatic finally turned off for the night, and I could see Simona and her long dark ponytail creeping out into the night.

One week. One week to prove she did it and save my bakery.

***

Pippa was still dead to the world as I pulled my sneakers on the following morning. To be fair to her, I was up at the crack of dawn, my body still set to baker's hours even though I didn't have a bakery to attend to.

I smiled down at Pippa's sprawled out body as I passed her on the sofa. It would have been nice to have her on board for the day's task, but I knew that I could handle it myself.

The flyer from the street fair dangled from my hand. On it, a list of every single food vendor from the day that Colleen had died. If the cops weren't going to investigate thoroughly, then it was going to be up to me to speak to every last one of them.

There were fourteen different restaurants and cafes

that had stalls that day at the Belldale street fair. I decided to start with the one closest to my own bakery, a sandwich place called "Deena's Deli" run by a woman, called—you guessed it—Deena.

"Hey there, Rach," she said with a jolly grin. Deena was in her mid-forties with a golden blonde bob and somehow always managed to have flour on her shirt despite the fact that I wasn't sure what she actually baked with flour in her sandwich store. "What can I do for you today? Are you after a sandwich?"

Not at six in the morning, no. Deena opened early to catch the tradesmen on their way to work, looking for breakfast sandwiches filled with greasy bacon, sausage, and eggs. But that kind of thing so early in the morning churned my stomach.

"No, Deena, not today. They all smell delicious, though," I said, nodding towards the sizzling bacon concoctions flattened beneath the iron of the sandwich press.

Deena sighed. "Business has been a little slow this week." She lowered her voice and looked around as though she was about to say something forbidden. "You know, since the 'incident' at the street fair."

Hmm, so it wasn't just my shop that had been

affected, though I seemed to have been the worst hit. "Actually, Deena, that's what I wanted to talk to you about."

"You did?" Deena brushed her hands against her apron, leaving even more flour there. Where did it all come from? "Rachael, I know a lot of people are saying that you did it, but I just want to say, hand on my heart," She placed her hand against her chest in another cloud of flour, "that I don't believe you did it."

"I didn't do it. Deena, that's what I'm trying to clear up. Tell me, that day, did you see anything suspicious at all?"

Deena screwed her face up in great concentration. "Not that I can remember, dear. Oh, and I do wish I could help you. It's an awful shame what that man did to your window."

"Woman," I corrected her. "I already know who did it."

"Oh." Deena looked confused. "My mistake then, dear. I'm sure you know what you're talking about."

"I do." I cleared my throat and smiled. "So you really can't remember anything strange happening that day? Did you see the woman—the victim—Colleen Batters at all?"

"Ha!" Deena shook her head as she let out a hollow laugh. "She never deigned to stop by my stand, just like she always turned her nose up at my shop. Yet people are still avoiding my food this week. Just goes to show that she can have a negative impact after her death! I don't like to speak ill of the dead, Rachael, but that Colleen Batters was a real snob—a real piece of work."

I glanced around and noticed that the bacon sandwiches were burning. "You might want to check those." As she hobbled over, I watched Deena carefully. "So you didn't like Colleen then?"

Deena laughed again as she pulled out a charcoal sandwich and threw it in the trash with a sigh. "No one did, dear. That's why I keep saying: anyone could have done it; any one of the people running those stands could have wanted her dead." She turned to me with a hand on her hip. "Don't tell me you're in here accusing me of having something to do with it?"

"Deena, I'm just trying to get to the bottom of what happened. Eliminate suspects."

The jolly look had drained from her face. "What are you, a cop now?"

Although I already knew who had killed Coleen—or, at least, I was 99% sure—I still needed to make sure I was being thorough. Besides, I still needed the smoking gun, the proof that Simona had actually done it. And I could see that I was rubbing Deena the wrong way and if I didn't start to butter her up, she would likely kick me out of her store.

"Deena, I'm just trying to make my rent. You can appreciate that. I don't believe you killed Colleen. But can you remember seeing her eating anywhere in particular that day?"

Deena softened a little. She nodded. "Yes. She ate a fish pie from Carl's Fish Shop. I remember that clearly because she took joy in telling me how much better his savory selection was compared to mine."

"Sounds like Colleen." I patted the counter, sending flour flying. "Thanks, Deena. I'll let you get back to work."

***

"What are you talking about?" Carl said, pouring more water into his kitchen mixer. "Oh, darn!" he shouted. "Now I've gone and poured too much liquid into the darn pastry! You happy now?"

No! I certainly wasn't happy with the reception I'd gotten when I'd walked into Carl's Fish Shop. It seemed that he was another of the vendors who was hurting in the wake of Colleen's death, so I tried not to take his grumpiness too personally.

"That day at the Belldale Street fair," I said again, walking along the other side of the counter to follow him as he turned and threw battered fish into a deep fryer. "Do you remember serving a woman named Colleen Batters?"

He spun around. "You talking about the woman who died? Obviously I'd remember a thing like that. She never ate any of our fish, if that's what you're suggesting! Don't you think I've lost enough business as it is without people speculating even further, and without you coming in here and sticking your nose into other people's business?"

"Carl," I said, as calmly as possible. "I have a witness who says she did see Colleen eating one of your products, a fish pie, on the day in question."

He shook his head. "There's no way that's possible."

"How can you know that for sure? Did you keep track of every single person who ate from your stall that day?"

"Of course I did. Do you think I'd forget serving a woman that died?"

I sighed. "Why would Deena make that up?"

"Deena?" Carl said, leaning over the counter. "Oh, she's just trying to pass the blame! It was probably one of her bacon and egg sandwiches that killed the woman! After all, her food made me sick as a dog a few days ago." He stopped short all of a sudden.

I frowned. "When was this, Carl? When were you sick?"

He shrugged. "I don't know exactly," he muttered. "A few days ago." He picked up a washcloth and busied himself wiping a bench that was already sparkling clean.

"Three days ago?" I took a step closer to the counter. "Is that when you were sick?"

He shrugged. "I suppose so. It might have been."

"People don't forget getting food poisoning, Carl. Was it three days ago or not?"

He nodded.

"So, the day before the street fair." I raised an eyebrow and looked him up and down. "And yet, you were still able to get up in the morning and work a full shift at the Belldale street fair? A shift where you were so alert that you are able to remember every single customer you served?"

Carl just kept wiping the bench top. "I was feeling a little better once the morning rolled 'round."

"Carl. Be straight with me. You weren't at the street fair, were you?"

After a bit of hesitation, he shook his head. "No, miss, I wasn't there. I was so ill after eating one of Deena's contraptions that I was knocked out for two days straight. I just started feeling better today."

I sighed. "So why did you tell me you were at the fair?"

He shrugged again. "Because, if I wasn't there, how can I know for sure that Colleen didn't eat any of my food?" He shook his head. "But I know, miss, deep down, that it couldn't have been my food! I been here on this street for thirty years, miss. Why, this place is practically a local institution! And not once in thirty years have I ever made a single customer sick. I only have the best standards here. Unless the fish is fresh that day, I won't sell it."

I had always admired poor old Carl's commitment to freshness and quality. And I'd never heard anything bad about his store before. Any time I'd eaten from there myself, the food had always been piping hot, delicious, and never with an unpleasant super-fishy taste that some deep fried seafood gets. His batter was always golden brown, a result of regular oil changes. No wonder he was getting his back up. His thirty-year reputation was on the line.

"Carl, I know the possibility might be hard for you to fathom, especially with your high standards, but if you weren't there that day to supervise, anything could have happened."

"I don't care if I was there or not," he snapped. "I know what happened. It was Deena's food. It had to have been."

I sighed and tried to remain calm. "Carl, who did you leave in charge of the stall that day?"

He shook his head. "It was supposed to be the boy I get in to help me out on weekends, Tim, but he had some baseball game or something and couldn't be there for the whole day. He said he left the stall under the care of someone he'd found online. I can't even remember her name, to be honest with you."

"Her?"

Carl nodded. "That's about all I know of her. I didn't

even see her myself, but Tim said she was a real airhead." Carl stopped and looked up at me. "But that don't mean anything bad happened." Worry flashed in his eyes.

"It's okay, Carl. Do you remember any other details about her? Do you have a number, or an email address for her?"

He shook his head. "Tim was the one who posted the ad. Maybe he has more details for you. We just paid her cash on the day. She only worked for that one day, you see. Hey, you won't tell on me, will you, miss?"

I shook my head. Even though I made sure all my employees were paid by the book and got their regular breaks they were entitled to, Carl's slightly dodgy, under the counter payments were my last concern at that moment.

"So where is this Tim fella right now?" I dug my phone out of my coat pocket and opened the note app, ready to take down the address.

"Well, miss, he's actually gone back to college this week."

Great.

I sighed. "Do you have a phone number for him?"

Carl frowned and began to rummage though a stack of notebooks sitting beside the register. "I do somewhere, miss. Just give me a minute to find it."

"You don't have his number in your own cell phone?" I asked, growing impatient with his fumbling.

Carl shook his head. "I still use a landline, I'm sorry to say."

And I was sorry to hear it. "Look, maybe I'll come back later," I said, heading towards the door. "There's other people I need to talk to. If you could find Tim's number by the end of the day, that would be great."

"Wait, miss."

I paused, my hand about to push against the door. "What is it?"

"I do remember one thing Carl said about the girl who helped him that day."

I took a step back into the shop. "What do you remember about her?"

"I remember Tim talking about her hair, how it was a real crazy color. Bright red, and curly."

I swallowed. "Thank you, Carl," I whispered, hurrying to get out of there.

***

"Pippa?"

No answer. I stepped in the door and placed the keys back in my coat quietly. "Pippa?" I called out again softly.

There was an empty space on the sofa where she'd been, the imprint of her body bare, surrounded by empty takeaway containers and discarded drink bottles.

I sat down on the seat opposite.

Oh, Pippa.

I closed my eyes. *Come on, Rachael, it's important not to jump to conclusions. Just because the girl working with Tim had wild, red curly hair and was a little air-headed, it doesn't mean it was Pippa.*

And even if it was Pippa, it doesn't mean that she was the one who killed Colleen.

But if it was her, why didn't she tell me she was working at the fair that day? She knows how worried I've been! She saw the paint on the bakery window! How could she keep this from me?

I opened my eyes and looked at the mess Pippa had left on my sofa. Storming to the kitchen, I grabbed a trash bag and began to toss the items into it. *I let her sleep here, free of charge, and she can't even be bothered to tidy up after herself.*

One of the empty soda bottles rolled onto the floor and under the seat. I bent down to pick it up.

My hand felt something soft under there and I pulled it out, wondering what I could have left underneath there.

It was the visor that Pippa had taken off that night after the street fair, the one she'd thrown onto the ground right before we'd started to watch Criminal Point.

I turned it over slowly and looked at the writing embroidered on the front of it: "Carl's Fish Shop."

All the life drained out of me and I slumped down. So, she had been working for Carl's stand that day. I shut my eyes and tried to recall what had happened that night when Pippa had come in through the door.

I sighed. I told her I didn't want to talk about the day I'd had and then she'd thrown the visor off before I ever saw it. That might explain why she hadn't told me about her day working for Carl's Fish Shop.

But what about the day after that, and the day after that?

I'd sent her to spy on Bakermatic.

When all along, she might have been trying to cover her own tracks.

Oh, Pippa, what have you done?

I heard the sound of the front door opening and quickly shoved the visor back under the chair.

"Hey, Rach! Didn't think you'd be back already? How'd the sleuthing go? Did you find out who did it yet?"

Maybe.

I stood up and shook my head, barely able to look Pippa in the eye. "Not yet," I said quickly before hurrying towards the kitchen. Pippa followed me.

"Sorry about all the mess, Rach. I did intend to clean it up before you got home."

"It's fine." I shoved the trash bag in the can.

"Hey, is everything okay?" Pippa sounded worried. "You're not mad at me or anything, are you?"

I shook my head. I was still looking at the floor. "No. Why would you say that?" I finally dared to look at her.

Trying to gauge any flicker of guilt that might cross her face. "Why would I be annoyed at you, Pippa?"

She shrugged. "I don't know. You just seem weird. Oh well, if you say you're fine, I'll take your word for it. I'm gonna go watch some TV."

"Wait."

Pippa spun back around, her big blue eyes staring at me. Was there innocence in there? I couldn't bear to think that Pippa could be responsible for a woman's death.

She's always been irresponsible though. "Airheaded," that was the word Carl used. She easily could have used the wrong fish, not checked the used by dates, or left the fish sitting out in the sun. Anything could have happened with Pippa in charge.

"What is it, Rach?"

She batted her eyelids, long black fake lashes that framed the blue pools in between them. Pippa was airheaded, yes, but capable of killing a person? Even accidentally? No, not my best friend. She couldn't have.

And if she knew I suspected her, that could cause a rift between us that could never be mended again. Thirteen years of friendship down the drain.

"Nothing, Pips. Go and watch TV." I gave her a brave smile and she shot me an odd look as she turned around and headed back to the living room.

I stared down into the trash. I'd thought the only thing at stake was my bakery, and possibly my own reputation. I knew I was innocent. But could I say the same thing about Pippa? Now Pippa's freedom was at stake.

I didn't know if she was innocent. And if the cops found out that Pippa had been working at the fair that day, off the books, she was going to become a prime suspect. I knew how bad it looked for her. I didn't trust Detective Whitaker to go easy on her, or even to look at all the facts.

I tied up the bag and gave the can a little kick. Shaking my head, I realized that now, no matter how unglamorous the whole thing got, how unlike being a detective on TV it all was, I couldn't give up now. If Pippa was innocent then I was going to have to be the one to prove it.

Chapter 6

"Detective Whitaker, what are you doing here?"

"Can I come in?"

I took a step back into my house. It was difficult to make out the expression on Jackson's face in the dark of night, which, that evening, was not even lucky enough to be graced by the moon.

"What is this about?" I asked, pulling my sweater tighter around me. "Are you arresting me again?"

"I've never arrested you before," Jackson pointed out. "Simply questioned you."

"Yeah, well, it didn't feel that different from being arrested." I rubbed my arms against the autumn chill. "So you still haven't answered my question. Are you arresting me? Or just here for more questioning?"

Jackson clenched his jaw for a moment and for a second looked as though he was going to turn and leave. "I just wanted to check in on you. See if you were all right."

"All right?" I was stunned that he would just turn up

like this, to check on my wellbeing. There had to be some sort of a catch. "Are you on duty?"

He held his hands up. "This is all off the books."

"Hmm," I mused, looking him up and down. He was still in his expensive looking navy suit. "How can I be sure?"

He grinned at me. "You'll have to take my word for it." His smile faded once he saw that I wasn't returning it.

"Do you really think I'm all right?" I asked him. "After everything that's happened." *No thanks to you,* I wanted to add.

"Look, Rachael, I'm not here in a professional capacity. In fact, I really shouldn't be here at all." He glanced around furtively as though someone might be following him. "It's a clear conflict of interest. I just wanted to drop by and make sure you are okay." He took a step back. "I'm sorry. I should go. Forget I was even here."

"Wait," I said. "Do you want to come in for coffee or something?"

He hesitated, but I could tell from the way his eyes lit up that he did want to say yes. It was just going to take a little persuading on my part. Usually I could tempt people, men especially, inside with the promise of one of my cakes. I always had a spare batch lying around the house. But under the circumstances that was probably not the best tactic—especially if Jackson still thought I did it.

I narrowed my eyes. Perhaps this was the best way to figure out whether he still thought I was guilty, whether I was still a live suspect. "I've got a fresh batch of fudge brownies in the fridge," I said, checking carefully for his reaction.

No clear indication that he thinks he is going to die from taking a bite.

Jackson let out an uncomfortable laugh. "Are you trying to poison me?"

I just stared at him. "That isn't funny. Never mind." I tried to push the door shut, but he put his foot in the way.

"Sorry, I just meant that because I'm a cop, and...never mind. It was a bad joke. I don't think there's anything wrong with your cooking."

"Yeah?" I raised an eyebrow at him. "Come in and prove it then."

He glanced around covertly. Luckily for him, it was pure blackness out there and no one was going to see him sneaking into a potential murderer's apartment even if he had been followed. "I really shouldn't."

"Come on," I said, stepping back. "I'll heat them up for you. I promise you, these are the best brownies you will ever taste in your life."

"Well. Now *that* I do have to investigate."

Jackson followed me in and sat at the table while I warmed up a brownie for him. He sniffed the brownie and after I assured him there was no rat poison in the mixture, he finally took a bite.

"Mmm," he said, nodding. "Rachael, this is amazing. Just as good as the cake I sampled from your stand on the day of the fair."

I sat my coffee mug down with a bang.

"Sorry," Jackson said quickly, wiping the crumbs away from his mouth. "That was the wrong thing to say, wasn't it?"

"No. I mean, it wasn't exactly the best thing to say if you're trying to get back on my good side."

"I was in your good side at one stage?" he asked me with a mischievous grin. "Good to know."

"You know, you did eat one of my products that day," I pointed out. "And you didn't get sick, or die. I remember worrying at one stage that you might."

"You were worried."

I let out a large, over exaggerated sigh. "Can we just stick to the subject again, without any flirting going on?"

"I didn't know we were flirting. Are we flirting?"

"You're doing it again."

"Sorry."

I brushed my skirt down, playing with the hem for a moment. "I only meant to say, surely that must count in my favor as far as the investigation goes? Give me some brownie points, so to speak."

Jackson sat his brownie plate down, his face now dark and serious. "Rachael, you know I can't talk to you about any of this."

I swallowed. "Jackson, do you know what's happened to me since you brought me in for questioning?"

He looked down at the carpet. "Yes, I saw the paint on your shop window. That's partly why I dropped by here, even though I know I shouldn't have. I'm sorry, I've already said too much."

He stood to leave and I wanted to drag him back down onto the sofa. "Wait, Jackson. You don't have to go just yet, do you?"

"If I don't want to damage this case any more than I already have. Sorry, Rach. I just wanted to make sure you were still in one piece."

"Still in one piece?" I jumped up after him as he started heading out of the room. I grabbed him arm. "Jackson, what does that mean?"

He shook his head. "Nothing," he murmured. "Just meant, I wanted to make sure you weren't falling apart."

I raised an eyebrow and stuck my hand on my lip. "I don't fall apart quite that easily. It takes more than a little red paint."

"I really ought to go."

Jackson stopped talking as his eyes seemed to be transfixed by something behind me.

"What is it? What are you staring at?" I turned around and saw it. The red visor sticking out from underneath my designer chair.

Quickly, I stepped back and kicked the visor back under the chair. "You were just heading out?" I said to Jackson with the most casual tone I could muster, pushing him towards the front door. "Let me see you out. You better be careful out there tonight, it's pitch black and...and you're on a sugar high." I was rambling.

"What was that?" He stopped and I realized that my strength against his was nothing. I couldn't budge him.

"What was what?" Still as casual as can be.

"That object you just kicked under the chair." He placed a hand on my shoulder and gently but forcefully moved me out of the way.

"It's my private property, is what it is!"

But Jackson was already kneeling on the floor, inspecting the visor. "Just what I thought it was, the logo from Carl's Fish Shop."

Jackson turned to look at me with heavy eyelids. "Did you know this was here? Why do you have a visor from Carl's Fish Shop in your house?"

"I don't. I don't know how that got there."

Jackson stood up, the visor hanging from his hands, as though it was important evidence that he had to be careful not to dirty with his own fingerprints.

"Is this yours?"

I shook my head.

"Then why is it in your house?"

I put both hands on my hips. "What, I'm not allowed to have a visor from Carl's Fish Shop in my house? Why does it matter how it got there?" I took a step towards Jackson. "Unless, of course, Carl is a suspect in the Colleen Batters case."

Jackson's face clenched. "I told you not to do any more digging around. You need to be careful, or else..."

"Or else what?"

"You just need to be careful, Rachael!"

Jackson took a step back and rubbed his temples. "You need to tell me what this visor is doing in your home."

"I think you ought to leave. And you can drop that visor as well," I said, stomping towards the door.

"I can't just leave it, Rachael This is official police evidence now."

"I knew it!" I shouted, spinning around. "I knew you didn't just drop by for a casual chat, checking to see if I was okay."

Jackson looked hurt. "Rachael, I did, you have to believe that. It's just that I could hardly stop my mind from working on the case, could I? Especially when you are hiding evidence in your apartment."

I scoffed in offense. "I was hardly hiding evidence. I didn't even know that hat was there."

"Really?" Jackson asked. "Come on, Rach, do you really take me for a fool?"

"It was hidden under my chair," I said indignantly. "I never saw it till you pulled it out."

"Then I'm going to have to ask you to come down to the station with me again."

***

The night was so black I couldn't even see out the front of the car window until Jackson snapped the lights on, blinding me.

I sat back against the car seat and pressed my eyes shut. I didn't think I could stomach another trip to the police station.

"Last chance." Jackson turned the key in the ignition. "It can all end here, Rachael. Just tell me, why were you hiding that visor? Were you working with Carl that day?"

My eyes flew open. "No! You know I was too busy running my own stall!"

"You might have taken a break, helped him out for a while. You weren't exactly overwhelmed with customers that day."

I shook my head. "Real nice, Detective."

The ignition was still running, but we hadn't moved an inch.

"Who's that?" Jackson asked, pointing to the front of my apartment. "Who's going into your home?"

"No one," I said, trying to get his attention away from the red-haired figure, clearly slightly tipsy, trying to get her key to work in the front door. "Let's just get to the station. Come on, bring me in for questioning again."

Jackson flipped the engine off again so that we were in total silence as well as pitch-black darkness. He leaned forward, gripping the steering wheel as he watched Pippa struggle with the front door. "She's not breaking in, is she?"

"I don't know," I said, shrugging in an exaggerated manner.

"She clearly has a key." Jackson turned to me sharply. "I didn't know you had a roommate, Rachael."

"She's just staying with me temporarily."

Even though I could only see Jackson out of the corner of my eye, I could see him putting the pieces of the puzzle together, could see him figuring out how many lies I'd told him. Why did I feel so guilty about them? He was the enemy, after all. He was the reason I had "Killer" scrawled in blood-red paint over the front of my bakery. He was the reason I was about to get evicted from my shop.

Jackson tapped his fingers on the steering wheel. "So the visor belongs to your roommate."

I didn't say anything.

"What's her name?"

I still didn't say anything.

"Rachael, I'm going to find out with or without your help, so you may as well tell me. You might think you're helping your friend by staying silent, but believe me, you're not."

"Her name is Pippa," I said quietly.

"And was Pippa working for Carl's Fish on the day of the Belldale street fair?"

For some strange reason, in that moment I thought about poor old Carl, how I'd promised not to turn him in for paying Pippa under the table. Was he going to get into trouble now?

"Yes," I said finally. "She was working there. But Jackson—Detective Whitaker—you've got to believe me, *please*." I reached out and grabbed Jackson's arm. "You've got to believe me that Pippa had nothing to do with any of this."

Finally the clouds cleared a little and there was the slightest sliver of moonlight draping us. All I could see was Jackson staring back at me. "As I've told you numerous times before, Miss Robinson, you're going to have to leave the investigating to us. We'll decide how guilty or not this roommate of yours is." He picked up his radio and began to talk into it, giving his name and location to whoever was listening on the other end.

"Wait," I said, reaching out to try and stop him as Jackson glared at me. He switched off the radio for a moment.

"I won't hesitate to put you in cuffs if I have to, Miss Robinson."

"Please, just don't make that call yet. I can help you. I can help you solve this case. You don't need to involve Pippa in any of this."

Jackson shook his head in disbelief and scoffed as he

said, "How many times do I need to tell you..."

"I know, I know. Not to investigate. But you have to admit that I've done a better job than you have so far. You didn't even know about Pippa working for Carl, even though you've clearly already considered him as a suspect."

Jackson's face was stormy. I could tell I'd hit a nerve.

"Listen," I said, hurrying on, quickly trying to take advantage of the fact that I had him off balance. "I already know who did it, Jackson. The person, the woman, is named Simona. She works at Bakermatic down the road from my bakery. And she's trying to cover it up by making me look guilty. She's the one who painted "Killer" on my window."

Jackson frowned. "How do you know all this?"

"Because I investigated, of course. How else?"

Jackson rolled his eyes a little. "I mean, how do you know for a fact that she did it? Do you have proof? Proof that she killed Colleen? Proof that she vandalized your bakery?"

"Well, I have some pretty good evidence,"I said weakly. "She had red paint on her hands."

Jackson scoffed. "Didn't think so. See, that's the

difference between being an amateur sleuth and an actual detective, Rachael. You need to follow the cold, hard facts. Not decide who is guilty and then make the evidence fit it. We actually use our heads. Our brains. Not our personal prejudices."

I felt like a naughty school child who had just been chastised by a teacher. "I'm not prejudiced," I tried to protest.

"Oh please, Rachael. You have a personal grudge against Bakermatic that is clouding all of your judgment. You are so hell-bent on proving that they're guilty that you can't even see what's right in front of your face." Jackson pointed towards my apartment building. "Or what is right inside your own home."

I had fallen totally silent. I thought back to all the episodes of Criminal Points where one of the detectives had become too personally involved and been taken off the case. Did I need to take myself off the case? Had I just been screwed over so often by Bakermatic that I couldn't even take a step back and consider that someone else might be to blame?

I turned my face back to my apartment. Pippa had managed to find the light switch at long last and had plonked herself back onto my sofa.

Was I so close to Pippa that I couldn't see the worst in her? It was true that every time my brain even drifted towards the conclusion that she might be guilty it was as though there was an electric fence there that shocked me and wouldn't let me cross it.

"You're right," I murmured. "I've taken this case too personally."

Jackson let out a soft sigh. His reply was gentle. "It's okay, Rachael, you were just trying to protect your friend, and your bakery while you were at it. I can't fault you for that. You're a good friend, and a darn fine cook. But you'd better leave the detective work to those of us who are actually qualified."

"Can I get out of the car now?" I asked quietly.

Jackson nodded and I pressed the button to free my seatbelt.

Jackson was hot on my heels as we walked back to my front door, but I felt as though I was moving in slow motion.

"Are you going to arrest Pippa?" I asked him.

He gave me a reluctant smile. "Just bring her in for questioning."

I nodded. "You do what you need to do then."

Before I knew it, Pippa was being led out by Jackson, now Detective Whitaker again, as I kept my eyes fixed firmly to the floor, unable to make eye contact with her.

This is for the best, Rach. If Pippa did it then it's better for her—not to mention you—that she comes clean now. And it's better that you take a step back. Your interfering is only making matters worse.

But as I slumped down on the sofa, Pippa now taking my place in the police car, I couldn't quite manage to convince myself.

As I stared at the blank TV in front of me, I kept thinking about one thing.

You know those detectives on Criminal Point, the ones who got too close to the case, took it all too personally, and had to be removed? Most of the time, they ended up being right.

Chapter 7

"Pippa?" I called out gently, flicking on the light in the living room. Her spot on the sofa was empty.

Swallowing, I shuffled to the kitchen and boiled some water. I was going to need a strong cup of tea if I was going to get through the day that lay ahead. And I was going to need something solid in my stomach.

I opened the fridge. Apart from my plate of brownies, the only items in there were one solitary egg and a quarter of a carton of sour milk.

Brownies weren't going to cut it, and the milk may actually give *me* food poisoning. I slammed the door shut and grabbed my keys, deciding to risk it. I was going to have one of Deena's breakfast sandwiches.

I was trapped in line behind half a dozen tradesmen in overalls and woolen caps, waiting for their bacon and eggs and cups of Deena's terrible, burnt-tasting coffee.

At least her business seemed to have picked up.

I glanced over my shoulder at my bakery, the front of which was just visible outside the window. There was no one lining up to get in there.

"Rachael!" Deena said, beaming at me. "I'm so glad to see you. I didn't like how we left things yesterday."

I held my hands up in a show of mercy. "I'm just here for a breakfast sandwich," I said, nodding towards the sandwich press. "You got any double egg, single bacon sandwiches?"

She shook her head. "No, but I can make one for you."

"That would be great. Extra butter, please."

The rush of tradesmen ended as I leaned against the wall and yawned, keeping an eye on the press. Deena was watching me carefully and she kept opening her mouth and then shutting it again as if she was going to say something to me and then changed her mind.

"Hey, Rachael," she said, lowering her voice as she leaned in to whisper to me. "I was thinking about our conversation yesterday, when you were asking me all those questions about the street fair—and Colleen."

"Deena," I said, interrupting her. "I'm not sticking my nose into that anymore. I never should have in the first place. I apologize for asking you all those questions yesterday, it wasn't my place to do so."

"Oh." Deena's face fell a little. "It's just that..."

I pointed to the sandwich press. "That's burning, Deena."

"Oh!" She hopped over to the press and pulled out the sandwich. It was only a little charred on the sides but I could see that the eggs were now well done, while I prefer the yolk a little runny.

"Oh dear," Deena said. "I have a real habit of doing that."

"It's okay," I said, seeing her crestfallen face. "A little barbecue sauce will fix it up, if you've got some."

Out in front of the shop, I leaned against the wall for a moment, applying my sachet of barbecue sauce while some tradesmen—painters, by the looks of their overalls—loitered beside me.

"She's always burning these darn things," one of them complained, a younger man in pale blue overalls, who shook his head.

"Come on, man, give her a break. She's been having a tough time ever since that woman left those awful reviews online. It really ruined her business."

"Excuse me," I said, butting in. I gave both the men my biggest, cheesiest grin. "Sorry, I couldn't help overhearing. I think Deena's food is great, some of the best I've ever eaten!" A lie. "I can't imagine why someone would ever give her a bad review. When was this?"

The younger man shrugged. "It was about a month or so back now, a bunch of really bad reviews in a row, but Deena reckons they were all from the same woman. Some woman with a grudge against her."

"Do you happen to know the woman's name?" I asked, trying not to sound too eager to know the answer.

"Sorry, love, no idea." Both men chucked their half-eaten sandwiches into the trash before strolling off to their waiting van, leaving me to wonder: did I really need to butt out of this case? Or was overhearing this a sign that I should ignore Jackson, and follow my own gut after all?

***

There were several review sites online that the men could have been talking about, but by far the most popular, and influential, was Trip Advisor—the same site that brought me my floods of tourists. Or, used to, anyway.

But it had been a while since I'd scoped out the reviews of my local competitors. Back when I'd first opened the bakery, I used to spend hours every day getting lost in all the reviews—checking my own, checking Bakermatic's, then checking for any recent reviews for the other restaurants and cafes near the bakery, making sure my ranking hadn't slipped. But I soon figured out that it was a giant time suck, and that my time could be better spent improving my own baking, my own recipes, and my own business.

So it must have been at least two or three months since I'd even looked at the reviews for Deena's Sandwiches.

Frowning, I sat down in front of my laptop with another strong cup of tea and saw that Deena's average rating had dropped to 2.1 out of 5. Ouch. Last time I'd checked, it had been at least a 4. What on earth had happened?

Scrolling down, I quickly got my answer. There was a spate of reviews all from the same week, all with very similar comments, all giving Deena's Sandwiches 1 star out of 5. Even though all the reviews had different usernames besides them, it was clear from the wording and the fact that the same complaints kept being repeated over and over again that this was one person operating under a dozen different sock puppet accounts.

"The worst food I have ever tasted in my life!"

"This food made me sick to my stomach. I have been throwing up for the past 48 hours!"

"Never eat here! That is a warning that you dismiss at your own peril."

I sat back and thought about Carl getting sick from one of Deena's sandwiches earlier that week. I was grateful now that I'd thrown my sandwich in the bin after a few bites of the rubbery egg and burned bacon.

But was this person telling the truth? Had Deena's food really made them sick? Or were they just trying to slander Deena's name and reputation?

There was no picture next to the usernames and every time I clicked on the username, it always showed that the 'reviewer' had only left the one review. It was clearly someone who wanted to remain anonymous. It was also someone who was clearly nasty and had a vendetta out against Deena's shop. Someone antagonistic enough to come back again and again, who wanted Deena, and everyone else, to know just how unhappy they were.

And I knew just the kind of person who would do that.

Colleen Batters.

***

The door opened and then closed with an angry thud, causing me to jump out of my seat.

"Pippa, come and have a look at this! Come look what I've found out."

I could hear Pippa throw her keys down on the bench before she slowly walked into the spare room I used as an office. She had a scowl on her mouth and a face like thunder.

"What have you found?" she asked in a low growl. Far from the usual perky, high-pitched voice she normally used.

"Pippa, what's wrong?"

She let out a snort of disbelief. "What the heck do you think is wrong? I've been down at the police station, Rachael! They think I gave Colleen the fish pie that killed her! And where have you been all day?"

"Sleuthing" I said with smile, attempting to put her in a good mood. "I was on my way to the station to find you, really I was, but then I stumbled across this new information. Pippa, where are you going?"

She stormed out of the room as I chased after her. "Pippa, please, don't be like this!"

She spun around. "How do you expect me to be, Rachael?! You're the one who told that detective that I was working at Carl's that day! How could you?"

I held my hand up. "Hey. You're the one who kept that from me, Pippa. I'm the one who ought to be mad at you! You knew I was being blamed for Colleen's death, and you kept this from me? When it could have helped me?"

Pippa looked away as the anger drained from her face slightly. "That night when I got home, you didn't want to talk about it," she mumbled. "Besides, I wasn't supposed to go mouthing off about it or Carl could get into trouble. I know how seriously you take proper business procedures. I knew you'd ask me if I got paid properly, if I got my regular meal breaks."

I sighed. "Fine. Whatever Pippa. So you're telling me that you didn't keep quiet because you knew you might be a suspect?"

Guilt crept onto Pippa's face. "I dunno, Rach. Maybe." Her head was still hanging, like a puppy that has been scolded for going to the bathroom on the kitchen floor. "I'm sorry, I should have been honest with you, I should have told you I was there." She lifted her head and I saw how tired her eyes were. "But I honestly didn't see anything that day that could have helped."

"Think, Pips. You didn't see Colleen Batters at all? There are witnesses who saw her eating a fish pie from your stall."

Pippa rolled her eyes. "You sound like the cops. I don't even know what this Colleen Batters looks like! Maybe I served her, maybe I didn't." Pippa threw her hands up in the air. "Who knows!"

"It's okay," I said, patting her arm. "Don't worry about that now. I'll get you some tea."

"But I am worried about it, Rachael. The cops think I'm guilty."

"They think everyone is guilty," I pointed out. "That's their job. Look, I've got something that might make you feel a little better."

"You do?"

"Follow me."

Pippa flopped down on the bed in the spare room after she'd read through all the reviews and I told her what I'd overheard about Deena. "Don't you see, Pips? Deena had the perfect motive to murder Colleen. She was ruining her business."

Pippa sat up. "Yeah, but she said Colleen didn't eat from her stall that day."

"Of course she would say that. But she's been losing business for months, not just this week like the rest of us. Sure, she's been a little hurt by Bakermatic, but..."

Pippa let out a little laugh.

"What?"

"It's just the first time I've heard you mention Bakermatic in a while. Usually you're obsessed with them. Are you finally willing to admit that they may not be the bad guys?"

"Hey, they're still the bad guys. Let me be very clear on that. But maybe Jackson was right. Detective Whitaker, I mean. Maybe I was too focused, too biased. Now that I've taken a step back, I think the real suspect has become a lot more obvious."

Chapter 8

"Can I speak to Detective Whitaker, please?"

"He's not at the station right now," a bored voice on the other end of the line said. "Is this an emergency?"

"Not exactly an emergency."

"Well, is it or isn't it?"

"I'll call back later."

Pippa was looking at me expectantly as I ended the call. "What happened?"

"He's not there." I let out a sigh. "Even if he was, I don't think he'd want to listen to anything I have to say. He thinks I'm obsessed with blaming Bakermatic. He probably won't even listen to my new theory now. I'm like the girl who cried wolf."

"Well, you *were* a little obsessed with Bakermatic," Pippa said teasingly.

"I know. And look, I still haven't completely crossed them off my list. But, if Deena is to blame, then I'm willing to accept that. I still think Bakermatic should be closed down, though."

"Come on," Pippa said, grabbing my arm. "Speaking of the devil, I need to go down there to pick up my paycheck from the day I worked there. And you're coming with me."

Despite my groans and protests, I somehow managed to end up in front of Bakermatic's sickly yellow shop front. "I'm not coming inside, though," I insisted, arms crossed.

"Yes, you are," Pippa said. "Come on, I don't want to face Simona on my own. You owe me at least this, Rachael."

I sighed. "Fine. Let's just get this over with."

Expecting to have to wade through an avalanche of customers, like usual, I was shocked to find that Bakermatic was almost empty, like a pastel yellow desert. "What's going on?" I spun around as Pippa shrugged at me.

"Haven't you heard?" Both Pippa and I stopped at the sound of Simona's voice. She was holding a broom, clutching it like it was a weapon and we were her prey. "Word's got out that Colleen's death was no accident. She was poisoned." Simona banged the broom on the ground and began a slow, angry sweep. "So I guess that means we're all screwed now." She shot me a low scowl.

"No thanks to you."

"No thanks to me?" I asked. "You're the one who has been trying to make me look guilty!"

"Because you are," she snapped, holding the broom up straight as anger flashed in her eyes. "I'm going to lose my job if things don't pick up," she said, taking an ominous step towards me.

"Maybe we should leave," Pippa whispered, tugging at my sleeve.

"Yeah, you ought to," Simona snapped. "Before I call the cops on you."

"No," I said firmly. "Pippa needs her money. We're not leaving until we get it."

Simona let out a laugh that was so giddy it almost amounted to a giggle. "What, for that one day you managed to last here, before you screwed it up?"

"Yes," Pippa said, crossing her arms. "I worked for that money, and maybe it would be cool if I was rich enough to just let it go. Believe me, I certainly never wanted to see your face again, but I need that hundred bucks."

Simona shrugged and dropped the broom. "Whatever. Wait here while I go to my office."

"Well, this is humiliating," Pippa said as we waited for Simona to come back with the paycheck.

"At least we get to see Bakermatic empty of customers," I pointed out. "I'm quite enjoying the sight."

"Rachael, look," Pippa said, grabbing my arms. She spun me around so that I was looking out the window.

"What the heck is Deena doing?" I asked, crouching down a little so that I was out of her line of sight should she look around. "Pippa, get down," I whispered, pulling her after me.

We both watched as Deena crept up to the front of Carl's Fish shop and glanced around before pressing her face against the glass of the window.

"What is she looking for?"

I shook my head. "She's probably heard the news that Colleen's death was no accident and realizes it's only a matter of time before she is arrested. She's probably getting desperate."

Carl came rushing out of his shop, startling Deena, and they had an argument before she scurried off, leaving a puff of flour in her wake.

"What are you two doing?"

Pippa and I both bumped our heads on the table as

we jumped up at the sound of Simona's voice.

"Still creeping around, I see." Simona held the check towards Pippa and told us to get out.

"Why?" Pippa said. "You don't seem exactly rushed off your feet with customers."

As I saw Simona's face fall, I actually felt kind of bad for her. I understood the feeling, and even though Simona didn't own Bakermatic (she would have been quite far down the food chain in the grand scheme of things) it still sucked to feel responsible for a business that was failing.

"Hey," I said to Pippa gently. "Don't go rubbing it in."

Simona looked up at me in surprise. "I thought you'd be the first to revel in this business's failures." A note of bitterness crept into her voice. "I thought you'd be dancing on our graves."

"I just know how it feels, that's all." I sighed. "If I did have anything to do with it., well, I'm sorry."

Pippa's mouth was wide open.

Simona held my gaze for a long moment then shrugged. "It's not just you," she admitted. "In fact, it's not just the Colleen Batters thing either. We had all these bad reviews on line in the past couple of days, saying that our food made all these people sick."

Pippa and I turned and looked at each other.

"Hang on," I said. "What do you mean, 'all these people'?"

Simona frowned. "There's a bunch of different reviewers. But they're all saying the same thing."

"Do you have a computer in here? Can I take a look at it?" I asked, already walking towards Simona's office. I knew where it was, after all.

"Er, sure," Simona said, chasing after me.

"Here we go." Simona pointed over my shoulder as she showed me all the reviews on Trip Advisor.

"Oh my gosh," I said, glancing over the comments.

"Stay away from this place!"

"Ignore my warnings at your own peril!"

"This place will make you sick—or worse!"

The same syntax as the reviews left on Deena's Sandwiches all those months ago.

All the user reviews had been posted in the past two days. I turned to face Pippa. "Don't you see, Pippa? These were all posted this week. Meaning, after Colleen died."

Pippa nodded, a grave look coming over her face. "That means they can't have been posted by Colleen."

"And neither could those comments on Deena's Sandwiches. Colleen isn't the mystery reviewer."

There was a flash of dread in Pippa's eyes. "Then who is?"

***

"Come on," Pippa said, "You can call Detective Handsome later. It's not like you've got anything solid to tell him anyway."

"But I'm starting to piece this all together, Pippa. I think I should tell him what I've learned." I pulled my phone out of my pocket and began tapping in the number for the Belldale Police Station again.

"It can wait five minutes, can't it?" Pippa asked as we crossed the road. "I need you for moral support again when we go to Carl's."

"What for?" I asked, pulling the phone away from my ear. "Didn't you get paid by him already? It was cash under the table, right?"

Pippa nodded a little as she rolled her eyes. "Yeah, but he only had half the cash for me that day and told me to drop by any time and collect the rest. I've been putting it off because of everything that happened, wondering if he'd throw it in my face if he saw me again!" She took a deep breath. "But I'm feeling brave since I faced Simona, so I'm gonna do it now!"

I nodded. "Right you are, Pips. You should get what you're owed. Let's go!" I said brightly, pushing the door open to Carl's, expecting to find another wasteland. But the place was bustling with customers and Pippa and I had to squeeze past them as we tried to make our way to the counter.

"Hey, no cutting!" one angry young man with a sleeve of tattoos yelled at us.

"We're not cutting in line!" I said back to him. "We're not ordering any food, just calm down."

He scoffed. "Well, you ought to, it's the only place around here that's safe to eat at."

Carl's eyebrows shot up as he saw Pippa approaching the counter. "What are you doing here?" he scowled.

"I need the thirty bucks you owe me from the street fair," Pippa said boldly.

Carl shook his head. "You've got some nerve coming in asking for that."

"If you don't give it to me then I'll have to tell the authorities that you paid me off the books that day." She nodded towards the rest of the staff. "And that you avoid paying taxes on your regular employees' wages as well."

Carl scowled at her. "Well, I'm run off my feet here at the moment, missy. You're going to have to go out the back and wait."

"Can't you just take it out of the till?"

"Out the back!"

Pippa sighed and I told her it was okay as we stepped out the back door to wait until the rush was over. There was a strong fishy smell in the lane and I wished we'd just left and come back later. But I knew that Pippa might not have the nerve to come back again if we left now.

I tried to ignore the smell, bopping up and down a little to try and keep warm. I took my phone out of my pocket.

According to the receptionist, Jackson still wasn't at the police station. I sighed and asked if I could leave a message then. "Tell him to please call Rachael Robinson back. No, I don't want to leave any further details. Thank you." I shivered and shoved the phone away again.

Still no sign of Carl.

"Why didn't Carl have the money to pay you the other day anyway?" I asked Pippa.

Pippa titled her head. "Apparently, the business has been suffering for a long while. They were a bit strapped for cash that day and they'd only be able to pay me half of it. I mean, whatever, I needed the job so I didn't argue with them." Pippa started hopping from foot to foot. "I hope he's actually going to give me the cash today."

I nodded towards the full shop. "Doesn't look like he has a problem with cash right now. I think you'll be fine."

Pippa let out a short laugh. "Yeah, he seems to be the only shop on the street who doesn't have a problem with bad reviews."

Pippa stopped talking as we stared at each other.

"Pippa," I said, realizing something. "How come Carl recognized you when you came into the shop?"

"What do you mean? I've met him before. At the street fair. He's the one who told me to come and collect the cash!"

I swallowed. "He told me he wasn't at the street fair. That he'd been suffering food poisoning after eating one of Deena's sandwiches."

Pippa let out a little laugh of disbelief. "I don't think anyone could ever get sick from one of Deena's sandwiches! She overcooks them all to the point that not even the strongest of bacteria would be able to survive!"

"You're right," I murmured. "Yet she got all those bad reviews a few months ago."

I glanced over my shoulder at Carl, who was eyeing us carefully. "Pippa, I think we ought to get out of here," I said, pulling her towards the door.

"What? Why? I need to get my cash."

"We have to go," I whispered to her. "Deena isn't the one who killed Colleen. And her food's never made anyone sick, unless they are allergic to charcoal."

"What are you saying, Rachael?"

I kept one eye steady on Carl as I began to plan our escape. "I'm saying, Pippa, that we need to get out of here, right now! Or losing thirty bucks is going to be the least of your problems, or mine."

Chapter 9

The back door slammed shut behind Carl as he stomped into the alleyway after us. The stench of fish had become almost unbearable.

"Just where are you two going then?" Carl asked us, focusing first on me, then on Pippa. "Don't you want your money?"

Pippa clutched her purse close to her as she took a step backwards. "Um, no you know what, I just realized that there's somewhere else I really need to be. I can come back for the money some other time, since you're so busy." She tried to step in front of Carl as he cut her off. He was a bull now and Pippa was the red flag. I could practically see his nostrils flaring as he closed in on poor Pippa, who was inching closer and closer towards the brick wall of the alley.

Carl kept switching his gaze between Pippa and me. "I didn't realize you two were so cozy," he growled menacingly. "This certainly makes things interesting."

At the last moment before she was about to hit the wall, Pippa tripped over a box of old discarded fish guts and bones, shrieking as she went over backwards, her backside landing in the pungent materials.

"Pippa!" I ran over to her but Carl grabbed me by the collar of my peacoat. "I think you girls better come with me." He reached down and snatched Pippa up as well, dragging us both to what looked like a small shed at the end of the alley.

He stopped before he reached the door and I thought for a moment that we were saved, that he had realized that throwing two young women into a shed was insane. "Carl, please, this is only going to make things worse for you," I reasoned with him, thinking he already knew that and he was ready to agree and let us go.

But instead, he reached into my coat pocket and grabbed my phone.

"Yours too," he said to Pippa, holding out his hand as she placed her cell there with trembling fingers.

"Get in here!" Carl said, shoving us into the small building with a strength I'd never have guessed he possessed. He shut the door and suddenly we were engulfed in darkness.

"Hey!" Pippa said, banging on the wooden door. "What do you think you're doing?"

Carl's muffled voice travelled through from the other side of the door. "I'm making sure you can't cause any more trouble! Or talk to the cops. Ever again."

We heard the sound of a lock turning and then Carl's footsteps walking away.

"Help us!" Pippa called out, banging on the door. "Carl, you can't keep us in here!"

"It's no use," another voice called out, causing Pippa and I to both jump out of our skins.

"Deena?" I asked, squinting in the dark. If only Carl hadn't taken our phones, we might have had a flashlight.

And a way to phone for help.

I heard Deena groan and as my eyes adjusted, I could see that she was bleeding from a cut on the top of her head, blood inching towards her eyes. "My gosh, Deena, what did Carl do to you?"

"Nothing," Deena said, shaking her head. "Well, he threw me in here, so not exactly nothing, but I hit my head once I was already in here. I can't see a darn thing since Carl took my phone!"

"But why did he lock you in here?" Pippa asked.

Deena shook her head again. "I was just coming by to get some money that Carl owed me."

I heard Pippa let out a scoff.

"But he didn't answer the front door, so I pressed my face up against the window," Deena continued. "That's when I saw him, on his laptop, and guess what he was doing?"

I shook my head and tried to catch Pippa's eye in the dark. "I don't think we need to guess," I said. "Writing bad reviews?"

Deena nodded. "Writing a bad review of *my* shop, no less. I thought those days of a hundred one star reviews were all behind me! Business had just started to pick up again! I thought it was a disgruntled customer who'd made all those reviews. I never in a million years would have thought a competitor was writing them!"

"You're too trusting, Deena," I told her. "What happened after Carl saw you?"

"He came running out the door after me, chasing me down the street."

I sighed. "We saw the argument from Bakermatic," I told her. "Sorry, Deena, I never thought he would lock you up. I thought it was just a simple argument amongst neighbors."

"You don't have to apologize. We're all in the same

boat now, after all. But, Rachael, my dear! What are we going to do?" Now that my eyes had adjusted to the darkness, I could see the terror forming in Deena's. "Is he going to do to us what he did to Colleen?"

I gulped. "Not if I have anything to do about it," I told her with a confidence I didn't actually feel.

***

Pippa leaned against the wall, knocking over a mop that had been standing upright against it.

"I can't believe this is happening," Pippa said. "Rach, how long do we have before Carl comes back for us?"

I loved that she thought I knew. "Let's just hope that rush hour in the shop lasts a little longer."

I glanced over at Deena, who was slumped against the floor. "Deena?" I knelt down and give her a gentle tap on the face. "Deena, you need to keep your eyes open! You need to stay awake!" I looked up at Pippa. "We need to get her out of here."

"We all need to get of here," Pippa pointed out. "Or we're all dead."

I checked Deena's pulse before I stood up. She was still alive—for now. "Well, you got any ideas?"

She didn't answer. "Pippa?"

"Sorry, Rachael. I was just thinking about something that happened on the day of the fair. Oh, Rachael, this is all my fault," Pippa whispered.

"Pippa, what are you talking about?"

"I didn't think anything of it at the time," Pippa said, her voice getting more high pitched with every word. "I thought we were just innocently chatting."

"Pippa, just tell me what you did."

Pippa gulped. "It's just that we weren't selling many products and Carl started grumbling that Bakermatic was taking all the customers from all the other stalls with their free promo giveaways."

"Well, they were," I said with some indignation, before I realized I was defending a killer. "Go on."

"So I mentioned that it seemed like everyone hated Bakermatic and I sorta mentioned that you did specifically, considering that you sell almost the same products," Pippa said. "Oh my goodness, Rachael, I'm so sorry. I didn't say we were close friends or anything, but I was telling Carl about how Bakermatic was stealing all your customers and undercutting your prices, and that you were having trouble making rent."

I sighed. I think I could see what happened next. "It's okay, Pippa," I tried to say.

She kept talking. "Carl was listening really intently, kept saying, 'well, isn't that interesting.' Then a woman walked by with a piece of your cherry pie in her hand. I recognized it, of course, as it's my favorite. It might have been Colleen Batters. I never met the woman before! But she threw your cake away before she'd even had a bite. I remember thinking that was very rude. And then Carl quickly asked me to take the trash over to one of the dumpsters, like he was trying to get rid of me. I remember being put out by the request because I wanted to tell the woman off for throwing one of your cakes away."

"So you didn't see what happened next?"

Pippa frowned, deep in concentration. "Once I'd returned back from the dumpster, she was already gone." Pippa suddenly gasped. "But I do remember him grinning like a lunatic afterwards, and, Rachael, that's when he took off. I never saw him again after that for the rest of the day."

"Hmm, must be when he got 'sick'," I said, putting

finger quotes around the 'sick' despite the fact that it was too dark for Pippa to see me properly.

Pippa's voice was full of guilt. "I'm sorry, Rachael. He must have heard me talking about you and Bakermatic and decided to take advantage of the fact that Colleen had one of your pies, knowing that you were under stress financially and would be one of the top suspects. I didn't know that she was Colleen Batters, the woman who had been making all your lives hell."

"She did annoy all of us, that's true," I said. "But I never wanted to kill Colleen! Well, I suppose sometimes I *did*, but I never would have actually done it. I'm sure Deena felt the same way."

A groaning sound came from the ground and I was relieved to discover that Deena was still conscious. "Carl was in deep debt," she said, trying to sit up.

"Deena, don't move suddenly," I scolded her. "Just hold tight until..."

"Until what?" Pippa whispered. "How are we going to get out of here?"

Deena didn't heed my warning and kept talking. "He was getting more and more desperate all the time, cutting corners, not paying staff properly, even borrowing money from me, as I told you." Deena pulled herself to her feet. "A few months ago, when things were really bad for him, he agreed to do an interview for Colleen's food blog."

I rolled my eyes. I remembered Colleen's promise to review my black forest on her blog. I guess that never happened.

"She promised Carl that it was going to be a positive review, but then she ripped him apart, gave him one star, and things just got worse for Carl from there on." Deena let out a loud sigh. "I thought it was Carl I saw painting 'Killer' on your store front. I couldn't be sure, but I did think it was him at the time."

"That's why you said 'he' when we were talking about it," I said, realizing.

"Rachael, all of this is what I was trying to tell you when you came to see me yesterday. But you said you'd given up investigating."

"So he decided the best way to right his business was to follow Colleen's lead and give every business in the area a bunch of bad reviews. And then, when the opportunity presented itself to get revenge on Colleen, I guess he took it. I'm sorry, Deena. I should have listened to you. Maybe I'm not so great at this detective stuff after all."

Deena shook her head. "No, you *are* good at it. You figured out it was Carl, even without my help. You just shouldn't have stopped, that was the problem."

Pippa reached out and gripped my arm. "Rach, can you hear that?"

I nodded. "Footsteps."

I glanced around the closet. "Okay, you take this," I said to Pippa, handing her a block of wood.

"What are you going to take?" Pippa asked frantically.

I took off my red peacoat. "I'll wrap this around his neck, and you hit him with that. You ready?"

"No?!"

The lock turned swiftly and suddenly bright sunlight streamed into my eyes as I stumbled back into the closet, blindly throwing my coat at the body there. "Go on, Pippa, hit him!" I shouted.

"I wouldn't do that if I was you, ma'am," a deep voice boomed. "Or you'll be guilty of assaulting a police officer."

"Jackson?" My eyes adjusted to the sunlight and I threw my arms around his neck as Pippa looked on with her mouth wide open.

"Ahem, sorry," I said, pulling away. "Not sure what came over me then. I'm just glad to see you Jackson—I mean, Detective Whitaker—I'm really glad to see you right now."

He grinned at me. "It's okay, 'Jackson' is fine under the circumstances. Are you ladies all right?"

I stood back and allowed him to take a look at Deena, while Pippa and I were helped outside by a pair of uniformed police officers.

"I got your message," Jackson said once he'd finished with Deena. "I knew something was wrong. I tried your bakery first, then Bakermatic, then they told me you'd come here. One of the customers told us that they'd seen Carl pulling you and Pippa down the alleyway. But we didn't know about Deena."

I glanced over my shoulder as one of the paramedics attended to Deena. "I'm sure glad she's okay," I mentioned to Jackson, as he reached over to adjust the blanket on my shoulders, which someone must have given me at some point.

"I have to admit, I'm glad you're okay," Jackson said. "We've suspected Carl right from the start and when I saw that paint on your bakery the other day."

"I know, I know," I said. "Carl did it. That's why you

came to check on me. You thought I was in danger."

Jackson nodded. Checking first that no one was watching, he reached out and gently squeezed my arm. "That's why I told you to stop snooping around. To let us do our jobs. Not because I didn't think you were any good at it, but because this is exactly what I was worried would happen."

I looked up at him. "I assume you've arrested Carl. But do you know that he was writing fake reviews for all the businesses in this neighborhood? About the fact he underpays his employees, or doesn't pay them at all?"

Jackson shook his head. "No, we didn't know about any of that. I have to admit, your snooping will help put him away. Not to mention the fact that we can get him on a bunch of other charges now." Jackson raised an eyebrow.

I smiled at him. "When do you get off duty, Jackson? Can I perhaps interest you in another one of my brownies?"

Jackson looked over his shoulder again before turning back to me. "Sounds great, and I would love to sample one of your many treats, but I'm afraid, for the time being, that will have to be as a customer only—at least until this case is wrapped up. I hope I can trust you not to get involved in any police matters in the future, Miss Robinson."

Jackson shot me a wink before he began to walk away.

"I can't quite go promising that just yet, Detective Whitaker," I said quietly, once I was sure he was out of earshot.

I walked back over to Pippa, who was standing there, grinning at me from ear to ear.

"What was that all about?" she asked, punching me in the arm.

"I don't know what you're talking about," I replied coyly.

Pippa laughed and grabbed my shoulders, looking me square in the face. "You get in a lot of trouble, Rachael. Are you sure you want a cop following you around on a regular basis?"

She was right. But maybe it wouldn't be so bad if that cop was Jackson Whitaker.

Epilogue

I cleared my throat. "Ahem. I would like to welcome to Rachael's Boutique Bakery, our newest member of staff: Pippa McDonald!"

I clapped as Pippa spun around and bowed to the crowd of one. Placing the pink apron over her head proudly, I said, "I can finally afford to have an employee, now that business is booming again. And I couldn't be more pleased that my first employee is my best friend in the whole world."

The smile on Pippa's face faded a little. "Oh, Rach, are you sure? I hope I don't screw things up for you."

I placed my hands on Pippa's shoulders. "You're going to do fine."

We both spun around as a person wearing a yellow polyester shirt walked sheepishly through the door. "I just wanted to wish you guys good luck on your reopening," Simona said, before pulling something out from behind her back.

She handed me the basket of muffins. "It's a good will gesture," she explained. "I was hoping in the future our stores could work together, rather than competing all the time. After all, you did help to clear our name as well. And you got all those fake negative reviews removed from online."

I smiled at her. Even though I had no intention of eating those prepackaged cakes, I did appreciate her extending the olive branch.

She turned to face Pippa. "And Pippa, even though you were a terrible employee, I wish you good luck in your new job." Simona shot me a look before she walked out the door. "You too. You're gonna need it."

We both stopped and stared, watching Simona's ponytail bounce behind her as she walked down the street.

"Hey," I said, turning to Pippa. "What was up with that red paint on Simona's hands that day?"

Pippa's mouth dropped open. "You know what? I don't know. Maybe she was throwing red paint at her ex-boyfriend's car or something? Or, maybe, she was the one who did it."

I glanced up at the spot on the window where the paint had been. Even though it had been well scrubbed a dozen times, I could have sworn I still saw a pink sheen to it. "After all, Deena was never one hundred percent sure it was Carl she saw that day."

"I guess we'll never know if we can ever really trust Bakermatic," I said, setting the gift basket down on the floor behind the counter. "But I've got bigger things to worry about now." I leaned against the counter and pondered as Pippa starting piling a tray high with glossy donuts.

"I'm starting to wonder, Pippa, if this should be my new calling."

She glanced up at me, a donut stuck on the end of her tongs. "What, running a bakery?" she asked.

"No!" I said, laughing as I stuck my tongue out at her. "I mean, solving mysteries."

"The Bakery Detectives," Pippa laughed.

I nodded. "The Bakery Detectives."

Donuts, Antiques and Murder

Chapter 1

Blood red jam seeped out as I pressed down on the pastry, causing it to drip from the center of the donut.

The smell of fresh cinnamon sugar sprinkled all over the donut hit my nose. *I need to taste test it for the good of the business,* I justified to myself before I popped the soft, warm donut in my mouth. *Mmm.*

I started coughing and Pippa had to thump my back as the first customers of the day started to pour into my shop, Rachael's Boutique Bakery. I straightened up and put on my brightest smile, my eyes still watering from my near-choke-experience. It probably served me right. I looked down at the trays of jam donuts and then at the line of early bird customers. We'd be lucky if we had enough to last the morning rush.

One after another they came, flooding the shop and making my heart leap for joy. Only a few months earlier I had thought my poor little bakery was going to perish, but now it was flourishing more than ever before.

Only one little teeny tiny problem: success can lead to complacency. Worse than that, it can lead to boredom.

My fingers were itching, and not just to knead dough, but to solve a mystery.

"Oi!" Pippa reached over and gave me a playful shove. "Stop daydreaming about solving mysteries!" Her hair was bright blue this month and it was often a talking point for customers when they came into the shop. "It's blueberry," she would say with a wink, before trying to sell them one of our fresh blueberry muffins. At least she was creative.

"I'm not," I said, standing up quickly, embarrassed. "That's all in the past. I'm one hundred percent focused on the bakery now."

Pippa shot me a skeptical look as a lock of bright blue hair fell into her eyes. "Doesn't look that way to me." She took off her apron, the morning rush over, and began to count the money in the cash register, one of her new tasks as assistant manager. "Besides," she said with a cheeky lift of her brow. "You know I've got plenty of real mysteries for you to solve, if you're into paranormal stuff."

I groaned. "I wouldn't call those 'real' mysteries, Pippa. I wish you'd stop hanging out with those people." I couldn't care less about hunting cryptoids or chasing ghosts, or whatever it was that Pippa and her new friends were into. I'd had a taste of the real thing; solved a real life murder. And, although I've never wish for harm to fall on anyone, I couldn't help missing the rush that had come with being an amateur detective. Belldale had been quiet—and, yes, boring—for the past two months.

"Our best morning yet!" Pippa announced with glee as she pushed the register closed again. "A new record."

We high-fived and I grinned.

Sure, solving mysteries was fun, but it didn't put money in the bank. The bakery did. I had to remember that.

Besides, a new record day meant I could finally take the plunge and do something even more exciting than solving a murder mystery.

I took a deep breath and followed Pippa over to an empty table as she took her break. I let her eat anything she liked on break and today she had chosen a Danish pastry.

"Guess what, Pippa?" I sat across from her, too

excited to eat anything as I readied myself to tell her the exciting news.

I could see her mind already starting to work as she looked up at the ceiling and poked her tongue out of the corner of her mouth.

"Hmm, you're finally going on a date with Detective Whitaker!"

"Pippa! No! Don't be silly."

"Well, has he called you yet?"

"Pippa...no...that doesn't matter. That's not my news and I wouldn't be excited about it if it were. Keep guessing."

She put her Danish down and chewed on it, still pondering.

"You've found another mystery to solve? Is that it? I know that would make you excited."

I shook my head. "That's not it."

She threw her hands in the air and said she was ready to give up. "Besides, cookies need to come out of the oven," she said, hurrying over to the oven to pull out the tray before she gave one last wild guess. "You've won the lottery?"

"Nope!" I said, pleased that she hadn't guessed. "Pippa, we're expanding the bakery. I'm purchasing the antiques shop next door!"

The tray of cookies she was carrying crashed to the ground.

Not exactly the reaction I was hoping for. Was she happy? Excited? Her wide eyes said otherwise.

"Rachael," Pippa whispered as she gripped the collar of my shirt. "You can't purchase the antiques shop!" Her face was as white as a ghost.

"Pippa!" I shook her off and brushed at my shirt. "Why-ever not? I thought you would be pleased for me? For us." Pippa had a...let's just say 'issue' keeping a job longer than a week. Her tenure at my bakery, two months now, was the longest she had ever stayed at a job. I thought she would be thrilled to know that she had secure employment in a blossoming business.

"I'm pleased that the bakery is successful." Pippa stopped and glanced over her shoulder in the direction of the antiques shop, as though she could see through the brick wall. She shook her head slowly. "But you can't buy the shop next door." She turned back to face me, her eyes still as wide as pies.

"Rachael, that place is haunted."

I scoffed. "Oh, come on, Pippa. I know you believe a lot of outlandish things, but this is too much."

"Rachael!" Her voice was high and indignant. "You must have heard the rumors."

I walked back to the counter in a little bit of a huff. I felt as though Pippa was raining on my parade. "No, I haven't heard any rumors." I shot Pippa a look. "But I don't really frequent the same places you do."

I was talking about the Belldale Haunted House tour and the Belldale Paranormal Club. Pippa had recently joined and had attended several of their tours, which took place after dark and involved dragging locals and tourists alike around Belldale's 'most haunted' locations. Pippa had come back to our apartment following these tours and given me several breathless accounts of how amazing and eye-opening they were, while I tried to listen with a straight face.

Pippa let out a deep sigh. "Well, yes, the haunted house tour *was* very informative when it came to the antiques shop."

"Pippa, that whole tour is just a scam to get money. It's a bit of entertainment. You can't take the stories too seriously, and you can't let them impact a business decision."

"But the rumors have been around for way longer than the tour has been running!" Pippa caught my skeptical expression and lowered her voice. "You know that painting that's been sitting in the corner for years—the one of the young girl and boy."

I swallowed. I knew the one she meant. A large watercolor in a bronze frame of a pair of children, painted like they were in the 1940s, but cartoon like. Both children had been painted with large cartoon-like eyes that dwarfed their faces, and the eyes seemed to follow you. I always hurried past it, it gave me the creeps. The painting had been in the store, in the same place, in the front window, for as long as I could remember.

"What about it?" I picked up a cloth and began to wipe the tables, as though I wasn't really interested in what Pippa was saying, when actually I had my ears keenly pricked, waiting for her response.

"They say that painting is haunted. That's why it never sells. No one wants it in their home."

I stood up straight. "Well, that's the silliest thing I've ever heard." I shook my head. "That painting doesn't sell because it's over-priced. Not to mention ugly. Besides, the painting won't be there once I buy the store, none of the antiques will."

Pippa shook her head. "The rumors say that the boy and girl live in the painting..."

"The boy and girl are painted onto the canvas," I corrected her.

Pippa ignored me. "The story goes that they live in the shop. They've lived there for decades. That's why the painting never sells. They don't let anyone buy it. They can't be moved from their home. Rachael, if you buy the shop and try to get rid of the painting, then the children will be very upset. They will curse you."

I stood there staring at Pippa like she had gone out of her mind. "Okay, Pippa, that's a great story. But unfortunately, some of us have to live in reality. Some of us have a business to run."

"Rachael, I am warning you. If you buy that shop, and try to get rid of the painting, you will pay the price!"

***

I told Pippa I needed to run to the post office so that she wouldn't try to stop me, but as soon as I was out the door, I went off in the opposite direction, towards the mortgage firm where I was meeting the landlord of the antiques shop--a tall, thin man named Bruce who had a pencil thin mustache and eyebrows that always looked raised.

He pushed the contract over to me and I gave it a look over. "That should all be in order."

Yes, I decided. *This is the right time to do it. Time to take the plunge.*

"Great," I said, smiling at him. "I'll give it to my lawyer to look over, and then sign it. I should have it back to you by tomorrow."

"Tomorrow?" he asked nervously, his raised eyebrows disappearing even further up into his forehead. "Why can't you sign them now? I can assure you everything is in order."

I stood up as a show of confidence. "I just need to make sure everything is in place. Tomorrow will be fine, won't it? Not much can change by tomorrow!"

As soon as I stepped out of the bank, the heavens opened and I stared up at the sky, mouth agape, to find the sky, which had been a bright blue before I'd stepped into the bank, was now practically black, filled with angry swirling clouds that spewed icy rain all over the streets.

And I didn't even have an umbrella with me.

Using my purse as a shield over my head, I raced back to the bakery, cursing the fact that I hadn't looked at the weather forecast.

"It wasn't predicted by the weather weather man," Pippa informed me warily as I shook myself off, causing a small puddle to form in the entryway of the shop. "Where have you been?" She stopped frothing the milk for the cappuccino she was making and looked me up and down.

"I told you, the post office."

"The way to the post office is totally covered. You've been the other way."

Sprung.

"Okay, fine," I said with a sigh, pulling the contract out of my bag to show her.

"Oh, Rachael..." Her face was grave. "Aren't you going to listen to anything I told you?"

"Pippa, it will be fine. I can't be put off by a silly superstition."

She handed the contract back to me and crossed her arms. "It's more than that, Rachael." She shivered and looked up at the ceiling. "You've set events in motion now by taking that contract."

"I haven't signed it yet," I pointed out. Not that I believed anything she was going on about.

"That doesn't matter, Rachael. It will already be starting."

I sighed and took off my soaking wet red peacoat and hung it on a hook by the door. As I stepped back towards the counter I heard a snapping sound and heard my heavy coat fall to the floor, the hook taking off a chunk of paint and plaster with it as it tumbled after the coat.

"It's just an old hook, Pippa," I said, staring at it. "And the coat was heavy from the rain."

"I'm telling you..."

There was a crashing sound and all of a sudden we were encased in darkness. Outside, the sky was so dark that without lights in the shop, there was no light at all.

Pippa let out a shriek and rubbed her arms as though she had the worst case of the chills the world had ever seen.

"It's just a blown fuse, Pippa," I said, catching the gleam of the whites of her eyes. I could tell what she was thinking before she even said it. "Or a power line has come down in the storm. Calm down, Pippa. Think rationally."

"It's the curse, Rachael. It's already started."

Chapter 2

Curses were just going to have to wait. As soon as I had confirmation from my lawyer that I wasn't getting ripped off, all it required was my signature.

My hand hovered above the blank line. It wasn't Pippa's curse getting in my head. It was a different kind of fear. Fear of the unknown. Fear of failing.

It hadn't been that long ago that I'd thought my bakery was going to go under. Could I really take a risk like this? What if disaster struck again?

What if there really was a curse?

I shook myself off. That was the dumbest fear of them all. Trying not to let my worries get a second look in, I scrawled my name across the dotted line.

"There!" I said proudly. "Done." Now it was just a matter of handing it in. "See," I said out loud as I grabbed my coat. "I knew nothing would happen between yesterday and today."

Pippa was still fast asleep on the sofa. She had enough money now to afford her own place, but she'd said she'd gotten into the habit of sleeping there and was in no hurry to hunt for apartments yet and my sofa was a great rent saver. Truthfully, I thought the stories from the paranormal club had gotten to her and she was too scared to live alone but didn't want to admit it. Anyway, I didn't mind her living with me, I only wished I had a second bedroom. I glanced down at the contract, hot in my hands. All my extra funds had to go into the business for the time being, not into a bigger apartment.

"Come on, Pips, I can't wait for you forever," I called out.

Pippa lifted her head off the sofa and pouted with her arms crossed over her chest. "Well, you're going to have to. I'm not coming. I can't be a part of this curse."

I stood there with my mouth wide open. "What do you mean you're not coming? Thanks for the support, Pip. This is kind of a big deal for me, you know. I was counting on my friend for moral support."

A look of guilt interrupted Pippa's pout. She tossed the covers off and stood up with a sigh. "Fine. I will come with you to hand over the papers. But if anything spooky or scary happens, I am out of there."

"Nothing spooky or scary is going to happen, Pippa. Come on."

I had spoken far too soon.

"What the heck is going on down there?" Pippa stopped short in the middle of the street while I stood next to her, shivering and wanting to get a move on. There was a definite winter's chill in the air and I was keen to get indoors.

"Don't get distracted, Pippa. We've got to get to the antique shop."

Pippa pointed. "That's where all the fuss is, Rach. Look."

I stopped and looked towards where she pointed. In front of the antiques shop was a bunch of police vans, and the entire store had been taped off with police tape.

"What the..." I murmured. I began to hurry towards the shop, but Pippa grabbed my sleeve and pulled me back.

Please just let it be a break-in, I thought.

"Rach, I told you, if anything scary happens..."

"Pippa, I'm about to be the owner of that shop that is surrounded by police! I need to find out what is happening." I broke free of her grip and hurried towards the scene where I saw a familiar face.

"Detective Whitaker," I said, coming to a stop.

Uh-oh. If he was here, that meant it was serious. It was unlikely to be just a simple robbery.

It seemed to take him a few moments to register who I was. I tried not to take it personally.

"Rachael," he said as he stopped whatever he was writing on his notepad.

"Jackson, what's happening?" My voice came out far more vexed and breathless than I'd intended it to. I tried to push past, craning my neck to get a better look at what was happening inside the shop, but Jackson stopped me.

"This is police business, Rachael. You can't get back there."

"But I'm the owner of the store. At least, I'm about to be." He frowned so I pulled the contract out of my coat pocket and waved it around in his face, as though the act might grant me access to the crime scene.

"But you're not the owner now?" Jackson looked very serious.

"Well, no," I said helplessly. "But I'm buying this

shop. Please, you need to tell me what is going on. I need to know if I've made a huge mistake." I looked up at him and made my best damsel-in-distress face. "Please, Jackson," I whispered. "As a friend."

I wasn't sure that's what we were, exactly, but he looked left and right at the crowd and then nodded at me slightly.

"There's been a body found inside," he said quietly, not quite looking at me as he spoke. He glanced all around him to make sure that no one overheard us. "A young man by the looks of it."

"A body?" My heart froze and I could feel a hard lump in my throat.

Not again.

"Like...a dead body?" I whispered.

I saw the look on Jackson's face. Okay, dumb question. But I couldn't believe what I had just heard. I leaned over and grabbed onto the police tape, which did little to steady me and I almost ended up face first on the concrete.

"Whoa there," Jackson said, reaching out for me. A few people in the crowd tittered amongst each other at the sight of my almost fainting.

"Come with me," Jackson said, leading me to the back of a police van. I could feel everyone's eyes on me and I was vaguely aware that this made me look like I was guilty, but my legs were so unsteady and my head was swimming so fast that I didn't care. I just needed to sit down.

Jackson wrapped a blanket around me and offered me a Styrofoam cup filled with water. I took it with shaking hands and tried to take a sip.

"I'm sorry. I'm so embarrassed..." I said once the ringing in my ears had stopped. "I don't even know what came over me. I'm just...shocked. That's all."

Jackson shot me a small smile and a sympathetic look. "Seems like a lot of this sort of thing is happening around here lately."

I stopped sipping my water. "A lot of what, exactly?" I asked cautiously.

Jackson shrugged. "Murder."

My heart clenched up again. "Murder?" I whispered. "So that body you found...it wasn't an accident?"

I saw a look of dismay take over Jackson's face and a faint blush crept up his cheeks. "I...I shouldn't have said that." He coughed. "The details are not clear yet. We're still investigating."

"But you think it's a murder."

"Rach, I didn't..."

"Detective Whitaker," a stern female voice called out. "We need you back inside."

Jackson shot me an apologetic look and promised to check on me later. He made me promise to wait there a while and rest. But as soon as he was out of eyeshot, I stood up and threw my cup in the trash.

"Pippa," I called out breathlessly, running back to where she still stood, seemingly frozen in shock. "Pippa, someone was murdered in the antiques shop."

She turned to me slowly. "Now are you going to believe me, Rachael?"

"Believe you about what?" It took a moment or two for me to figure out what she was going on about. "Pippa, you have to be kidding me..."

Her voice was low and foreboding. "I told you, Rach. The children in the painting. They won't let their home be taken from them."

I placed my hands on my hips. "So what are you saying, Pippa? That the children in the painting have *killed* someone? Seriously, just think for a second about how ridiculous that sounds..."

Pippa gave me a long, low look. "I've already warned you twice, Rachael. First the storm, then the hook coming off the wall--on the side of the bakery that is next door to the antiques shop even!"

I rolled my eyes.

"Then the blackout that was confined to our building."

I shifted from one foot to the other. Now that one was a little harder to explain away. We'd checked the fuse box and it had been fine. And no other buildings on the street had been affected. The lights had mysteriously come back on three hours later, but by then, we'd already lost all our preparation time for the following day, costing me a great deal of time and money. Still, there had to be a logical explanation.

Didn't there?

Pippa was still standing with her hands on her hips.

"Now the twins are sending you an even more serious warning. Are you really going to buy that shop, Rachael? Are you really going to work in there? Run your business from that place?"

I stared up ahead as a stretcher with a body bag

lying on top was pushed from the shop into a waiting ambulance.

I gulped and reached into my pocket to feel the contract still waiting to be handed over.

If I was still going to buy the shop, I was going to have to figure out who killed that young man.

Pippa was still staring at the shop. She was so blue and pale that she was practically translucent. Her eyes were glazed over, but there was a distinct look of fear frozen inside them.

And I realized: more than anything else, I was going to have to prove that the killer was human.

Chapter 3

I leaned over and inspected the rows of flaky pastry topped with thick, hard vanilla frosting. My personal favorite: Vanilla Slice.

But not my personal recipe.

Pippa held her breath. "Well?" she finally squeaked. "What's the verdict?"

"Hmm, they smell good, but I think I'm going to have to sample one just to make sure." Pippa almost turned blue as she waited for me to sample the dessert. The pastry was perfectly crisp and flaky, and the custard was soft but firm without being gelatinous.

I narrowed my eyes at her as I leaned against the counter, stringing out my verdict like I was the judge on a reality show.

"I give them a nine out of ten."

Pippa heaved a sigh of relief. "Thank goodness. I was so worried that Romeo wouldn't be up to the job. Oh, I'm so glad you like them, Rach."

Romeo was Pippa's first hire in her role as assistant manager. One of the perks of expanding was that I could hire an apprentice baker, and one of the other perks was that I could outsource some of my managerial duties. I'd been a little nervous leaving Pippa in charge of hiring, but not as nervous as she had been about finding the right person. Romeo was a talented baker, even though he could be a little grumpy, but that could have just been due to the early hours that bakers had to keep. I could cut him a little slack on that. Been there, done that. I was grateful that I occasionally got to sleep in these days.

Speak of the devil, Romeo trudged out of the kitchen, wiping his flour-covered hands on his apron as he scowled at the two of us. His dark curly hair was sticking out from underneath his cap and I could tell from the bags hanging under his eyes that the 3:00 A.M. alarms were already taking their toll on him.

"Good morning," I said, smiling brightly at him.

"I need coffee," he said back, heading straight for our espresso machine. I placed my hand gently in front of the machine, stopping him.

"You don't need to do that. How about I run and get coffee for all of us from that new place down the road, the Red Ribbon, I think it's called, as a treat?" I asked cheerily. "They've got some amazing flavors..."

Pippa nodded eagerly and told me she'd take a cookies and cream iced coffee. Romeo was still scowling but he reluctantly said he'd take a short black. "You sure you don't want anything a bit special?"

"Short black," he said gruffly.

Pippa and I looked at each other as he stomped back to the kitchen and we both burst into laughter as the door swung shut behind him. "He's only twenty but he acts like a grumpy old man."

Pippa agreed. "Sorry that he's so...tempestuous, though. I swear, at the interview he was a lot more friendly."

"You don't need to apologize for his every action, Pippa. You can't be held responsible for his attitude. Besides, as long as he keeps baking like this, he can give me all the attitude he likes...just don't tell him that," I added, before I grabbed my purse to head out the door. "I'll be back in ten!"

***

There was a long line at the Red Ribbon when I arrived. Maybe I was going to be little longer than ten minutes. I glanced over my shoulder at the bakery, wondering if Romeo could go that long without his coffee before he started murdering people.

Poor choice of words.

"Hey!" a voice called and I jumped. "You look like you're a million miles away there."

"Jackson...Detective, I mean," I said, straightening up. "Just hoping that everyone at the bakery is okay without me." Not thinking about murder.

He grinned at me. "I'm sure they'll manage just fine without you. Why don't you sit down and join me for a little while?"

I really shouldn't.

But I did have an ulterior motive for wanting to chat with Jackson, and it wasn't just to sit down and take a break. I was hoping that he might let some details of the case slip out if I could get him to relax a little. I couldn't just come straight out and ask him for police information, but over coffee, I might be able to get something out of him.

But I kept thinking about Pippa being stuck on her own with Romeo on a rampage.

Jackson seemed to sense my hesitation. "Come on,

I'll even buy your coffee."

He placed our order and I ordered Romeo and Pippa's to-go in half an hour.

I settled into a booth. "I'll just tell them the line was long. Really, really long."

"You don't have to feel guilty for taking a few minutes to yourself, Rachael," Jackson said as he slipped into the seat across from me. "You've worked non-stop the last few years to get that bakery to the point where it can take care of itself."

"It's not that," I said, stirring even more sugar into my vanilla latte. Romeo wasn't the only person that morning who needed a pick-me-up, but I relied on sugar over caffeine for my morning hit.

I chose my next words carefully. "I'm just a little on edge after everything that happened yesterday."

Jackson sat his coffee mug down. "Right," he murmured. "That would be a huge thing for you right now. Has business been affected?"

I shook my head. "Not like last time." Last time someone had been murdered on this street, I'd almost gone of out business. But last time the murder weapon had been a pie. This time it had been...that was just one detail I needed to get from Jackson.

I waited for Jackson's reaction. "The last time. Right. Trouble sure does seem to be following you lately."

"So how was the man killed?" I interrupted him, speaking far more bluntly than I'd intended. *Great, Rach,* I scolded myself. *Way to be subtle about getting info.*

He narrowed his eyes at me. "We don't know that yet." He picked up his mug again and took a sip, watching me closely. "Do you?"

"Of course not," I replied quickly. "How would I know that?"

He shrugged. "Like I said, trouble seems to be following you lately."

"Pippa has this crazy idea that I am being haunted," I said, rolling my eyes.

I expected Jackson to laugh, but instead he just gave me a long look. "Weird things do seem to happen around you, Rachael." Now he looked suspicious. "Things like people getting killed."

I was outraged. "Are you suggesting I might have been in some way responsible for that guy's death?" We'd been down this road before. Last time a person had died on this street, I'd been a prime suspect in her murder, until I'd been able to solve it and clear my own name.

Jackson sighed. "I would have already brought you in for questioning if you were. Don't worry, you'll know about it if you become a suspect."

That was reassuring. "I have an alibi you know. I was with Pippa all night." This wasn't exactly how I'd wanted the conversation to go. I'd wanted to get information from him, not become a suspect.

He told me to take a breath, relax. Which was easier said than done.

It wasn't that I believed Pippa's haunted house stories. But Jackson was right: death seemed to be following me.

I shivered.

"Here, I'll order you another coffee."

I shook my head. "I need to go," I said, standing up abruptly. Jackson looked disappointed. "Sorry, there's just something I need to do."

***

"Shoot," I said, stepping through the door as I realized I'd forgotten Pippa and Romeo's coffees.

"Where have you been?" Pippa asked. "You've been gone for over half an hour."

"The line was massive." I threw my empty hands up into the air. "So I just gave up. I hope Romeo isn't going to kill me."

Pippa sighed and crossed her arms, glancing back over her shoulder at the kitchen with a worried look on her face. "Well, I think Romeo's coffee is the least of your problems right now."

"What do you mean?" I heard a crashing sound and then the back door slamming shut. "Pippa," I shouted, running towards the kitchen. "Is that the sound of Romeo leaving? What's going on here?"

She chased after me as I opened the door to find a kitchen in absolute chaos. There were overturned bowls everywhere, flour and pastry and cake mix covering every surface, including the walls and floor. "Has something exploded in here?" I asked Pippa.

"Yeah," she answered. "Romeo."

My jaw was open wide. "I've heard of people getting grumpy because they don't get their morning coffee, but this is just insane. Pippa, what happened?"

I turned to find her huddled against the door looking guilty. "I don't know, Rach, but I think whatever was upsetting him, it was something more serious than coffee. I don't think he got any sleep last night. He was in a rotten mood all morning. I mean, he's always a bit surly but today it was on another level."

I looked at the mess all around me in horror. "Well, is he coming back?"

Pippa threw her hands in the air. "I'm sorry, Rach. I don't know." She hung her head. "This is my fault. I should never have hired him."

I turned to leave. "Just try and get him back, by this afternoon preferably. Otherwise, we're going to have to find another apprentice baker. Or have nothing to serve this afternoon."

***

"It's the curse," Pippa said as our meager supply of cakes ran out shortly after lunchtime.

"What is?" I asked.

Pippa shrugged and looked down at the empty display cases. "This," she said, pointing to them.

I turned towards her slowly. "Are you trying to blame Romeo's unprofessionalism on a *curse?* I'm pretty sure that was all just due to him being a bad employee. And young. Not everyone can handle the stress of the early hours. There's nothing paranormal about it. In fact, it's very normal to react badly to poor sleep."

Pippa shook her head. "I told you, the twins will do everything they can to stay in their home." She grabbed me by the shoulders. "And they will do everything they can to stop you from taking over. Screwing with your staff, and your cash supply, so that you can't buy the store!"

"I am buying the store. One poor day of sales can't stop me."

Pippa turned white. "You're really going to ignore all this?" she whispered.

I had to turn the sign on the door to "closed," seeing as we had nothing to serve for the rest to the afternoon.

"Should I place another job ad?" Pippa asked quietly.

"Not just yet. Let's see if Romeo comes back." Even though he had acted atrociously, I was willing to give him another chance, based on his age and baking skills, and also largely due to the fact that we'd all been through a bit of a shock following the previous day's events.

"I can wait, Rachael, but I don't think Romeo is coming back. He's as freaked out as I am."

I stopped and stared at her. "What does that mean?"

"Nothing," she said quickly, picking up a broom. "Just that he was on edge."

"Does he believe this crazy story as well? Did you put these ideas in his head?" I took a step towards her. "Come on, Pippa, you better tell me what really happened this morning in the kitchen."

"Nothing," she repeated. "I don't know what was up with Romeo today. He just went crazy." She swept a bit of rubbish into a pile and brushed the stack into the bin. "But I wouldn't blame him if he was too scared to keep working here."

"Fine, Pippa. If you're so hell-bent on sticking to your crazy haunted painting theory, then come with me to the antiques shop and prove it to me."

Pippa's eyes were so wide that all I could see were the whites. With her bright blue hair, she looked a little bit like a circus clown. "Fine," she finally said. "But if anything happens while we're snooping around, you have to take it as your final warning. To stay away from the place. Deal?"

I hesitated. But what were the chances of something odd happening? "Deal," I agreed.

Chapter 4

It was 1:00 A.M. I'd been out on the back of the street at this time before, but that was only once when I had a mountain of pastries to bake and no staff to help me.

"Actually, after we finish this snooping around, I will probably have to start work," I grumbled. "On zero sleep. You thought Romeo was bad today. I'm going to be a match for him." I paused. "You haven't heard from him by any chance, have you?"

Pippa shook her head. As she spoke, the chill in the air caused her words to steam in front of her. "I'll find an even better baker for you, Rach, I promise. I'll make it up to you."

"Don't worry about that now," I said gently. "Let's just concentrate on what we're doing here."

Pippa shocked me when, instead of heading towards the back entrance of the antiques shop, she started walking around the front.

"Where are you going?" I called out in a shout that I tried to keep to a whisper.

She stopped for a moment. "The back is deadbolted,

I can't pick that. The front is just a regular lock."

I ran after her. The streetlights at the front of the shop suddenly cast a sobering light on what we were doing.

"We really shouldn't be going inside," I said, glancing at the yellow tape that still surrounded the antiques shop. "We could be arrested for tampering with a crime scene."

"It was your idea." Pippa pushed past me and began to search around with a flashlight.

I pushed the flashlight down and told her to keep quiet. "Someone will see us."

"Well, how are *we* supposed to see?" Pippa shivered. "I'm not going inside that place without any light."

"Fine."

We crept up to the door and Pippa took a pin out of her hair. I'd heard the rumors about her prowess with lock-picking, but I'd never actually seen her skills first hand.

"Keep a look out, Rach." She didn't need to tell me twice. Last thing I wanted was to get arrested for breaking and entering. Detective Whitaker would put me at the top of his suspects list for the guy's murder.

171

I told myself that we weren't there to cause any damage, or to even touch anything. We were there to help solve a crime. That helped ease my guilty conscious a little bit.

"What would I do without you, Pips?" I had to admire the way she'd picked the lock like a skilled pro. Although, as I stepped over the threshold and glanced at the popped lock, I couldn't help but think about the fact that I would have had the keys by now, if the slight problem of the murder hadn't taken place.

Pippa was stalking ahead with a confidence that surprised me. After all her stories, I'd been expecting her to cower behind me. "Wait up," I called, as she had the flashlight and it was difficult for me to see three paces behind her.

I coughed as soon as the heavy dust hit my nostrils and settled there. "I'm gonna have to give this place a good scrubbing before I actually serve food here."

"You're going to have to give it more than a good scrubbing," Pippa muttered. "I'm thinking more like an exorcism."

She shone the flashlight on item after item. Old paintings, vases, statues, trunks, furniture and more flickered into view before going dark again.

"I've never actually been inside this place before. There's so much junk." I moved around carefully, trying not to knock any of the tall vases lest they smash and give us away to anyone still awake and nearby. "I wonder where Gus is going to store all this stuff once he goes out of business."

"Probably in the garbage," Pippa said, then she stopped. She had the flashlight trained on...*it.*

"I can't believe this is still in here," Pippa whispered as she stared at the old fashioned painting. The twin boy and girl depicted in it, both around three years of age, stared eerily back at her.

"Well, where did you think it would be? Taken down to the station for questioning?" My joke was an attempt at easing the fear emanating from her, but Pippa just stared back at the painting, the flashlight trembling in her hand.

"What, Pippa? What is it?"

"Rachael, it's...it's moving..."

I stared straight into the eyes of the girl and boy depicted in the picture, almost expecting their eyes to be moving, for the picture to come to life.

Pippa really was getting to me. I shook my head and

closed my eyes. "Pippa, paintings can't move."

She looked at me like I was crazy. Then I saw what she meant. It wasn't the figures in the painting that were moving (okay, I have to admit that was a little insane) but the entire frame. It was shaking and moving from side to side.

Despite my better senses, I screamed and almost pushed Pippa over in my rush to get out of the shop. Still shrieking, I pulled frantically on the door, screaming for it to open before Pippa came up behind me and pointed out that I needed to push it.

We both spilled out onto the street, doubled over as we struggled to catch our breaths. I felt like there were razor blades in my lungs. And like my heart had been electrocuted.

"What the heck was that?" I finally asked. I could hear the trembling in my voice. I looked down to see that my hands were shaking. "Why the heck was it moving?"

I looked over at Pippa and noticed that she was empty handed. "Pippa! You dropped the flashlight in there!"

Pippa was shaking even harder than I was. "So?" she asked. "Let's scooch! We need to get away from this place before whatever is in there gets us." She was like a wild animal, up on her hind legs ready to flee.

I steadied my breathing. One of us had to keep our cool. "I agree that we need to get away from this place, but we can't leave the flashlight in there. Someone will figure out it's ours. "

Pippa shook her head frantically. "There's no way they'll know it belonged to us."

"Your fingerprints are all over it, Pippa."

"I don't care."

"We need to go back in there and get it."

Pippa just stared at me and backed away from the door. "Well, you'll have to go back in on your own."

"Pippa..."

I stared inside the shop in dismay. Total blackness. The thought of stepping back in there, with that thing moving around sent shivers up my spine.

"Well?" Pippa said. Even with the fear present in her voice, I could hear the tone of triumph shining through. "Are you really going back in there alone, Rach?"

I slowly turned back to her, shaking my head. "No."

***

I didn't get much sleep that night. And it wasn't just due to the fact I had to be up at 5:00 A.M. thanks to Romeo's sudden disappearance. Every time I shut my eyes, all I could see was that painting, rocking back and forth, taunting me. Heck, maybe those painted eyes really were moving!

"Hey," Pippa called out as I shuffled into the kitchen. I jumped a mile.

"Sorry, I didn't mean to scare you." Pippa dug a spoon into her bowl of cereal while she sat at the bench.

I tried to play off my nerves. "I'm just startled to see you up this early, that's all. You usually don't rise until well past midday if you can help it."

"I couldn't sleep either," she replied softly.

"Who says I didn't sleep?" I didn't know why I was so intent on proving to Pippa that I wasn't rattled. I just didn't want to admit that what happened the night before had actually happened. But there was no explanation for it. And that made me uncomfortable for more than one reason.

Pippa gave me a long, slow look before she jumped

up to rinse her bowl. "Well, I've got a plan," she announced. I popped a slice of bread in the toaster and waited. "I'm going to call an emergency meeting of the Belldale Paranormal Society."

"That's your plan?"

"Rachael, they'll know what's going on. They'll have answers."

I rolled my eyes. "Pippa, I really think you ought to stop hanging around with the people in that club. They are seriously messing with your mind, and now the craziness is rubbing off on other people." I reached for a carton of juice and slammed the refrigerator shut. The only reason I'd been freaked out so much the night before was because of Pippa's outlandish claims.

Pippa pouted. "So you think I've gone crazy?"

I looked at Pippa with her frizzy blue hair sticking out at crazy angles. I'd always thought she was a little crazy. But in a good way.

I smiled at her. "What do you mean 'gone crazy'? I think you're already there."

She gave me a playful push, then turned somber. "I know some of their ideas are a little wacky when you hear them for the first time, but if you'd just come along for a meeting..."

"Pippa, there's no way I'm coming to a meeting."

She looked hurt. "Why not?"

I didn't know. A hundred reasons. Too busy running a successful business, too concerned with logic...

Pippa tilted her head to the side when I didn't immediately answer. "Are you scared?" Her tone was teasing. And I wasn't about to fall for that tactic.

I sighed. "No, I'm not scared."

"Because some of them are witches," Pippa said with a bit of awe in her voice. I was glad my head was facing towards the refrigerator, as she would have taken even further offense if she could see the face I made. "But don't worry, if I say that you're with me, they won't do any harm to you."

That was the last worry I had. My primary worry was that I would lose my respected reputation if I was seen entering or exiting a meeting of the Belldale Paranormal Society.

"Please, Rach, at least think about it."

I was about to tell her that there was no way I was even going to think about it when we both heard something crash in the hallway. We jumped like startled cats and I could feel all my hair on edge as I crept into the hall to see what had made that insanely loud noise.

It was still dark outside and the hallway was black. I fumbled until I found the light switch and gasped when I stepped back and banged into Pippa.

"Sorry," she whispered.

Suddenly there was light and the whole thing didn't seem quite so scary, but then I saw what the noise was. There was a picture frame lying in the middle of the hall, smashed into a thousand different bits, with glass scattered everywhere.

My first thought was, *how in the heck am I going to have time to clean all that up before I start work?*

But Pippa was trembling as she approached it. "Rach... Look what this is a picture of..."

I had to follow her to see what she was talking about. My walls are lined with dozens of random photos and paintings. If you'd asked me before then to tell you what artwork was in a specific part of the house, I wouldn't be able to tell you. "What is it a picture of?"

Pippa seemed to know my own decor better than I did. She pointed at the smashed frame to the corner of the picture. At first glance, the picture was nothing more than a landscape, an oil color of an old fashioned scene, a golden field with an old house in the background and a bridge in the front of the house.

But in the corner... In the corner, so tiny you could hardly see them, were two tiny little children.

They looked about four years old. They looked like twins.

I looked at Pippa. Maybe a meeting of the Belldale Paranormal Society wouldn't be such a bad idea after all.

Chapter 5

Knock, knock.

A girl—woman—possibly in her late teens or early twenties stood there. She had long dyed purplish-red hair and pale porcelain skin. She was wearing a cape that made her look like Red Riding Hood, except that she was dressed in black.

"Is Pippa here?" she said in a tone so quiet I had to lean forward to be able to hear her.

I suddenly knew who she was. Or, at least, where she was from. The Belldale Paranormal club.

I shook my head. "She's at work." Pippa was covering for me because I was feeling quite ill with a headache and fever. Three days had passed since the incident with the painting in the hallway and—so far—nothing else unusual had happened.

Of course, Pippa was blaming my illness on the so-called 'curse.' Another sign that the twins would do anything to keep me from buying the antiques shop.

But I had another reason for wanting to take a little time away from the bakery. I just couldn't accept Pippa's explanation of events. There had to be a logical explanation for everything that had happened, so I had decided to use my sick day for something more than just lying on the sofa and watching Criminal Point: I was going to get to the bottom of everything.

I wasn't too impressed with the woman in front of me and certainly didn't want to waste my time on her. Hoping to end the interaction quickly, I started to close the door but she stepped in front of it.

"Maybe I should talk to you then."

I didn't really like the sound of that. "I'm a little busy right now," I said politely. "Fighting off a bit of the flu, actually. I wouldn't want you to get infected."

"Oh, I won't get infected," she said with eyes that opened so wide it was a little creepy. "I have a spell that makes me immune from all the winter bugs."

Oh boy.

"I can cast it on you if you like?"

"No, thanks. I've got plenty of aspirin and throat lozenges. Those are my magical spells."

She didn't seem amused. Her face had a ghostly, otherworldly quality. "Are you Rachael? Pippa's told me a lot about you."

I nodded. "The one and only."

182

"I'm Tegan," she replied.

The name was familiar to me. I now knew exactly who she was. She was the leader of the Belldale Paranormal Society. The one that called all the shots.

Most likely the one that had put all the crazy ideas into Pippa's head in the first place. I eyed her with suspicion.

"I really ought to go back inside. I'm feeling rather faint."

Tegan eyed me like she could see right through me. Literally. But also as though she could tell that I was lying. "Rachael, Pippa told me about all the mysterious things that have been happening to you."

"Did she?" I asked heavily.

Tegan nodded. "It sounds to me like you have had a curse placed on you, Rachael."

"Don't be ridiculous." I tried to close the door again.

She stopped me. "I can help you, Rachael, if you let me. I know what's going on."

She peered at me again with those eyes that seemed to see directly into my soul.

I gulped and shook my head. "I don't need your help,

thank you."

***

One little peek through the window couldn't hurt.

I leaned close to the window, cupping my hands around my face to get a better look. Suddenly, a figure started lunging towards me and I screamed. Pulling back, my breathing returned to something resembling normal when I saw it was the antique store's owner, Gus.

Gus was in his late fifties and always seemed a little gruff, his clothes were always as dusty as the antiques he kept in his shop. I'd seen less and less of him over the last few months as he'd been ill and mostly leaving the shop in the hands of his family. To tell the truth, I was glad I hadn't had much interaction with him, given that I was in the process of buying his store—effectively pushing him out of business.

"Gus!" I said, plastering a smile on my face as he opened the door for me. This was a little awkward. Even though my intended purchase of his store was nothing personal, he probably still resented me for the fact that I would be its new owner.

"Hello, Rachael." We'd always been on friendly terms since I'd opened the bakery three years earlier and I was relieved to find that he didn't seem, on the surface at least, to harbor any ill will towards me.

"Is everything okay?" I asked him. Stupid question. Of course it wasn't. Not only was the poor guy about to sell the business he had put his blood, sweat and tears into, there was now the problem of the shop being...well, literally filled with blood, sweat, and tears.

"Besides the fact that a man was murdered in my shop..." Gus started, and I braced myself. His forehead creased into a deep frown. "There was a break-in a few days ago."

I froze.

"A break-in?" I asked, trying to keep my voice steady.

"Some stuff was moved around. And they were stupid enough to leave a flashlight in here."

Yes, they were.

"Oh no," I said, pretending to be outraged. "That's terrible, Gus. Do you know who it was?"

Gus shook his head. "No. And strange as it is, it

185

seems like they didn't take anything. But it makes you wonder, doesn't it?"

"It does."

"Whoever it was that killed that poor guy, they might have come back to clean up after themselves."

"Well, if they left a flashlight behind, they mustn't have done a very good job of cleaning up!" I let out a forced high-pitched laugh that was far too loud.

He gave me a suspicious look. "You didn't happen so see anything that night, did you?"

I shook my head quickly. "No, I was home in bed early that night."

He narrowed his eyes. "I didn't tell you exactly what night it was yet."

I gulped and checked the time on my phone. "Shoot, Gus, I really gotta go. We're down a baker at the store and I've been doing double duty." That wasn't exactly true. If anyone had been pulling double duty, it was Pippa. But I had to get out of there.

But I stopped just as I reached the door. I could hear the rush of customers on the other side and even through the cracks, I could smell cinnamon and vanilla wafting out. And there was Gus next to me, dutifully, sadly, clearing out the remains of a dying shop—a shop that was a crime scene no less. I wondered if hearing my own full shop next to him was just like the final twist of the knife in his guts.

I snuck in and grabbed a Danish pastry without anyone noticing me. Pippa was running around and wouldn't have noticed if the president walked in at that moment. I couldn't do much to help Gus, but I could do one thing: offer him pastry.

I tiptoed back to Gus's shop, hoping to surprise him, but I stopped short at the door when I saw what Gus was doing. I made sure no one was looking before I pressed my face closer to the glass. He was tampering with the painting of the twins. I looked closer. It looked like he was pulling wire off the top of the frame.

Wire that could have easily been used to move the painting from side-to-side. Wire that could have been used to scare off trespassers.

Gus suddenly looked up at me, locking eyes on me like I was a target. I dropped the Danish pastry and backed away from the window, but he was already storming towards the door.

"What are you doing?" he growled. Then, with a small satisfied scoff, "Snooping around again, I see."

"Again?"

"I know it was you and your friend here the other night."

I steadied my breathing. "Oh yeah? How could you know that unless you were here as well?" I raised an eyebrow at him, daring him to come up with a good answer for that.

His lips moved silently for a moment. I'd got him. It must have been him in the shop that night, moving the painting around and trying to scare us off.

But why?

When he didn't answer, I backed away and left the pastry lying there on the ground, waiting for the stray cats to come and get it after dark.

***

"Pippa," I said, grabbing her as I ran into the bakery. "I've got to tell you something! It's urgent. I've had a major breakthrough in the case."

She opened her mouth in disbelief.

"Rachael, we're slammed right now, can't you see

that?" She pointed to the long line of customers snaking out the door. "You could lend a hand if you wanted," she said, a little too pointedly.

I nodded. "Sorry," I said, grabbing an apron. As we rushed to serve customers, I managed to whisper a few details to her, but it wasn't until we closed that I was finally able to tell her the information that was about to burst out of me.

"Pippa," I said, taking my apron off. "Listen to this." I waited until I had her full attention. "I think Gus is the one who killed that person in the antiques shop!"

Pippa frowned as she placed a tray of brownies back in the fridge. The sweet smell made my tummy rumble and I stopped the door before it shut, grabbing one and taking a bite of the heavenly brownie. "Boy, I was starving. Especially after the day I've had."

"Me too," Pippa said. "I didn't get a chance to take a lunch break." Again, her tone was rather pointed.

"Are you mad at me Pippa?"

"I just think..." She slammed the door of the fridge shut. "That you've been spending so much time on this investigation that you're neglecting your duties here. And I'm the one whose been left to pick up all the slack."

I placed my brownie on the counter. "You're the one who keeps telling me that there is a mystery to solve, Pippa."

"No. I keep telling you to stay out of it."

"So that's what all this is about? You're so scared of all this silly superstition that you want me to drop it? What are you so worried is going to happen to you, Pippa?"

"Rach," she whispered, "I'm worried that something really bad is going to happen to *you.*"

She didn't sound so worried about me right then. Sounded like she was more worried about being overworked. But I didn't want to say that. "Pippa, I really appreciate you helping me out. You know that, don't you?" We were getting well off track now. This was not how I'd imagined the conversation going in my head.

She nodded. "And I appreciate that you gave me this opportunity, Rach. I feel so bad about what happened with Romeo and I want to make it up to you. Sorry if I complained about feeling overworked."

"No, I'm sorry, Pips. How about I let you have tomorrow off and I cover both shifts?"

"But we still haven't gotten anyone to replace Romeo."

"Don't worry about it, I'll be fine. You take the day off and hang out with your friends from the paranormal society, if you like." I thought about telling Pippa about my run-in with Tegan earlier, but something about the whole interaction had creeped me out. I didn't really want her coming back to the house, but I figured bringing it up at all would only cause another potential argument.

I suggested we take a break. A proper one. "You need to eat, Pips. Anything you want is on the house."

***

"Okay, so tell me your theory about Gus then." Pippa had chosen to have a donut and a chocolate shake for her 'dinner,' which was fine by me. Though I couldn't help but think that it wouldn't hurt us to eat some vegetables one of these days. "Why do you think he did it?"

"Well, think about it, Pippa. He is the one with the most to lose out of the whole sale of the antiques store, isn't he?"

Pippa nodded and took a sip of her shake. "That's true."

I leaned in closer. "So what if he made up all these stories about the painting to try and scare off potential buyers. What if he even *killed* to keep potential buyers away?"

"I dunno, Rach. I don't think Gus was the originator of that story about the painting. That story has been around for years, and why would he make that up about his own shop while he was still trying to make money from it? Presumably, he wanted to sell that painting at some stage. The rumors would have done nothing to help him."

I was silent for a moment. Pippa was right. It was unlikely that Gus had invented the story. "There's still something that isn't right, Pippa. You should have seen the way he was acting before."

"Well, this must be a tough time for him."

Again, true.

"This isn't Scooby Doo, Rachael. Gus isn't pretending to be a ghost to try and drive potential buyers away. He's a middle-aged man. I'm sure he has a little more dignity than that. And I'm sure he could have come up with a better plan."

"Then what was he doing fooling around with that painting earlier? It definitely had some kind of wires hanging off of it. I didn't see enough before he caught me, but it looked like he was trying to remove them."

Pippa gave me a slow look. "Do we need to go back in there? Check it out? Maybe tonight after dark."

I picked up my latte and took a sip to buy me a little time. I knew, logically, that I wasn't cursed. I also knew, logically, that the antiques shop wasn't haunted. And I knew, more than likely, that it had been Gus screwing around with the painting that night.

So why was I still scared to go in there after dark? "I dunno, Pippa," I said when I finally gave an answer. "Gus already thinks we were snooping around the other night. If we get caught red-handed, it's not going to look good."

Pippa narrowed her eyes. "Are you sure that's all it is, Rachael? You're looking a little pale there."

"Just need to get some fruit and vegtables into my diet," I said quickly. "Still can't quite kick that flu from last week. I can't survive on brownies indefinitely by the looks of it. I just think we ought to back off sneaking around the antiques shop for a day or two."

Pippa shrugged and picked up her garbage to throw in the trash. I sat there for a moment trying to collect my thoughts while Pippa cleaned up. Once she'd taken the trash out back, I sighed and stood up to lock the front door. The sun had long disappeared from the sky and the street looked particularly eerie that night. I looked over my shoulder. I couldn't wait for Pippa to come back inside. Quickly, I grabbed my keys and locked the front door, pulling on it three times to make sure it was locked properly.

That's when I froze. There, standing on the other side of the street, staring straight through the window and into my soul, was Tegan.

Chapter 6

My cold seemed to be getting worse. I woke up with eyes so puffy that I could hardly see out of them and an awful pain in my gut.

"Rach, you look freaking terrible."

"Thanks," I said, pouring hot water over a peppermint tea bag. The smell was immediately soothing, even though I winced when I took a sip. The flavor always reminded me of being sick, as it's what my mom always used to give us kids when we had a flu or an upset stomach.

"I'm serious. You have to stay home." Pippa began to pull on her jacket, but I told her to take it off.

"It's okay, Pippa. I promised you the day off and I am going to stick to my promise. I'll be fine once I get there and the adrenaline sets in." I was actually hoping I'd be so rushed off my feet that I wouldn't have time to think about how rotten I felt.

Pippa pulled a face of semi-horror as she stared up at me. "Rach, you really don't look well enough to go to work. I'm worried about you."

"I'll be fine," I tried to reassure her, cringing at the

crackling in my voice. "It's just like I said: I need some more fresh fruit and veggies in my diet. I promise I won't snack on cakes and cookies all day."

But when I got to the bakery, those were about the only things I could stomach. As I forced a slice of brownie down, hoping to get my sugar hit to kick me into gear, I felt even worse.

What's happening to me? Doubled over, I clutched my stomach, wondering if I should go back on my word and ask Pippa to come in to cover me.

But then the morning rush began and I was right. I didn't even have time to think, let alone focus on my puffy face and labored breathing. And I managed to get through the day without throwing up.

But there was a downside to running around all day with no backup. I hadn't been able to clean as I went, and I was left standing in the middle of what looked like the wreckage of a tornado at the end of the day.

I grabbed a broom and mop and got to work. Now that I had time to think, all I could focus on was the aching in my limbs and the pulsing in my head.

The bakery's phone began to ring in a shrill pitch, cutting right into my headache. I limped over to it and picked up the receiver. "Hello?"

"Rach, it's me. You weren't picking up your cell."

"Battery's dead. Didn't have time to charge it. What's up, Pippa?"

"Are you going to be home soon?"

I glanced at the mess and chaos surrounding me. "Not for a few hours."

There was heaving breathing on the other end of the line. When she didn't reply, I asked if she was okay.

"I just don't like being all alone in the house after dark."

I glanced out the window. The days were getting shorter and shorter. 5:00 P.M. and the streets were completely dark. "I'll be home as soon as I can. You'll be fine though, Pippa. What do you think is going to happen to you?"

"Please, Rach, I'm really frightened."

"I've got a mountain of a mess to clean up. If I leave it like this, there'll be ants by morning, maybe even rats if we're really unlucky." I was growing a little impatient with Pippa. "You're stressing about nothing. I'll be home in an hour or two, I promise."

I heard her gulp on the other end of the line. "You're right," she whispered. "I'm probably just being silly. I have to go!" she added suddenly before slamming down the receiver. I cringed, the sound doing nothing for my headache. *Thanks, Pippa.*

***

"Okay," I said out loud to myself as I swept the last of the mess into the trash hours later. "It might be fun to be busy occasionally, but I really need to find some more staff. Today was just ridiculous."

I let myself out the back and locked the door, barely even aware of what I was doing as I stumbled towards my car.

Suddenly a body stepped in front of me.

I screamed. Boy, I really was jumpy these days.

"Sorry, it's only me," a gruff male voice called out. I could see him holding his hands up in the dark. "I came back to collect my final check."

I thought Romeo had some nerve coming back to collect money, but at the same time, I didn't begrudge him the money that he had actually earned.

I nodded and sighed. "Come on in, I just need to

unlock the door again."

He followed me back into the bakery and to my office where his check lay on my desk.

I paused just as I was about to hand the check over. "So are you going to tell me why you stormed out that day? You kind of left us in the lurch here. I'm asking because I am genuinely worried that we did something to upset you, Romeo."

He grabbed the check out of my hand and stared at the tiles. "I just wasn't happy here," he said, before glancing up at me with guilty-looking eyes. "Sorry that I left like that, though. I do appreciate you taking the chance with hiring me."

I sighed. "Something must have really upset you that day. Was it just because I was late getting back with your coffee? I know the early hours can be a drag..."

Romeo let out a little laugh and shook his head. "It wasn't that, Rachael." He started to walk back out.

"Just tell me then," I called out. "Look, we're really overlaoded here lately. If you want your job back, I'm willing to give you another chance."

He spun back around. "After what I did?"

I sighed. "I know. I'm not a total pushover, just let

me make that clear. But I do believe in second chances. Plus, we're kind of desperate," I had to admit.

He stared at me for a long while before finally shaking his head. "Sorry, Rachael. It's nothing personal, but I can't work here."

"Why not?" I asked, chasing him as he left out the back via the kitchen. We were out in the dark alley before he finally answered.

"Why don't you ask, Pippa."

Then he spun around and disappeared into the dark night.

Ask Pippa? What did Pippa do to make him leave?

I threw my head back in a silent scream. I had a pretty good idea. She could frighten anyone away.

Maybe it wasn't Gus who was making up the ghost stories to drive people away. Maybe the real culprit had been living in my home the entire time.

***

"Pippa!" I called out as I stormed into the apartment. I threw my coat onto the hall table and stepped over the broken glass shards that were still lying in the hall, even though I could have sworn we'd cleaned all of them up. "I need to talk to you!"

But Pippa wasn't in her usual spot on the sofa. "Pippa?"

I found her shivering on top of my bed with only a lamp on besides her. "What's happened, Pippa? Have you caught my flu?" She was holding the blanket up to her face, and she was white and pale and clammy when I felt her forehead.

"Rachael...I...I..." Her teeth were chattering too hard for her to be able to speak properly.

Shoot. Something was really wrong with her. "Do you need to go to the hospital?" I wrapped the blanket around her tighter, hoping that would stop the shivering.

She shook her head. "I'm not sick, Rachael."

I sat down besides her, understanding now. "Pippa, what's frightened you so much?" I felt a stab of guilt over the fact I hadn't come home as soon as she'd called me. "Sorry, Pips. I should have left the mess to clean up in the morning."

Pippa was still shivering as she stared off into the

distance. "I saw something, Rachael," she whispered.

I stood up, thinking about the glass shards in the hallway. "Did someone break in?" I asked, terrified as well now.

"Not someone," Pippa whispered. "Rachael, the thing I saw wasn't alive, it wasn't human."

I stomped over and turned the lights on properly. "Come on, Pippa," I said. "You're freaking me out."

"I don't mean to," she whispered. Her eyes were filled with tears now. One of them spilled down her cheek. "I'm not making it up, though. Rachael, there was a ghost in the house. I heard something in the hall. I went to investigate, and I saw it."

I was fighting not to show that I was scared as well, but I was losing the battle. "Pippa, I think you've just caught my flu," I said gently, completely forgetting about all the drama with Romeo earlier. "Maybe you're just hallucinating?" I asked hopefully.

She shook her head. "I feel fine. Besides, have you been hallucinating?"

No, I had just been feeling sick to my stomach. No ghostly apparitions.

"Rachael." Pippa tried to steady her voice. "It told me

to stay away from Gus's shop."

I just stood there staring at her.

I wasn't sure what I believed at that moment.

"Pippa," I said gently, but firmly. "I know you're scared right now, but you have to admit that sounds a little ridiculous. After all the crazy stuff you've had in your head, don't you think it's possible that maybe you just imagined it?"

She shook her head. "That's it, Rachael, I'm out."

"Out of what?"

"The investigation for one thing. No more snooping around at night, no more asking questions. I'm done with all of it. And if you want my advice, you should leave it alone as well." She shot me a look. "And if you decide to go ahead with buying Gus's shop, then I am done with the bakery as well."

Chapter 7

So now there was one. Just me, alone, trying to solve this mystery. Gus was still my prime suspect.

I had found out earlier from another shop owner on our street that the guy who was murdered was someone named Jason Hamilton. I knew a lot of people in this town, with my business and living here as long as I have, and I was thankful that I didn't know him. The shop owner from the yarn store, Knitwit, had told me that the police weren't releasing his name, but she had found out from her brother-in-law that works at the station. That explained why Jackson wouldn't answer any of my questions about the murder victim. It was supposed to be all hush-hush.

I sat down at my kitchen table and got out a notebook. It was still hours before Pippa would rise so I knew I had a little time before she caught me. I started scribbling down the ideas I had so far.

Access. Gus owns the shop, so he had the opportunity to kill Jason.

Motive. Gus has a big motive for killing Jason. He wants to keep his shop. The murder—and the freaky stories surrounding it—means that no one will want to buy the shop.

I paused and put the pen to my lips. Hmm. *In fact, the stories could actually attract more attention to his store. People like antiques with a story. And it would also buy him a little time before he has to sell.*

I glanced at Pippa sleeping over my shoulder. All of a sudden, I was desperate to wake her up and tell her my theory. She'd thought that Gus wouldn't make up ghost stories because it would be bad for business.

But what if they were actually *good* for his line of business?

But Pippa had said she was done with the case. Sadly, I turned around and let her sleep. I was going to have to do this on my own.

"What are you doing?"

"Nothing!" I slammed the notebook shut. "Just writing down a list of stock we have to order for the wedding reception."

Pippa frowned. "The reception? The one that's today? A little late to be ordering supplies, isn't it?"

"Just a few last minute things I need to get. The bride had some special gluten free requirements for some of the guests."

"Oh," Pippa said, nodding. "We don't want to poison any of the guests." She cringed. "Sorry. Poor choice of words." The memory of a customer being poisoned—and one of my pies being to blame—was still a little too fresh. But I told her not to worry about it.

"We need to get going. It's big days like this that can really make or break the bakery!"

***

"Hey, you guys are opening really late today," a man wearing an army jacket and a bright yellow hat said as he waited by the bakery door. I pulled out my key, struggling as I juggled boxes of the gluten free supplies I'd been forced to buy while Pippa accompanied me to the specialty store. That's what I got for lying: three hundred dollars out of pocket. Oh well, the reception we were about to host would make up for that little loss.

"Sorry," I said, putting on an apologetic face as I struggled with my boxes. "We're closed for a private function this afternoon. Hence the late start. A wedding reception."

"Oh," the man said, scowling as he craned his neck to try and get a look through the window. "That sounds mighty interesting. Is anyone welcome to come along?"

Out of respect for my guests' privacy, I stood in front of him. "No, sorry." But I couldn't help thinking what a strange request that was. Who asked that? "We'll be open to the public again tomorrow morning. I hope to see you then!"

I wasn't sure I really was, but I watched him trudge away.

"Who was that?" Pippa asked.

"An unwanted guest," I said. "Wow!" My breath was almost taken away by how beautiful the inside of the bakery looked, all decked out in pink, silver, and white. "You did an amazing job, Pippa."

She grinned at me. "Let's get ready this wedding reception!"

I was dressed to match the decor in a short pink and silver dress, partly because I wanted to blend in with the scenery. I was there as staff, not as a guest. Still, it was exciting to see the bakery come to life like that, to see it full of people dancing and eating and enjoying themselves. I cast a glance next door. If only we'd been able to use the second store, we could have fit in even more guests.

"What are you thinking about?" Pippa nudged me and nibbled on a cupcake.

"Nothing," I said quickly, straightening up. "Just admiring the shop."

"Why don't you take a break?" She winked at me, though I had no idea why. "Something tells me that you might want to have a dance soon."

"Does it?" I asked incredulously. "Pippa, I'm here to serve food, not dance it up!"

She nudged me again and then pointed at the crowd before scooting away. I turned to see what on earth she was pointing at.

My eyes widened and I straightened up immediately. How long had he been standing there?

"Jackson!" I'd seen him in a suit before, his detective suit, but this was different. Usually he wore dark colors but today he was dressed in a rather festive light grey with a salmon colored tie. It suited him.

"I had no idea you were going to be here."

"The groom and I are friends from way back," Jackson explained. "But I don't know too many of the guests, I have to admit, but when I saw the reception was being held here, I just had to tag along."

He did know how to make a girl blush.

"Would you join me for a quick dance?"

I glanced around. Would it be incredibly bad form for a server to join in? But the bride nodded at me and I took that as a sign that I had her permission. However, I was still a little nervous about dancing with Jackson for some reason.

"Hey, you never told me why you ran out of the coffee shop the other day," Jackson said as we gently swayed to a mid-tempo pop song.

I shot him a look. "I just didn't like being accused, that's all."

"I told you, I wasn't accusing you of anything." He was silent for a moment. "Though there were some rumors that you were sneaking around the crime scene shortly afterwards."

I pulled back. "So you *are* accusing me then?"

"Not of having anything to do with that man's murder."

"What are you accusing me of then?"

He raised an eyebrow. "Trying to solve the case

yourself."

I felt my face go red and we began to dance again.

"Am I wrong?"

I shook my head. "No," I admitted softly. "But I have a personal stake in this, Jackson. I was already supposed to be the owner of that shop by now. Then all this happened."

Jackson frowned. "You do realize you're not a detective though, Rachael. Do you have your PI's license?"

"No," I had to admit. "But anyone can be an amateur sleuth, can't they?"

He sighed. "I just don't want you to get into trouble again.

I wondered if it was already too late for that. There was no way I wanted to get into all the paranormal stuff—sorry, alleged paranormal stuff—with Jackson, but so much creepy stuff had happened lately that I was starting to wonder if I really should back off and listen to Pippa.

"You've gone awful quiet."

"Just enjoying a bit of peace," I said quietly.

The DJ started playing a more upbeat song and I took that as my cue to pull away again. "Sorry, I just need to run out for a second. See if we have any cakes left in the back." Really, I needed to go to the bathroom, but he didn't need to know that.

"Okay," Jackson said, looking disappointed.

As soon as I finished in the bathroom and headed back to the counter, Pippa shot me a look. "What are you doing? Go back over to him!"

I turned around. Jackson was dancing a little awkwardly by himself in the middle of the floor. "I don't know." Just as I was contemplating going back over to him, there was a loud crashing sound.

That's when we all heard the screams coming from next door.

***

"Move away," Jackson commanded as all the guests spilled from my shop to Gus's, all trying to rubberneck and see what was going on.

I tried to push through the crowd. "What is it?" I asked Jackson.

"You too," he commanded. "Rachael, you need to step back." It seemed like the intimacy between us had faded away already.

I looked past him anyway. I had to see what the heck was going on.

I brought my hands to my mouth and gasped as I saw it: a dead body lying in the center of Gus's Antiques. From the looks of it, a young woman.

Another murder victim.

***

"Well, that kind of put a dampener on the whole wedding reception." Pippa sat next to me while I tried to soothe my nerves with a cup of ginger tea. It wasn't working. The guests had all cleared out and I hadn't even collected payment from the bride and groom.

"What a total disaster," I groaned, throwing my head on the table.

"Not to mention a tragedy," Pippa pointed out.

"I know, I know." I looked up. "You can go if you like. Jackson said he only needed me to stick around."

Pippa wasn't above making a joke in that moment. "I bet he did."

"He just wants to ask me a few questions."

On top of everything else, I was incredibly nervous about why he wanted to speak to me. But I told Pippa I was fine and that she ought to go home.

It seemed like I was waiting hours for Jackson to finally come speak to me. "Thanks for waiting. Sorry your event got ruined."

"You ought to tell that to the bride and groom."

He sat down across from me and pulled a notepad out of his breast pocket. "Did you see anything suspicious today before you started work?"

I thought for a second before shaking my head. "I was in a rush. Nothing that I can remember." I paused. "Jackson, how did she die?"

"I told you earlier, we can't give out that information to the public."

I'd been hoping I was more than just 'the public.' "But how can I help you if I don't know any of the details of how she died?"

"And I've told you that already as well: you don't need to help us in that way. You can help by answering my questions."

I leaned forward. "Did she die the same way as the first victim? Do you think we are looking for the same person?"

What I really wanted to ask was, *Do you already have an idea of the suspect? Because the first person you should be looking for is Gus.*

He glared at me. "Rachael, 'we' are not looking for anyone. The police are looking for a suspect. You'd do better to stay out of it. Now, can you remember anything suspicious happening today?"

I shook my head and stood up. "I really should be getting home, if that's all."

He looked at me gravely. "It's not, actually."

I turned back to him in surprise. "I've already told you I didn't see anything. What else do you want from me?"

"I'm sorry to do this, Rachael. But if you don't want to cooperate here, I'm afraid I'm going to have to ask you to come down to the station to ask a few more questions. Officially."

I just stared at him. "You've got to be kidding me, Jackson. I was here the whole time!"

He stared at me. "Not the whole time."

I rolled my eyes. The bathroom break. Right before the screams. I shook my head. This was just great.

"Fine. You lead the way."

Chapter 8

I felt like I had been in the back of the police car for an eternity. Jackson mentioned something about the storm coming and I stared at the dark clouds above that looked like they were about to engulf the entire town of Belldale with one swallow.

But all I felt was numb. I pressed my cheek against the glass to try to feel something. "Can I roll down a window?" The heat in the car was suffocating.

"It's about to start raining," Jackson replied, sounding slightly curt.

I took it as a no.

Guilty. That's the way I felt. A second body? I glanced down and played with the bracelet on my wrist, spinning it round and round. What if I really was to blame?

What if Pippa was right?

Either way, it seemed like everything I'd worked so hard for was slipping away again. Just when things seemed to be going well, disaster struck again.

What if I really was cursed?

***

The seat was plastic and digging into my back. Now I was freezing. Would it have killed them to put on the heat? It was the middle of winter, after all, and we were about to be hit by a storm.

But I supposed cops didn't really care about making their suspects feel comfortable.

"Gus Sampson is the person you should be questioning."

It was a different detective interviewing me this time, a woman in her early thirties with a rail thin frame and curly red hair. "Where is Detective Jackson, by the way?"

She paused from the notes she was jotting down and shot me a look. "He's busy. You don't need to worry about him."

I wondered if he'd asked this woman—Detective Emma Crawford, apparently—to conduct the interview because he had a conflict of interest concerning me.

"So," Detective Crawford said. I wondered how long she had worked at the station. If her and Jackson were

217

partners. If they ever worked cases together, long nights on stakeouts...

"You were in the bathroom?" She raised a thinly manicured eyebrow. "That's a convenient story."

"Not very convenient seeing as I am in here," I pointed out.

"Can anybody confirm you were using the bathroom?"

I shook my head. I didn't want to say anything else. I wanted to speak to Jackson. Or get a lawyer.

Detective Crawford continued.

"And weren't you also a suspect in the murder of Colleen Batters?"

"Emphasis on suspect. For about a minute. I actually helped to solve that case," I said pointedly.

A look of amusement crossed her face. "Did you? That's nice that you think that."

I felt like I had shrunk to the size of a mushroom. Maybe I wasn't a cop, and maybe I didn't officially have a P.I's license, but I had helped to solve that murder fair and square.

I crossed my arms. "You can ignore what I have to

say about Gus Sampson, but if you do, it's at your own peril." I knew how ridiculous that sounded before I'd even got to the end of the sentence and immediately wished I could reach out for the words and swallow them.

Detective Crawford's amusement only grew wider. "I think we'll be okay."

I nodded, silent again. After everything that happened, I wasn't sure I was doing much good towards the case anyway. I hadn't been able to stop the second girl from dying.

"Did you even come into contact with Bridget Lassiter before?"

"Bridget?" I asked, confused.

Detective Crawford blinked slowly. "That's the name of the woman who was found dead today."

I ran the name through my head, foraging for a connection, but I just ended up shaking my head. "Was she the same age as the other victim?"

Another long blink. "Roughly the same. Don't try to solve this case for us. Detective Whitaker said you had a habit of that."

I raised an eyebrow. So he talked about me to her.

Maybe to others.

I leaned forward. "With all due respect,Detective, there are two people dead. Will there be more to come? If you want my opinion, the sole person you should be looking at is Gus Sampson." I told the detective about what I had seen him doing in his store that morning, with the painting and the wires.

She frowned. "You saw him jiggling a painting around? Sounds very suspicious." I could tell she was biting her lip to keep from laughing now. I realized that without context, without explaining to her everything about the painting and the so-called 'curse'—and, most importantly, without explaining that I had broken into his shop the night before—that Gus playing with the wires on the painting added up to exactly zero evidence against him.

I leaned back. Maybe what I'd seen did mean exactly nothing.

But Gus had to have done it. "It's not just the painting thing," I pointed out, worried that I sounded totally stupid now. "He's the only person with access to the store." I saw the look on her face. "Well, apart from the other employees of course," I added quietly. Maybe I really was out of my depth here.

"Don't you think we, as detectives, have already thought of that?"

"Most likely," I mumbled. "Yes."

Detective Crawford stood up and opened the door for me. She had a small smile on her face that seemed genuine. "You're free to go, Rachael."

"I am?" I asked, surprised, as I stood up after her. I buttoned up my coat. "I take it this means I am no longer a person of interest."

She cast me a long steely gaze. "Just make sure you come to us if you see anything else interesting or suspicious. You do run the bakery next door to the crime scene, after all."

I stopped buttoning. "Does this mean that you'd like me to be your eyes and ears out there?"

"We don't need your help with solving the case, if that's what you're getting at, Miss Robinson. And don't try to solve it yourself. Just tell us if you see anything."

I did try to tell you what I saw. But you weren't interested, I thought as she showed me the door. *You practically laughed at what I'd seen.*

But I knew that what I'd seen—Gus tampering with that painting—meant something. I just didn't know what that was yet.

But I couldn't quell that nagging feeling in my stomach that it *was* important and that Gus needed to be brought in off the streets before anyone else ended up dead.

But if Detective Crawford wasn't going to listen to me, what more could I do?

I should have been relieved at being set free and taken off the suspect list, but I only felt stupid as I stumbled out of the interview room, like I was a little kid playing at being a detective and a grownup had told me off and told me to stop pretending.

That's why I almost stumbled into the figure heading towards me. He was super familiar, but it took me a moment to place the dark-haired man staggering into the interview room after me.

"Romeo?" I whispered out loud. "What the heck is he doing here?"

I spun around only to see him being led into the room.

Maybe he saw something.

But if he was at the bakery, why? Was he snooping around again? I thought about the night I'd bumped into him out back when I was closing up. He'd claimed he was there to get his paycheck, but he could have been doing anything and just used that as a cover when he was caught.

I shivered at the idea that I'd ever let him work in my bakery as I stared at the closed door of the interview room.

"Can I help you, miss?" a weary-looking uniformed police officer asked, grabbing my attention. "You look a little lost there."

I straightened up. "I'm just looking for Detective Whitaker. To say goodbye to him before I leave." Sort of true. I was thinking that, if one detective wouldn't listen to me, maybe another one would. I'd already *slightly* tested the waters with Jackson regarding the curse, and I figured that if I explained the entire thing to him, he might be a little more open-minded to listen to the curse as a theory.

Boy, I was starting to sound like Pippa.

"Can't help you, sorry. I think he's busy at the moment." The uniformed officer returned to the magazine he was reading.

Really busy or just 'doesn't want to see me' busy? I wondered.

"Thank you."

"Exit's that way."

Right.

I bumped into him as I was exiting the station.

"Jackson!" He looked a little pleased to see me, I was sure of it, but he looked around uneasily to check if anyone was watching us. "I have to tell you something. Detective Crawford wouldn't listen to me about something I saw."

He looked at me blankly. "She should have listened to you, if you had some kind of witness evidence to put forth."

I didn't want to get her into trouble. "No! It's not like that. I suppose I don't really blame her for not listening. Do you have five minutes?"

I wished Pippa was with me as I unraveled the entire story to him, ending with the way I'd seen Gus jiggling around the 'haunted' painting the following morning. "I'm not going to be arrested for trespassing, am I?"

"Trespassing?" he asked. "No. What you did was breaking and entering."

My face turned white. "I was only trying to help. The

door was open when Pippa and I went in, anyway, so it wasn't breaking in." A quick lie to try and save us from getting booked.

Jackson shook his head. "That's besides the point right now. Obviously, we had Gus Sampson as a suspect."

My ears pricked. "Did you say 'had'? Why the past tense?"

Jackson glanced into the station. Boy, he really did not want anyone to see us together, did he?

Jackson sighed. "I shouldn't really be telling you this, but given everything." He placed his hands in his pockets. "Gus is out of town right now, meeting up with an antique dealer in Pottsville. We have confirmation of his alibi already. He's been out of town all weekend." Jackson stared down at my face draining of more and more color by the second. "Gus wasn't there, Rachael. He couldn't have done it."

My head started spinning.

"Okay," I said unsteadily. "I need to go then. Sorry." I hurried away, pushing my way through the glass doors, but I didn't think the apology was really necessary. I doubted he was very sorry to see me go at that point.

I gulped for air when I finally got outside.

If Gus Sampson hadn't killed those two people, then who? Or what?

Detective Crawford might have said I was free to go, and I doubted I'd be called in for questioning again, but I couldn't help the feeling of guilt that twisted in my stomach.

Was I responsible for those people getting killed?

What if...what if the curse was real? What if my decision to purchase the antiques shop had set in motion a chain of events that had lead to the deaths of two innocent people?

I glanced back at the police station right as thunder cracked overhead. I wanted to run back in there, turn myself in, present my wrists, and say 'Lock me up, I'm a hazard to the community.'

But that would be insane. I backed away.

Perhaps there was somewhere else I really needed to go. A place I had been avoiding.

And dreading.

But I needed answers.

Chapter 9

I wasn't sure I'd ever even BEEN in this area of Belldale before. The town had a population of only about fourteen thousand, but it was divided by a small highway that split the two into two distinct halves and this half was one I was unfamiliar with. There were coffee shops I didn't recognize, and the streets seemed wider with the shops more spread out. It was at least a ten-minute drive from our apartment, but Pippa seemed to know exactly where she was going.

She'd been there many times before.

'Downtown', I suppose the area would be called.

We finally pulled up behind an innocuous-looking building.

"This is it?" I wasn't sure if I was disappointed or relieved.

The meeting place didn't look anywhere near as spooky as I was expecting it to. I had imagined the club met in a cave surrounded by cobwebs or something.

But this was just a spare room in the back of a regular-looking church on a Monday night. There were a few cobwebs, sure, and there was a musty smell like the place hadn't been aired out in months or years, but there was nothing gothic or scary about it.

"I know. I was a little disappointed at first as well. But it does the job we need it to."

I took in a deep breath. I wondered if it would do the job I needed it to. Or whether I was finally losing my mind, going down the rabbit hole that Pippa had already been dragged into by Tegan and her ilk.

"We have to pay fifty dollars to use the space every week," Pippa explained as she began to unfold chairs. "We take donations of people when they come through the door." She set me up at a little folding table with instruction to take people's money and put it in an old pickle jar. Around here, Pippa was my boss.

"Why don't you just meet at the house of one of the members?" I asked.

"You'll see," Pippa said, raising her eyebrow.

I did see. I was expecting a handful of people at the meeting, five or six at the most. But as soon as the clock hit 4:30, people began streaming into the small room and within twenty minutes, the entire place was full wall to wall of members of the clearly very popular Belldale Paranormal Society.

I gulped.

I get claustrophobic around large groups of people and suddenly wasn't sure this was such a good idea.

"Rachael," an eerie voice called out. Tegan had finally sauntered into the room right at five. She still had her cape on, but some of the purple had faded from her hair, revealing blonde roots.

Pippa raised an eyebrow at me. "You two have met before?"

"I'm so glad you finally decided to join us at one of our meetings. I think you will find it very enlightening. I've been hoping to see you here for quite some time." Tegan closed and locked the door behind her and everyone went quiet as she swished her way to a small podium in the middle of the back wall. "

Pippa quietly took the jar from me and quickly counted it. When she was done, sh nodded to Tegan.

I shivered. Now that the sun had gone down, a kind of spooky quality had taken over the room. It was freezing and Pippa had to set up a tiny space heater in the corner, which barely did anything but did add an interesting smell to the room, sort of like burning plastic but slightly more sinister.

Or maybe it was just Tegan's presence that had changed the make-up of the room. She had a knack for doing that.

There were all sorts of people in the club. Some were relatively normal-looking, still wearing suits and ties from work, but the majority of them wore items that would immediately get them labeled as 'alternative' to onlookers. Necklaces with pentagons and other symbols that I didn't quite recognize, hair dyed in various bright, unearthly shades.

I suddenly saw how well Pippa fit in here. And she seemed very 'at home,' milling amongst everyone, talking and chatting and catching up with gossip that I wasn't privy to. I couldn't help but feel a little jealous that Pippa had friends she was just as close with, or even closer to, than me.

I settled into an empty seat beside her. The others were being friendly enough, saying hello, introducing themselves, but I still felt distinctly ill at ease. I was so far out of my element it wasn't funny.

"You don't need to look so nervous, Rach. These people don't bite. They are just interested in discussing and learning about all the unexplained paranormal happenings in Belldale." She gave me a grin. "Just a bunch of amateur detectives, kind of like you!"

She patted my hand and I nodded. Maybe that was true. Everyone in the club was here because they had a thirst to solve the unsolvable, an interest in puzzles and the unknowable. But I still felt uneasy as I waited for Tegan to begin.

Before she'd started talking, I had no idea there were so many unexplained mysteries in Belldale. We were just one little town, but apparently we had a very storied history. This week, there was a lot of discussion focused on this so called 'mystical big cat' that many members of the town—and specifically the club— claimed to have seen, but no one had ever actually caught or taken a proper photo of. Belldale's very own Bigfoot. Apparently, this creature was black with bright red eyes and was capable of disappearing right in front of a person's eyes. There had been fresh sightings this week.

"I saw it dissolve into thin air," a young man named Aaron, with long dark hair and a sleeve of tattoos, piped up. "While I was trying to take a photo of it." A little too convenient for my tastes.

But others had similar stories.

"All of this can't possibly be true, can it?" I

whispered to Pippa. She returned an eager nod.

"Of course. You see why I like it here now?"

I had to admit there was a certain appeal to it all. The human mind is drawn to mysteries and, by extension, the paranormal. All the stories were fascinating, but I had to remind myself to keep a skeptical mind. But as I listened to the club discuss everything from large cats to haunted houses and even alleged UFO sightings, I felt my nerves dissolve a little. In fact, I totally forgot myself for a while and just sat there and listened.

"See, Rach?" Pippa whispered to me. "You'll never have to worry about being bored and not having a mystery to solve ever again—if you just keep coming to these meetings!"

She was probably right. Maybe I would have to keep coming along.

But I wasn't sure this was entirely where I belonged. I felt like a tourist in that room, listening to everyone's strange stories but feeling two steps removed from them all.

Tegan eventually drifted the topic onto the next part of the meeting, and I was still so distracted thinking about all the mysterious 'cases' that had been brought up that I jumped when I heard my name mentioned.

"Now, Rachael is going to tell us all a very interesting story!" Tegan placed her hands together and nodded at me while everyone clapped.

I am? I thought. "Pippa, you never told me I had to stand up in front of people and talk to them."

"Then stay seated while you talk," she answered, rather unhelpfully. "Come on. This is what you came for, right? For help? How are you going to get any if you won't tell your story?"

I sighed a little and stood up. I took a deep breath. Public speaking isn't that bad...is it?

Yes, it is. It's basically the worst thing imaginable.

I headed up to the podium. Tegan's eyes were still boring into me. I tried to relax and ignore her—and everyone else in the room—and just focus on Pippa in the audience. She was grinning at me and nodding her support.

Here goes nothing.

Everyone looked enraptured as I unleashed my story. I told them all about the day I'd decided to buy Gus's antiques store, and how the—I paused before I said the word '*curse*'—seemed to have started right after then.

"And, Rachael, have you been feeling sick all the time?" Tegan's voice called out.

I paused for a second. "Yes," I had to admit. "Almost constantly, actually."

Tegan nodded and I could hear her murmuring, "A clear sign of a curse."

Was it? I took a moment before I got to the really juicy detail of the story; the salacious events that I knew everyone was really there to hear about.

I gulped right before I spoke. "Then, of course, there are the murders."

There were a few gasps and murmurs in the crowd.

Tegan's eyes drilled into me as I told them about the two bodies that had been found in Gus's antique store. First the man Jason, then the second, a woman named Bridgett. "They were both found in the antique shop next to her bakery. It looks as though the killer was the same person."

I could have sworn that Tegan was shooting me a judgmental look. The severity of it took me off guard and I stammered for a moment as I tried to remember what I was talking about. I felt as though I should clear something up for the crowd. "Even though I was taken in for questioning, I was quickly released. Er, thank you." There was some thin applause as I scampered back to my seat.

Tegan looked grim as she retook to the podium. "As you can see, something rather terrible has befallen Rachael. A curse!"

Everyone nodded and half the crowd turned to look at me. I could feel my face growing red. "And we can help her," Tegan added. "Don't worry, Rachael." She turned her full attention to me now. "You're in the right place now, a safe place. We can remove this curse that has taken over your life. If you will accept our help."

She seemed to be waiting for an answer or confirmation from me. The room was silent as everyone stared at me.

I sat very still. Eventually I nodded, and a sly smile spread over Tegan's face. I was willing to try anything.

At this stage, I was willing to believe just about anything. After all, anything could be possible. And I was running out of rational explanations for all the weird stuff that had been happening to me.

Pippa reached over and squeezed my hand. "You'll be fine now. Everything will go back to normal if you just follow their instructions."

But little did I know, I was NOT about to like the advice that Tegan was going to give me.

"First of all," she announced. "You are going to have to go back and undo any of the actions you made that caused the curse to be placed on you."

"Well, I don't have a time machine," I half-joked, though no one seemed to find this amusing. So I sat still and silent again.

"Do you still have that contract you signed?" Tegan looked at me pointedly.

Did she mean the sales contract? I nodded uneasily.

"Good. Burn it."

Burn it? That seemed a little extreme and melodramatic.

I turned towards Pippa, who was nodding enthusiastically. I bet she was loving this advice. Her eyes did seem to be lighting up.

Tegan continued, "Next you have to go into the shop and apologize to the twins' spirits."

"You mean the painting?" I asked, slightly incredulous.

"I mean the spirits that placed the curse on you." She meant the painting, though. I sat back in my seat.

"Take back all the intentions you made to buy the property and try to offer them something in order to remove the bad karma. A gift or a sacrifice."

But I was still caught up on the first point. "Take back all my intentions? Burn the contract? You're telling me..." I shot a look at Pippa. "That I can't buy the store?" I started to get this little nagging feeling in the pit of my stomach that Pippa had put Tegan up to this. It all seemed to align exactly with what she had been nagging me to do.

Tegan looked outraged. "Why on Earth would you still wish to purchase the store after there have been two murders in there? You need to cancel all your plans immediately."

She had a fair point. I'd been considering that myself. Who wants to eat in a bakery where there have been two murders?

I'd been trying to tell myself that if I could just prove that the killer was human, that there is no curse, no ghosts, it isn't so bad.

I hung my head and whispered to Pippa. "Maybe she has a point. Maybe you have a point. Maybe I really have to rethink my business plan."

I glanced up to see Pippa exchanging a wink with Tegan, and mouthing the word "thanks."

I stood up. "So you did put Tegan up to this then? You told her to say that to me?"

Pippa looked aghast. "Rach, what are you getting so upset for? You know this is the right thing to do. What, where are you going?"

"I'm leaving, Pippa. I came here for real advice, not to be set up. You know what? It sounds to me as though you've been against my plan from the start! What is it, Pippa? What is really going on? Why did you tell Tegan to say all of that stuff?"

"Rachael, I can explain." She looked startled as I started to stomp out of the room. She shrugged apologetically at Tegan and started to chase after me. "Please, just stay for the rest of the meeting. These guys are really cool once you get to know them, I promise."

I pulled on my coat. "No. You can either come with me now or stay with these guys and catch the bus home later."

"You need me to drive," she pointed out. My old car didn't have GPS and I'd had to rely on her to get to the meeting.

"I can find my way."

Pippa sighed. "I'll just come with you. Hang on."

I was still fuming once we got to the car. "So are you going to tell me what is really going on?"

"I've already told you a thousand times before," Pippa said, "There's an evil spirit behind all of this! Or spirits. How else do you explain everything? I thought you were willing to keep an open mind." Pippa's face crumbled in distress. "I was so excited when you told me you wanted to come to the meeting. I thought you were finally willing to accept that all this stuff is true."

***

We didn't talk much during the car ride home. Of all the people I could possibly lose trust in, Pippa was the worst. We'd always been there for each other. But now I was starting to think there was some other reason she didn't want me to buy Gus's shop and she was just using this so-called 'curse'—and Tegan—to scare me off.

I finally broke the silence once we were back in my kitchen. "I'm not sure which is worse, Pippa: you lying to me about this curse, or you actually believing all this crazy stuff."

Pippa stared back at me for a long while. "Okay, yes, I did tell Tegan to advise you not to buy the shop! But I was trying to protect you, Rachael!"

I shook my head. "I knew it."

"I do believe in all this stuff that you call crazy," she finally whispered, a little sadly. "I just wish you could see it. I wish you would listen to Tegan."

"Pippa, can't you see? This club is getting in your head. And worse than that, it's getting in the way of our friendship." I shook my head. "We've been bickering for weeks now, and it's always about the same thing. I wish you would just use your brain for a second and see how illogical all of this crazy stuff is."

I stomped over to the fridge and grabbed some leftover cake from the shelf. That plan to eat more fruits and vegetables had been a failure so far. "From now on, I'm going back to solving this mystery the old fashioned way. Looking for suspects... human suspects! And finding evidence. See, Pippa, there's one crucial aspect that has been missing from all these paranormal theories, and that is evidence! These so-called friends of yours are not your friends, Pippa, if they make you lose touch with reality."

Pippa was just staring at me with her hands on her hips. It seemed like she was trying to get up the guts to say something to me.

"Maybe if you actually had a little time for me lately, Rachael, I wouldn't have needed to make these new friends."

"What are you talking about?"

My stomach had begun to ache again and I stumbled over to the sink for a glass of water. I took a large gulp, but it did little to ease the pain.

"You've been so busy with the bakery the last year or so," Pippa started to chide. "Which I don't blame you for, of course. You had to take the time to build your business up. I get that. But I was hoping that when I started working there, it would be a chance for us to spend time together again. But you've barely even been at work! You've been so preoccupied with solving this case."

"Pippa, that's not true! We live and work together, for crying out loud! How much closer do you think we should be?"

"You didn't even know about my break up!" Pippa

blurted out. She immediately looked like she regretted it.

"What break up? I didn't even know that you were dating anyone."

How would she even have found time for that? And how could she have dated someone without me even knowing about it.

I suddenly realized.

"You were going out with Romeo?" My jaw was practically on the floor. Now his little fit made sense. It had nothing to do with the early mornings or the lack of caffeine in his system. It was a lover's tiff.

So that's what he'd meant that night when he'd told me to 'ask Pippa.'

Pippa was turning bright red as she looked at the floor. "I didn't think I could talk to you about it." But her voice was full of guilt, not accusations.

"You didn't think you could talk to me about it because you knew it was unprofessional of you to hire your boyfriend."

She nodded. "I thought that if you could just see what a good baker he was, you would be so pleased to keep him that you would overlook his questionable hiring."

I sighed. "That's why you were so nervous about me liking his baking." I shook my head. I wasn't angry with Pippa; I was just kind of hurt that she wouldn't be honest with me. Especially after I gave her the assistant manager job and bestowed the extra responsibilities onto her. I knew she'd always been kind of a flaky employee at the other places she'd worked, but I would have thought she'd know better than to hire her boyfriend at my bakery...and not even tell me about it.

"Rach?"

I sat down at the table and took another nibble of my cake. Pippa pulled out the chair besides me. "Aren't you going to say something?"

I stared at the table. "I was really worried about why Romeo had quit Pippa. I thought maybe I had done something to upset him." I shook my head. "I thought he'd been scared off by the tales about the ghost. Or the curse." I let out a little bitter laugh. "But it was all a lot more simple than that."

"Rachael, I'm sorry."

I swallowed. "Didn't you care that you were screwing with my business when you hired your boyfriend? Pippa, I'm down a baker now and we've been really struggling lately. Well, I'VE been struggling!"

Much to my horror, Pippa burst into tears. "I've been struggling as well, Rachael! I've just been trying not to show it!"

My phone began to ring.

"Rachael?" a familiar voice said. "There's been a break-in at your bakery. You ought to come down here."

Jackson ended the phone call without even saying goodbye.

***

There was broken glass all over the place, but nothing seemed to be missing. All the money in the register was still there and nothing had been taken.

Jackson took my statement anyway. "Is there anyone you think might have done this?"

Yeah, several, I thought. *Gus, Romeo, take your pick of the litter.*

"Hey, Jackson," a voice called out. "We found something."

I spun around to see Detective Crawford standing

there holding a broken video surveillance camera in her hands. "Looks like they were looking for this."

My security camera?

"Where does that footage go to?" Jackson asked in a super serious tone.

"It gets sent to my computer, an old laptop that I keep behind the counter. It's not good enough for anything else."

We both hurried behind the counter. Gone.

Someone had wanted that footage.

"Which way did this camera point?" Detective Crawford asked.

"Towards the street," I whispered quietly. I was starting to get an idea of why the thief had wanted it.

Detective Crawford glanced at Jackson. "We need to find that footage."

He nodded at her and they walked out together after Jackson advised me to take the following day off and to keep out of harm's way. The two of them looked rather cozy as they climbed back into their police car, I thought.

I sat down with unsteady legs at a table towards the

back. "I saw Romeo down at the police station when I was called in," I said quietly as Pippa joined me.

"What?" Pippa sat down next to me. "Why didn't you say anything?" Then she hung her head in her hands. "Oh no," she groaned.

"Oh no, what?"

Pippa sat upright. Her tears had dried up by this stage. "Oh, Rachael, I need to admit something to you."

I braced myself for a revelation about Tegan and the paranormal society.

But she had something quite different to reveal to me.

"Please don't be mad at me."

"Okay," I said unsurely. "Pippa, just tell me what it is."

"That night when I called you late at work...upset and crying..."

"I remember."

Pippa hung her head. "It was because of Romeo. He was at your apartment. We started to argue and he got angry again just like he did that day he stormed out of the bakery."

"Pippa, why didn't you tell me that!"

"I was embarrassed about all of it, Rach. It was easier to pretend I was scared of something paranormal than to admit to anything else."

I placed an arm around her. "It's okay, Pips. I'm just glad you aren't with the wretched guy anymore."

She dried her eyes and sat up. "Do you think it was him that broke in?"

I shook my head. "I have no idea. But promise me that you will stay away from him from now on?"

She nodded.

"How did you meet him anyway?" I asked.

Another look of guilt snuck over her face. "You aren't going to believe this, Rach."

"Oh, please don't tell me he is a member of the paranormal club?"

She shook her head. "No, but I did meet him while I was investigating something to do with the club." Her voice trailed off as she frowned.

"What were you investigating?"

She was quiet for a second. "The painting," she finally said. "In Gus's shop. Romeo was looking at it as well. He seemed super interested in it. I thought he might want to buy it so I had to warn him about it. So I told him all about the curse. He seemed really sweet and interested, so I kept talking and talking. He asked me out and we started dating."

I had to ask. "Pippa, is the reason you don't want me buying the shop because it has memories about Romeo?"

She let out a little laugh and shook her head. "No. Come on. I am a little more resilient than that."

She suddenly grew deadly serious. "But, Rachael, I have to tell you something. Even though I love this job and appreciate everything you've done for me. I'm sorry, but I have to tell you this. If you buy that shop, I *will* quit."

***

"Bronson...is it?" I asked, glancing over the guy's resume. He was young, but at least he already had a few years experience working in a bakery. Plus, he was here at 6:00 A.M. for an interview. You've got to want a job pretty badly if you're up and going at that hour. Plus, I was desperate.

The young man with the carrot-colored hair and freckles nodded eagerly. "That's right, miss." He had a rather charming southern accent. "I'm a quick learner. I can guarantee that you won't regret hiring me, ma'am."

I couldn't, not with the run of luck that I was having. "Can you start right away?"

I was just showing him into the kitchen when I heard the jingle that let me know we had a customer. "Sorry, we're not open for another hour or so...Jackson." I straightened up. "Sorry, Detective Whitaker. I assume you're here in an official capacity."

"Are you okay, Rachael? You're looking kind of green around the gills."

Great. Now the curse was turning me green on top of everything else. "Just a bit under the weather."

"Still? You really ought to see a doctor."

"Like I have time for that."

"Really. You have to go to one."

I nodded and promised to make an appointment as soon as he left. Not that it would do a lot of good. If I was cursed, what was a doctor going to do for me? I didn't say any of this to him, though.

Jackson cleared his throat. "Have there been any further incidents?"

"You mean has anybody else broken in? No."

He glanced around the room. "I thought I advised you not to open today."

"I chose to ignore that advice. Is there anything else I can do for you?"

Jackson leaned against the counter, his lips slightly pursed. "Have you seen Gus Sampson about?"

I shook my head. "I thought he was no longer a suspect."

Jackson looked down at the ground. "He's not." I could tell he wanted to say something, but was holding back.

I took a step closer and lowered my voice so that Bronson couldn't hear us. "Then who is?"

Jackson cleared his throat. "No one." He turned to leave. "Please let us know if you see Gus Sampson."

I narrowed my eyes. "Why? Is he still in Pottsville? Seeing that antiques dealer, right?"

"That's right," Jackson said. "As far as we know, anyhow."

He was just about to leave. "Hang on," I said suddenly. Jackson turned back to me. "If Gus is about to sell his shop—go out of business—then why is he out of town speaking to an antiques dealer?"

Jackson stood still for a moment. "That's actually a very good question."

I thought about it. "I suppose he could be, theoretically, buying for his own private collection. But with all the unsold stock he has, and his financial position, that seems unlikely."

"You're starting to think like a detective," Jackson replied. There was a hint of admiration in his voice, which surprised me.

"I thought you didn't like me sticking my nose in police business," I said playfully. "I thought you didn't want me having anything to do with this case."

"I never said that." He paused to correct himself. "Well, not recently. Your help did prove to be invaluable last time. I have to admit that. If you come up with something of interest again, I'd gladly listen to it."

I frowned. "Then why were you acting so cagey around me down at the station? Like you were afraid someone was going to see you talking to me? Seemed like you were kind of ashamed to be seen talking to me."

A blush of red crept up the sides of Jackson's neck. "That wasn't the reason for my furtiveness."

He didn't seem to want to continue. "Oh?" I prodded. "Pray tell then."

"I didn't want Detective Crawford to see me taking to you. I was afraid she might get the wrong impression."

"Right," I said. Now it was my turn to start blushing. So, they were seeing each other then.

"It's only recent, Rachael. We've only been on a couple of dates."

"Hey, it's none of my business."

I turned back towards the counter, performing my old trick of pretending I was cleaning a really stubborn stain out of the counter. The awkward silence hung between us both for a few moments.

"Hey," I said all casually, just as I sensed that Jackson was about to leave for good this time. "What was the name of the antiques dealer that Gus was meant to be visiting?"

"Maureen Tatler," he answered. "Why's that?"

"No reason. Just curious."

I could see from the look on his face that he regretted being so candid, regretting the accidental spilling of information that he otherwise would have guarded, if not for the desperate need to cut the awkward tension between the two of us.

I forced a smile at him as he backed out of the door. I thought he might tell me not to go to Pottsville. To leave well enough alone.

But he didn't.

And I wouldn't have listened to him even if he did.

***

"Gus!" I said, stopping with my car key in mid-air, pointed towards my car. "You're back."

"You sound disappointed," he said gruffly, stuffing his hands in his pockets. "Still keen to throw me out of my shop then?"

"No," I said, shaking my head. "It's not like that. It's never been like that Gus." I put my hand down and walked over to join him behind his shop. "I hope you don't think that. It's never been anything personal. I just want to expand my business." I nodded towards he store. "And this is the most convenient location."

He leaned against his own car. "Ah, I know that, sweetheart. It's just hard."

I wanted to bring up his trip to Pottsville without letting on how much I knew. "You've been away then?" I nodded towards the rear of his car, which was filled with luggage. "Was it a vacation?"

He let out a scoff. "Not exactly." He narrowed his eyes and shot me a sideways glance. "Actually, I was meeting up with someone who might be a little competition for you, if you really want to know."

"What do you mean? You were meeting with a baker?"

"No. Someone who might be interested in buying this joint." He nodded towards the shop. "And keep it in tact, not fill it with cakes and pastries."

Maureen Tatler. "Oh. So...what happened then?"

"Wouldn't you love to know?"

I would, actually.

Gus stood up straight. "You don't have to worry about her, sweetheart. Turns out she was only interested in buying one very specific item."

"Which item?" I asked quietly.

He shrugged. "Some painting of two little kids. But I told her, that painting ain't for sale."

***

My keys were already in the ignition and my car ready to pull out when a figure stepped in front of me, forcing me to slam on the brakes.

"You nearly gave me a heart attack!" I called out.

The guy, wearing army camouflage and a yellow hat, gave me a weary look before he continued walking like nothing had happened. I stared after him and watched him go through the back exit of Gus's Antiques.

I recognized him from somewhere, but it took me a moment or two to figure out where I had seen him before.

"Huh," I murmured. "That's strange. That's that guy that was there the morning of the wedding. The one who wanted to come in, that we turned away."

He never did come back the next day.

"Well," I said out loud, as I finally pulled out of the

parking lot. "I guess we're going on a road trip."

Chapter 10

Finally, I had something to go off of. I could have kissed Gus, I was so grateful for the tidbit that he had accidentally let slip about Maureen Tatler. There had to be a reason she wanted that painting. And it had to be connected to the killings.

There was no time to waste now. Word about the two homicides had spread around all of Belldale and it felt like history was repeating itself as our customer numbers dwindled down to a small trickle. People didn't feel safe venturing down to our once safe and cozy little enclave. And I didn't blame them. That was why I had to restore our reputation quickly. We needed to put the killer behind bars.

But I wasn't sure I could travel out to Pottsville on my own. Not without backup.

I needed Pippa's help.

More than that, I needed her company. I knew that once we actually got out on the road, and actually arrived in Pottsville, that Pippa would enjoy herself. It could be a chance for us to repair our friendship. I was even fairly sure that she'd enjoy investigating again once she was doing it. Especially if she knew the painting was involved.

I just needed to show her that.

So I had to rely on subterfuge.

I caught her just as she was pulling on her boots, about to head to another meeting of the Belldale Paranormal Society. "Hey, Pippa, you know how I haven't been feeling very well lately? I was thinking that some clean country air would do me a world of good. What do you say we get out of town for a day or two? Go on a little road trip, just the two of us?"

She sat up straight, a smile curling on her lips. "Are you serious?"

"Yeah. We should pack an overnight bag, throw it in the car and just drive out to the county, see what we find. How about out towards Pottsville?"

Pippa nodded thoughtfully. "But what about the bakery?"

"Bronson will be fine on his own for a couple of days." Normally I would never leave a new hire in charge of my business, but there was something about Bronson I felt like I could trust. Plus, we had very few customers these days.

"So what are we waiting for?"

Pippa's eyes widened. "What, you want to go right now? But I have a meeting! "

"This early?" I asked, looking at my watch. It was barely 7 A.M.

"We're meeting at Stanton Park to see if we can catch a glimpse of the mystical cat," Pippa said as she stuffed her camera and extra batteries in her purse. "Everyone knows he hunts in the morning."

I waved my hand dismissively. "Come on, you can miss one meeting. We may as well go now, make a long weekend of it."

It took us about three hours to reach Pottsville, an even smaller town than Belldale with a population of roughly four thousand people and a heavy reliance on apples as the prime source of industry and tourism. Neither of us had ventured there before, so it was new to both of us.

I had the name, Maureen Tatler. And I was pretty sure of the location, even though the old website Maureen had up only had the street name, not the full address of the house that also doubled as her place of business. And even though I had to rely on memorizing a map of the area before we left so that I could make my discovery of the street look totally innocent, I figured I would take my chances on both those fronts.

Halewood Road. I thanked my lucky stars that I'd been able to find it without driving around for hours or needing to make an excuse for why I needed to check my phone.

I pulled the car onto the street and slowed down until I saw what I was looking for.

That has to be it.

"Hey," I said, trying to sound both chirpy and casual. "This place looks cool. Looks like an old antiques dealer or something. Why don't we pull over and have a quick look inside?"

"I dunno, Rach, I've kind of had enough of antiques lately. Haven't you?"

Oh my gosh, yes. But I didn't say that. "This could be interesting though. And, come on, it's not like there's gonna be a wealth of things to do in this town."

She sighed. "Okay then, you've twisted my arm."

There was only one way to describe Maureen Tatler's house, and that was...haunted.

"It looks like a witch's castle," Pippa whispered as she stared up at the grey, gnarled building. She sounded more awe-struck than scared, though. "Tegan would LOVE this."

I suppressed my eye-roll. "You'll have to take some photos for her then. And for the rest of the club, since you missed the meeting. Get something to show them. So, are we going inside?"

I knocked on the door. "Hello?" Tapped again. There was no sound of movement on the other side of the door.

Pippa read out the plaque that hung beside the door. "Maureen Tatler, PhD. Antiques dealer and artist." Pippa paused. "It says her open hours are weekdays 9 - 4. So she should be inside."

I knocked again, harder this time, and the door pushed open thanks to the extra force.

Pippa and I looked at each other and shrugged. "Should we just go in?"

"What the heck is this place?" Pippa whispered as we moved through the dark creepy hallway. A spider's web hit my face and I cringed as I pulled off the sticky thread, shuddering at the thought that there might be a spider making its way down my shirt. Maureen clearly didn't have many buyers through the house. In fact, it seemed like no one had walked down this hall in weeks.

Months.

"Can you smell that?" Pippa asked. She'd always had a far more sensitive nose than me so it took a moment or two for me to realize what she was talking about.

"What IS that?" I had to cover my nose with my hand.

"It smells like something died in here."

***

"Maureen?" I called out.

Pippa had to run back to the car for a flashlight. We needed it as we entered the back of the property.

"I think we located the source of the smell," Pippa said, grimacing as she waved her hand in front of her face. "It's all this junk."

As she shone the flashlight over the room, I took in the stacks of newspapers and piles of old junk. I'd expected the property of an antiques dealer to be full of valuable items, collector's editions, stuff like armor and war memorabilia and hundred year old furniture. But this was just junk. Garbage that was festering and rotting, lining every inch of the room.

I still wasn't convinced that was what the smell was, though.

"How are we going to get through to the next room?"

We'd come to a dead end, a wall of newspapers blocking our way in the maze.

The papers smelled as bad as anything else in the house.

"I think we should just get the heck out of here," Pippa said. "This is dangerous, Rach. I don't know what we're here for anyway."

She turned to leave, but I grabbed her arm. "Wait, you can't go yet, Pippa. We have to find Maureen!"

She stared at me. "What's going on, Rachael?"

I was going to have to come clean or she was going to run out of there, leaving me to locate Maureen under a pile of garbage on my own. "I'm just worried about her, is all," I tried to say. "What if she's hurt? Or worse? We can't just leave her in this house in this state."

"Rachael, she's the one who made the mess. Looks like this is just how she lives. She's clearly a level five hoarder. This is not our monkey, and not our zoo. I don't want to die in here."

She made a move to leave and I grabbed her again. "Okay, fine. Just wait, Pippa. I need to tell you something."

I kept half an eye on the pile of newspaper, just waiting for it to tip over and crush us.

"Don't be mad, okay?" I tried to make Pippa promise me. "I only did this for our own good."

It looked like Pippa would not be able to make that promise. "Hurry up and tell me before we get killed in this joint, Rachael!"

I nodded. "Okay...okay...I drove us here on purpose. I wanted to find Maureen Tatler."

Pippa's mouth dropped open. "Why would you want to?" She sucked her breath in. "Right. Antiques dealer. Is this related to Gus? To the case?!" She shook her head and threw her head back. "Oh, I don't believe this, Rachael! I told you I was out! That I wanted nothing more to do with it!"

"But, Pippa," I tried to tell her as she started to stomp back towards the hallway. "It's about the painting. Maureen wants to buy it, but Gus won't sell. Don't you want to know why?"

"No, I don't!" she called out, her footsteps heavy as

she stomped away. "I can't believe you tricked me like this, Rachael!"

"Pippa, I'm sorry!"

I started to chase after her when I saw a ghostly figure out of the corner of my right eye. "What the..."

I spun towards it, shrieking a little as I saw a dirty looking figure with wild curly hair, grey from either dust or old age, which one I wasn't entirely certain.

Pippa stopped at the sound of my shriek, but it was too late. The old woman was already lunging towards her, rasping in a voice that sounded like it had been mixed with gravel. "What are you doing trespassing in my home?"

Pippa screamed as the body flung itself at her. I only saw the long yellowing fingernails clawing at her.

"Quick! Run!" I tried to call out. But running in that claustrophobic room was not easy and Pippa had stumbled awkwardly in the direction of the wall of newspaper.

Surprisingly agile, the woman jumped out of the way before the wall came down. It seemed like she was used to dodging this sort of thing, but Pippa was not so nimble and not so lucky.

At first, only the top few newspapers slipped off, but pretty soon it was an avalanche, and there was no stopping it. I lunged out of way myself, coughing violently as dirt and dust flung up into my nostrils.

My eyes were enveloped in dust, and I frantically tried to push it away, along with the stench that grew stronger with the figure's presence.

"Pippa!"

The dust settled and I raced over to her. The witch-like figure, a woman I could see now, had grey hair and wrinkled, leathery skin that she shielded from the light coming through from the front of the house.

I could only see her head staring out the top of the newspapers. "Please just answer me, say something, let me know that you are still alive."

"I'm alive," she muttered, "but I am going to kill you."

***

"Maureen, I think we ought to get you to a hospital."

She swatted at my hand and pulled her tattered

266

shawl tighter around her shoulders as she hobbled away. Her body was all pointy joints and angles, and I wondered how long it had been since she'd last eaten a proper meal.

"I think it's me that needs to get to a hospital," Pippa said, still brushing bits of dirt and debris off her body. "Or at least a hotel for a long hot bath." She shot me a pleading look.

"Are you talking to me then?" I asked her, hopeful at her not-entirely-homicidal tone.

"You mean after you almost got me crashed to death?"

But my attention was snatched away by Maureen who was sitting, shivering, on her own curb.

"Maureen," I said gently, sitting towards her. "We can get someone to help you, maybe some help cleaning your house out."

Pippa shot me a look and shook her head. "That's the worst thing you can say to a hoarder," she whispered to me. "You'll just make her panic."

"That's my collection," she finally said. Her proper speaking voice shocked me. I was expecting a raspy old drawl, but she had a prim and proper English accent with a clipped and pronounced delivery of every word. "And it is not to be touched."

I glanced at Pippa before turning my attention back to Maureen. "And was there something you were hoping to add to your collection, Maureen?"

She looked at me with sharp, bird-like features. I could see now that even though dirt covered her face, underneath it was a rather pretty face with well-defined, high cheekbones and piercing blue eyes. "To what precisely do you refer to?"

"A painting," I said softly, "of two young children. Twins, probably." I glanced up at Pippa and she seemed to understand precisely now why we were here. "Gus Sampson told me you were interested in buying it off him."

She cast me a long steely glare like I should already know the answer to the question, as though I was foolish for even asking.

"I did not want to buy that painting off him," she said in her short, clipped, posh tone that still didn't match her exterior. "That is my painting!"

"Your painting?" I whispered. "What do you mean, Maureen?"

"That is a painting of my two children," she whispered in a chilling tone. "The twins that I lost many years ago."

I sucked in a short gasp. "Maureen, I'm so sorry."

Pippa looked aghast. "So why won't Gus give it back to you then?" She glanced back over her shoulder at the house. Suddenly a lot of things about the place were starting to make sense.

"That old man refuses to part with it," Maureen whispered bitterly. "No matter what I try to do to get it back." She looked away, gazing off into the distance. In that moment, she was no longer sitting there with us, but was far away, lost in some deep, dark crevice of her past. "Why he won't part with it, I have no idea. That painting..." She stopped to close her eyes. "In all my years of collecting items, antiques, objects, storing everything I could get my hands on, that painting is the one thing I truly want, and the one thing I can't add to my collection."

I glanced up at Pippa. It seemed like Maureen had been collecting and hoarding everything she could find in some desperate attempt to replace what she had lost: her children.

"Maureen," Pippa said, joining us by the curb. "Do

you know why no one has ever purchased that painting before? There are rumors that it is haunted, and that anyone who buys it will be cursed."

Maureen opened her eyes and bit her lip. "That comes as no surprise to me. Rumors created by me in order to keep others away, and spread amongst others, no doubt. I had no idea that they would grow legs, but at least it means that I know where the painting is."

Pippa's face was a mixture of distress and disappointment. "I can't believe Gus would be so selfish as to keep the painting from you."

The faraway look returned to Maureen's eyes. "No matter what price I offer, he claims it is not enough. I have no idea why that man is so intent on keeping the one thing I have as a memory of my children." Her voice began to crack and Pippa reached her hand out to cover the old woman's.

"We'll get the painting back for you, I promise, Maureen," Pippa whispered.

But there was something I had to ask Maureen. "Why was Gus here, visiting you over the weekend?"

Maureen shook her head. "He was warning me to stay away from his shop," she whispered bitterly. "Had some crazy idea in his head that I had been snooping around, that I would try to break into the shop to take the painting away. That's why I was squirreled away today, hiding out the back. I was afraid he might return with more threats."

Again, there was something I had to ask. "And had you been, Maureen? Had you tried to break in, to find the painting?"

She shook her head. "I don't drive, dear, not with my eyesight. How could I get to Belldale on my own?" She turned and looked me straight in the eyes, then whispered, "But my great nephew lives there, and he has been trying to secure it for me. But with no luck."

Pippa and I were just staring at each other.

I knew we were both thinking the same thing, but it was Pippa who finally said it out loud. "Maureen, is your great nephew's name Romeo?"

Maureen frowned and shook her head. "No, dear. His name is George."

We both stared at each other, the disappointment between us palpable.

***

Pippa still desperately needed a bath and I needed a warm bed.

"So I guess that's how the whole curse rumor got started," Pippa murmured as we headed back towards the car. "I'm not sure whether the paranormal club is going to be exited to hear this news or disappointed by it."

"Disappointed that it wasn't a real curse?" I shrugged. "In a way, it was cursed. Just not caused by an evil spirit."

Pippa shivered and looked up at the dark clouds that were circling above. "Maureen's story doesn't explain everything, though. We still don't know who killed Jason or Bridget, or what the heck Gus was doing scaring us away that night. Or who Maureen's great nephew is."

I could feel a smile creeping its way to my lips. "Are you saying, Pippa, that you would *like* to know those things? Does this mean that you are back on the case?"

She let out a heavy sigh. "We always work better when we are together."

"In more ways than one."

I wrapped my arm around her neck and did a little hop and skip in mid-air. "I knew you would be interested when I finally got you out here. I'm sorry I tricked you, Pippa," I said as I stopped skipping. "Seriously. That was terrible of me. But come on, you have to admit it was more than worth it." I nodded towards the house. "If we hadn't come along then Maureen could have died in there."

Pippa looked back at the house and nodded. "She definitely could have been crushed to death. Like I almost was."

My mouth dropped open and I let out the loudest gasp I had ever heard.

All of a sudden, I knew.

I knew who had killed Jason and Bridget.

Chapter 11

Our weekend away turned into a single long day of driving. Pippa still hadn't gotten her bath.

"Do you think Maureen did it?" Pippa asked while she was huddled up beside me in the passenger seat. "Do you think she was trying to get her painting back? Or trying to teach Gus a lesson?"

The longer I drove, the less confident I was becoming in my theory. I closed my eyes for just a second (I was driving after all) and told myself that I needed to trust my instincts.

"No, I don't think Maureen did it," I said quietly. "I think she is just a heartbroken old lady, not a cold-blooded killer."

"Not a cold-blooded killer now, but she seems to hate Gus. What if she tried to break in to steal the painting, accidentally killed Jason and thought, well, if Gus gets blamed for it, that's just too bad?"

"And what about the second body? What about Bridget? Maureen was in her home in Pottsville when that happened."

"Oh." Pippa slunk back against her seat. "I forgot

about that." She was silent for a moment. "Then what are you thinking, Rachael?"

"I need to get inside Gus's shop again, while he isn't there, to see if I'm correct."

When Pippa didn't give me any sort of response, I glanced at her to get a good look at her face. She was staring out the window. "I don't think that's such a good idea."

"Oh, come on, Pippa. This isn't still about the curse, is it? We know how the rumor of the curse started now, and it was a very sad story indeed. You can't still believe that painting is haunted."

She had her face pressed so hard against the window that it was entirely smooshed. "Just because Maureen started the rumor," she murmured, "doesn't mean it's not true. In fact, having heard her story, it seems even more likely that the painting could be haunted." She looked down. "I didn't know that the twins in the painting were based on real people. Or that they had died a long time ago."

I opened my mouth to say something, but closed it again. With her head pressed up against the window like that, looking so forlorn, Pippa reminded me of a small child. I could tell that she was truly upset about

Maureen's revelation, so I spoke gently. "She's a grieving mother, Pippa. She hasn't cursed the painting."

Pippa finally lifted her head to stare at me. "What about all the weird things that have happened to you then, Rachael? Do you have an explanation for all of them?"

"Some of them, I do," I muttered. "And I'm sure there are perfectly logical explanations for the rest of them as well."

We drove the rest of the way in silence.

***

"Shoot, Gus is in the shop." I leaned forward for a second. It looked like he was finally making moves to clear his stuff out and the butterflies in my stomach began to do a dance. This could mean that the sale of the property might be back on the table. And I would have to make a very big decision.

I quickly turned my head away as I sat in my parked car, so that Gus wouldn't spot me staring straight at him.

"What do we do now?" I asked.

Pippa unclicked her seatbelt. "I'm still up for that bath."

"I know," I said, ignoring her. "We'll wait in the back, in secret, 'til he leaves, then break in just like we did the other day!"

Pippa was shaking her head vigorously. "No! No way! You can count me out."

I was shocked. "But, Pippa, I know what happened! Or at least I think I do!"

"I don't care, Rachael! I may be back on the case, but I can't pick another lock! I am trying to stay out of trouble from now on. I don't need an arrest on my record. Another one, I mean."

I wondered if 'stay out of trouble' also meant staying away from the paranormal society. I had noticed a distinct change in her demeanor since our visit to Maureen's. Even though she was still talking about the curse, I could sense that she was ready to give up the ghost, so to speak. And I couldn't wait for her to come back down to earth.

But I desperately needed her lock-picking skills. Just one last time.

"Let's at least go into the bakery instead of just

sitting here," Pippa said. "We should at least check that Bronson is doing okay."

We each spilled through the doors and I thought Bronson looked slightly disappointed to see us. He was probably looking forward to an entire weekend in charge with the bosses away. "Ignore us," I said quickly as Pippa and I hurried into the kitchen. "Trip got cut short...long story." I glanced at the clock: 3:30. This day felt like the longest day of my life.

Bronson surprised me by following us into the kitchen. "Actually, I'm kinda glad you guys are back. We got a huge booking for this afternoon, short notice, and I'm not sure I can handle it all on my own. It's a birthday party. Apparently, the restaurant they were supposed to have it at flooded. I didn't want to have to tell them no." He glanced at the two of us, waiting for direction.

Pippa looked at me. "Can you put this mystery on ice for the afternoon? We need the cash, considering how quiet it's been recently."

Which one of us was the boss again? The lines had definitely become muddied. "Yes, Bronson," I said. "We can help out a bit." I caught the look on Pippa's face. "But please tend to the front counter while the two of us are out here. Thank you."

"Come on, Pips, you're the only person I know with nimble enough fingers to be able to pick a lock quickly." I shut the kitchen door so that Bronson couldn't overhear us.

"Don't try to butter me up." She nodded towards a tray of cookies. "Speaking of which, these probably need to go out on display. And, if you're done playing detective for the day, you could actually help me out with this party we're now supposed to be catering. I would really appreciate the help. Can't you just forget about this whole thing for one day?"

I picked up the tray and swallowed. I glanced over my shoulder in the direction of Gus's store. All I wanted to do was go over there and prove my theory correct. I knew Pippa and Bronson would be able to handle the function without me.

"Rach?"

Suddenly, there was the sound of a heavy thud and the front doors were pushed open as party guest began to spill in. I grabbed a donut and scarfed it down for a bit of energy.

I nodded. "I will stay and help, Pippa. Of course I will."

But half an hour into the function, my stomach seemed to have other plans. There was a smashing sound as I dropped the tray I was carrying and keeled over in pain. Clutching my stomach, I whispered for Pippa, who came running over to me. "Oh no. All my brownies, ruined on the floor!" I cried out.

"Don't worry about that, you knucklehead! Bronson, take over while I drive Rachael to the hospital! We'll be back before the end of the function. I hope!"

He nodded and threw down the cloth he'd been drying his hands with. "Can do, miss! You'd better go quick. She looks terrible."

"Thanks," I croaked. "Don't go asking me for a raise any time soon."

***

"How long do blood test results take?" I groaned, shielding my eyes from the glare of the fluorescent lights. My stomachache had subsided a little, like it always seemed to after an hour or so, but my entire body was aching. I began to imagine the absolute worst-case scenario. I'd had these aches and pains for weeks—or was it months—and that couldn't have been good.

The doctor was a chipper young woman named Doctor Shu Ng, who I quite liked, even though she was probably about to tell me I was dying.

"Well, Miss Robinson, you're not going to like the results much, I don't think, considering your line of work."

I could feel my eyes growing wide. "Oh no, what is it? Am I going to become paralyzed? Lose the use of my arms?" I leaned forward. "Be straight with me, doc, will I ever bake again?"

She allowed a smile of amusement to cross her face. "It's not as severe as all that. Yes, you'll be able to bake again. But as for how many of the items you'll be able to eat, that's another story."

I frowned and tilted my head. "You're going to have to be less cryptic, doc."

"You've got a gluten allergy. Quite a bad one, I'm afraid." She raised an eyebrow at me. "Are your symptoms worse after you eat one of your cakes, for instance?"

I thought back over my symptoms over the past few weeks. "Yes," I gasped. "It seems worset after I've eaten a piece of cake or a brownie." I threw my head back. "Oh, why did this have to happen to me!" I was half-joking, being melodramatic for the sake of it, but there was an element of truth to my dismay.

Pippa looked at me in horror. "Oh my goodness, Rachael, what are you going to do?"

I thought about all those gluten-free items I had bought the other day when I'd been fibbing to Pippa about what I was up to. I gulped. Maybe the only thing I was cursed with was bad karma...or irony.

"We might have to add a few new items to the menu, Pips." I sighed. "Or else, I'm going to have to leave the majority of the taste-testing to you."

She was trying not to smile. "I think I can handle that."

Doctor Ng gave me some tips and some brochures, and told me to see my personal physician for more blood tests and advice if my symptoms got any worse. "Feel better soon, Rachael."

"I hate to ask you this, Rach, but do you think you

could come back and help out at the function?" Pippa cringed apologetically as she waited for my answer.

I was weary and ragged, but I managed a smile. "Just try to keep me away."

"Shoot, sorry, Bronson. That took way longer than we thought," I said, rushing into the bakery. My stomach was rumbling again already and I instinctively reached for a brownie before Pippa smacked it out of my hand.

"Oh, right."

The man who was apparently in charge of organizing the birthday party, a 40-something year old man with an expensive suit and a matching attitude, marched over and asked who was in charge.

"That would be me, I guess."

He hesitated before he handed the check over. "We were expecting a far bigger venue than this. Something twice the size, in fact."

When I'd updated the website to include our new function facility, I'd assumed I'd have Gus's shop to expand into by now. I really needed to log in and fix that up.

Pippa and I exchanged glances. "We may be small in size, but that just adds to the cozy atmosphere! I'm sure your guests have all been able to get nice and close to each other. It would have made for some great socializing!"

Bronson nodded. "And everyone looks more than happy, sir."

The man looked a little skeptical, but he nodded and handed over the check. "I suppose that's true," he said. "Thanks, girls."

I heaved a heavy sigh of relief. I needed that check. Mostly so I could pay Pippa a big fat bonus at the end of the month.

We high-fived. "Thank God today is all over with. Hey, Rach, promise me one thing?"

"Anything."

"No more high-maintenance clients."

Now that was a promise I could keep. "Deal."

We both stared at the rows of leftovers. Pippa picked up a brownie and began to hand it to me before she realized what she was doing. Looked like we both needed to get used to my new dietary restrictions. "Oh. Shoot, Rach, I'm sorry. What are you going to do?"

I laughed. "You mean what am I going to eat from now on? I know it does sound crazy, but I have heard of people that eat foods besides cakes and cookies and donuts."

Pippa's eyes were wide. "That's no way to live. We are going to have to start stocking a very wide range of gluten-free products. Otherwise, you're going to starve to death."

I chuckled. I could deal with my gluten allergy later. Right then, I was just grateful that Pippa and I were back to being best friends again.

I took a deep breath. "Now, Pippa, if I could just ask you one big favor..."

***

"Okay, but I swear this is the last time I'm doing this." Pippa's tone was teasing as she reached for the pin in her hair.

"Maybe it's the last time I'm going to need you to do this. After all this, I'm thinking about giving up the detective work for good."

Pippa's hands worked expertly and soon the lock clicked open. The sun had set and the shop was empty.

I took a deep breath. There was only one thing left to do.

Chapter 12

"Why does he still keep this here?" Pippa whispered. It was the first time she had really come face to face with the painting, the first time she had not been completely afraid to.

"Even after he started clearing the other stuff out of here," I said quietly. "And why won't he give the painting back to Maureen?"

I knelt down. "Come have a look at this, Pippa."

She squatted down besides me. "Those are definitely wires." I ran the thin metal wire through my hands, letting them snake through my fingers.

I stood up again. "In the dark we wouldn't have seen them, of course. That night when Gus was trying to scare us away."

"What was he trying to scare us away from, though?" Pippa asked.

"From this." I pushed the painting aside.

"Holy crud!" Pippa exclaimed. What are those?"

The sound of the back door opening made both of us jump and I quickly put the painting back in position.

I grabbed Pippa and pulled her so that we were huddled behind an old statue that wouldn't stop wobbling. "Keep still or it is going to topple over," I whispered to her.

A large white figure that looked like it was floating came towards us and Pippa's knees only started jittering more and more.

"I can't...I can't stop shaking, Rach. I knew...I knew this place was haunted...and now the ghost has come looking for us!"

She made a move to run, but I pulled her back and reached for the flashlight she had dropped on the floor last time, which was still lying there, out of place amongst the expensive old relics.

Pippa was going to give away our position anyway.

I flicked the light on and shone it on the hazy white figure lunging towards us. "There's your ghost," I said.

"Romeo?" Pippa's breathing was short and ragged. "What are you doing? Did you break in here?"

"No," I said firmly. "Because he has a key."

"What?" Pippa whispered. "Romeo, what's going on?"

He gulped and glanced towards the painting. And

288

what was behind it.

He kicked the painting so hard that the frame split and cracked, causing both Pippa and I to gasp. While we both lunged towards it to check it was still intact, the statue smashed down around us and Romeo fled out the back door, kicking and knocking items over as he went, creating a gauntlet for Pippa and I to get through if we were ever going to catch him.

"Stop him!" I yelled.

Pippa tripped over the statue and cried out in pain, clutching her ankle. "Pippa!?" I knelt down beside her while she groaned for me to go after Romeo. "That is his stuff hidden behind the painting, isn't it?"

I nodded at her. "Did you ever ask who Romeo was when you first met him? Pippa, he wasn't just a customer here that day you two met. He *worked* here."

Pippa groaned in pain again. "You have to go after him. He's going to get away. He's going to get away with killing Jason and Bridget."

"But, Pippa..."

"I'm fine," she insisted. "You can come back for me later. Hurry, go!"

I took off after Romeo. Outside, it was already dark

and I immediately wished I'd thought to bring the flashlight. I turned back so that I could run and get it, but a hand reached out and grabbed me. I kicked at him. "Let me go!"

"Not if you're going to go back in there and reveal my secret." He placed his hands over my mouth. "Not if you're going to go back in there and tell Pippa."

I stopped struggling for a second. "What?"

I heard him gulp. "I don't want Pippa to know what I did."

"It's too late for that now, Romeo. She already knows. She already saw the stolen antique swords you are hiding in there." I swallowed. "I know that Gus would never put his business in jeopardy that way." I pulled hard and finally freed myself, but he grabbed me again by the wrist.

"Pippa is lying in there hurt, Romeo. If you care about her at all, you will let me go in and see her. What if one of your swords falls on her and hurts her, or worse, kills her the way they killed Jason and Bridget."

Romeo brought his hands to his face and stumbled forward as a sob escaped from his lungs. "I never meant for any of this to happen."

I yanked my wrist free. "You could have stopped it, Romeo. You could have stopped it after the first time. What the heck are you doing, keeping those things stored there?"

I heard him sniffling. Not so tough once he'd been caught. "There's a black market for them," he whispered. "When I moved back to town a month or two ago, I got into contact with some people who were interested in buying them."

"So what happened?" I asked. "How was Jason killed?"

Romeo hesitated at first, but then came clean. "It was a deal gone bad. The sword he wanted had been stolen from some history museum. I didn't steal it. I was just the middleman. When he came in to buy it from me, he got aggressive and I was afraid he was going to walk out with the sword without paying. I tried to get it back from him, but…" He stared off into the distance and I could tell he was picturing it all in his mind. "The sword was heavy," he said, shaking his head. "I couldn't control it. The next thing I knew, he was on the floor. It all happened so fast."

"What about Bridget?" I asked, not picturing her as the type who would be interested in black market swords.

Romeo sighed. "I hid the swords in my apartment until after the cops searched the antique store. When I thought it was safe, I brought them back to the shop to hide them. I knew that if I hid them behind that bloody painting that everyone is so afraid of, no one would ever see them there. No one would dare to move the painting. Not even my old man."

I narrowed my eyes. "But someone did move the painting, didn't they?"

Romeo nodded. "That lady, Bridget, she moved it and..." He couldn't finish his sentence.

"One of the swords fell on her," I said quietly.

Romeo nodded.

"What the heck are you two doing out here?" I jumped at the sound of Gus's voice.

I spun to face him. "Gus, I'm just..." I turned back to Romeo. "How could you do this to your dad?"

"I did this FOR my dad," Romeo cried. "The business was failing. This was my way of bringing in extra money for him. I was protecting him by not telling him about it...not telling him where the swords were stored."

I could see Gus's face growing heavy. "You did know,

didn't you?" I whispered.

He was still staring at the ground. "Of course I did. After that young man was killed, I found the swords and told Romeo to get out of my house and my business. He already had that new job next door with you anyway. Which he managed to mess up after a week! Like he always manages to do!"

Romeo took an angry step towards his father. "I was just trying to help you! You could at least show a little gratitude!"

"Help me? By completely destroying the business that I worked all my life to build? By killing a person in my store? Why should I be grateful for that! You should be grateful I tried to protect you instead of turning you in to the cops! But then you had to go and put the swords back there while I was out of town for the weekend! Which I had to rush back to remedy! Just like I've always had to clean up all your messes!"

Romeo raised his fist and took a step towards his dad, ready and aimed. I sucked in a sharp breath, shielding my face as Romeo prepared to strike.

Just then sirens sounded and Pippa came hobbling out of the back of the shop. "You may as well keep your hands up, Romeo! Because you're about to be arrested!

Not only are you the worst boyfriend and employee I've ever seen, you're the worst criminal as well."

***

Detective Crawford shoved Romeo into the back of the van while Jackson kept the engine running.

After a moment of hesitation, Detective Crawford strode over to me. "I've only got a moment. I just wanted to tell you that we found that missing video footage from your store. A young man confessed to breaking in and stealing it. Name of George Tatler. He said he was trying to catch an art thief or something. Thought something strange was going on at Gus's place. A very convoluted story about an old painting. I dunno, just between you and I, he was a little eccentric. Some stuff about a curse." She gave me an 'I don't know what to tell you' face.

"Another amateur detective, I guess."

Detective Crawford nodded at me and turned to leave. "Hey," she said. "Thanks for your help solving this case, Rachael." I nodded and caught Jackson's eye briefly as she jumped back into the car.

We exchanged nothing but a brief smile as they drove away.

Once again, I was left on the curbside with Gus Sampson as my only companion. Pippa had had the longest day of her life and she'd passed out with exhaustion in the back seat of my car.

"Gus, why did you do all this? Why did you cover for Romeo?" I stared out into the black night. "Why did you let everyone believe all the stupid superstitious stuff?"

"Because I was so desperate to save my shop, I would rather the police look for a killer on the loose, or the community blame a ghost, than blame my son and put us all out of business." Gus picked up a stick and dug it into the concrete.

"That night when Pippa and I..." I paused. "Broke in. That was you, wasn't it, trying to scare us away?"

Gus nodded reluctantly. "I used the curse to try and scare you away, get you off Romeo's trail. I already knew a little bit about the curse, of course, but Romeo told me all this extra stuff that little blue-haired friend of yours knew about it. All these details I never heard before. All came from some paranormal society or something."

I sighed and shook my head. "It all became a bit of a

self-fulfilling prophecy, I think."

I turned to face Gus. "So why wouldn't you give the painting back to Maureen?" I lowered my voice and spoke softly. "You know what that painting means to her, right? What the painting depicts?"

Gus dropped his head and nodded. "Yeah, I know. But if I gave the painting back, then I wouldn't have anything to attract customers, would I? I know the police would never take the curse theory seriously, but if enough regular people could be fooled... Well, people are interested in that sort of stuff.

"But you wouldn't stop snooping," he huffed.

I stood up. "Well, Gus, you can't put everything right. But there is one thing you can do."

He nodded. "I know," he whispered.

***

Pippa collapsed into my bed. I was going to take the sofa that night. "I can't believe all this time, there really was no curse. I guess you probably think I really am stupid and easily taken in now."

I sat down besides her and gave her a tiny wink. "At least, no curse that we know of for certain."

She gave me an amused, slacked jawed look and sat up. "You gotta be kidding me, Rachael. Our roles really have reversed now!"

I sat and thought for a moment. "There really is a lot we don't know about. I keep thinking of all those stories your friends told that night at the meeting. There really are a lot of unsolved mysteries in Belldale."

Pippa laid her head back against the pillow. "Does this mean that you will come to another meeting?"

I thought about it for a moment. "I think I might have to. After all, I'm going to need another mystery to solve now, aren't I?"

Epilogue

Two months later.

I tapped my champagne flute with my spoon. "Now," I said as the chatter died down. "I've already had one grand opening three years ago, but this feels like another big moment. A second grand opening." I nodded at Pippa, who ran to pull down the curtain.

"Ta da!"

"Ladies and gentlemen, can I present to you: Rachael's Boutique Bakery, part two!"

The crowd clapped and Jackson, stranded amongst them, caught my eye and winked at me. "Congrats," he mouthed, before he turned his attention back to Detective Crawford.

Gus slowly walked up to me and extended his hand. "Congratulations, Rachael. I mean it."

I grinned at him. "I'm just glad that the sewing shop on the other side decided to sell up! So it was great timing for both of us. How is your store going, anyway?"

Gus nodded. "It's still a little slow, as you can

understand. But since I've started to move into restoration, things have picked up a little." He suddenly grew very serious. "Rachael, if you have a moment in the midst of all your celebrations, can I borrow you for a minute?"

I nodded and asked Pippa to supervise as I followed him into his store. No longer dark and drab, it was bright and airy, with fresh coats of white and yellow paint that made the whole place look light and inviting. "You can see all the artwork I'm restoring now."

I nodded, slowly walking along the rows of paintings. "I'm a little surprised, after all..."

"Miss Robinson?" a posh English voice interrupted.

I spun around to see Maureen Tatler standing there.

"This is why I invited you over, Rachael. I think you ought to be here when I present this."

Gus reached behind his counter and pulled out the painting of the twins. The broken frame was now replaced with fine silver, the ripped canvas painstakingly put back together, and the ruined paint restored back to its original quality.

Maureen's eyes filled with tears as she took the painting from him with shaking hands.

"My collection is finally complete after all these years," she whispered, running her withered hand over the painting, gently caressing the faces of the twins, lost in a cloud of memories.

Back at the bakery, I closed the door quietly behind me.

"Pippa," I called out quietly with a small grin. "Come here. I want to ask you something."

"What is it, Rach?"

"Since we are expanding, I want to give you a promotion: to head manager, equal with me."

She reached over and squeezed my arm. "Nah," Pippa said. "I appreciate the offer so much, Rach, you know that, but you know it's not like me to stick around in one job for too long. Sorry to say this, Rach, but I just booked a ticket for a paranormal mystery tour of the midwest with the paranormal society, so I'm not gonna be around for a while!"

My face fell a little. "But when will you be back?"

"In a few months! Don't worry, though, I'll be back before you know it. But I'll probably look for a new job when I get back. Change is good for the soul."

I nodded. "Well, good luck, Pips. I'm going to miss

you. But I understand."

As the party continued, and guests ate and socialized, I moved towards the window. Maureen Tatler was hobbling to her car with the painting under her arm.

"Here, let me help you," I said, slightly out of breath from running to catch up with her.

"Thank you, deary," she said, climbing in to the passenger side. I nodded to the driver, her great nephew George.

Maureen grabbed my arm with her bony fingers just as I was turning to walk away.

"The curse is lifted now, Rachael."

Death by Chocolate Cake

Chapter 1

Belldale, Summer Time

"Are you ready for your close-up, Rach?"

"Huh?" I asked, leaning closer to the camera. "I thought this was just a test run! I haven't even got my makeup on yet! Don't tell me this is actually going to go to air?"

"Relax," Justin, the producer of *Baking Warriors*, said as he rolled his eyes at me. "I'm just teasing you. We'll shoot the proper intros tomorrow. This is just to test the lighting."

I let out a sigh of relief. Not only was my make-up not 'reality TV star ready', I hadn't even memorized the script. Yes, reality shows have a script. And even though I hadn't been officially cast yet, I still had to shoot the dreaded intro shot where I gave my name, age, and some pithy quote about how the other contestants needed to watch out for me and my supreme baking talents.

Justin ushered me away from the cameras and placed his arm around my shoulders. "Rach," he whispered, "about the age thing."

I stopped. "About what age thing?"

He peered at me through his thick-rimmed glasses with his hand perched on his hips. "Your age thing. We're thinking...instead of saying that you're twenty-six, we go with twenty-two. Hmm?" He looked me up and down. "You could just about pass. For a 'TV' twenty-two anyway. Not in real life."

I just stared at him. "Twenty-six is old now?"

Justin shrugged. "Twenty-two just sounds better, doesn't it?" He waved his hand. "That way we can showcase you as the young contestant, the wunderkind that runs her own bakery at just twenty-two." He glanced down at his tablet like it held more interesting content to him than the conversation. "After all, twenty-six is not all that impressive, is it?"

I thought it was. And if he really wanted some kind of interesting angle to my on-screen personality, well, there were always the recent murders I had solved. For just a second I considered telling him everything, but there was a reason I had left out my history as an amateur sleuth when I'd auditioned. I had to remember that was not what I wanted to be known for if I did end up being cast on the show. "Why not just shave off a few more years then? Why don't we just tell the viewers I'm eighteen, go all the way with it?"

Justin glanced up from his tablet. "Oh, honey, we've got to be realistic here."

I'd only sent in my audition tape to *Baking Warriors* on my best friend Pippa's insistence last year. When I hadn't heard anything back eight months later, I'd totally forgotten about it. Then I got the call: the show was doing 'round the country auditions for its fourth season and they were coming to Belldale to film an audition episode. Of course, the producers had already whittled down the auditionee list to a final ten but they were still putting on the pretense of an open cattle-call style audition the following day, where any amateur baker in Belldale could come along and 'audition' to be on the show.

"You'll be here at 5:00 AM tomorrow, right?" Justin called out to me, temporarily removing the earpiece that I thought was a permanent addition to his head.

I nodded. "5:00 AM. I really need to get out of here now though." I stopped, my hand poised on the studio door as Justin listened to something in his earpiece. He held his hand up, a sign that I was to stay put.

"We just need to do one last test."

"Justin!" I double-checked the time on my phone. Yep, I was already late. Pippa was going to kill me if I left her stranded. "I really, really have to go."

He ushered me back over to chair. "We must leave nothing to chance. Trust me, honey, it is my neck on the line here."

I sat back in my chair and groaned inwardly. Was the chance of becoming a reality TV star really worth all this hassle? We hadn't even started shooting yet—heck, I hadn't even gotten *cast* yet—and it had already taken over my life.

I sat there for a few minutes then jumped to my feet. "All right, is that it?" I grabbed my purse and ran for the door before Justin even had the chance to look at me again, let along drag me back to that chair.

"5:00 AM!" I heard him calling through the swinging doors as I bolted for my car. "5:00 AM, Rachael, and not a moment later!"

***

"The 10:10 flight from Oregon has been delayed."

Groans came from the arrivals lounge. Personally, I couldn't decide whether I was relieved or annoyed. A small delay I would have been pleased with, as I was already twenty minutes late, but an hour's delay? I kept looking at the time, trying to figure out how much sleep I could get before my call time. "If the flight gets in at 11:10, and it takes twenty minutes for Pippa to find her luggage, and it takes an hour to drive back to Belldale, and Pippa and I take a half-hour catching up, and I need a half-hour to get ready in the morning, and there's a forty-five minute drive to the studio..."

Great, that was about two and a half hours of sleep.

I tapped my foot nervously as I waited for the check-in list to finally light up yellow over the delayed flight's name to show that the plane from Oregon had touched down. I wasn't even sure why I was so nervous. I was acting more like I was waiting for a long lost lover than a long lost best friend. It was just that Pippa always had a habit of surprising me.

But in her last email, she had promised me that there were no great shocks awaiting me when she stepped off the plane. "Honestly, Rach, no new piercings, no crazy new hair style. I'm not pregnant and I haven't adopted a kid! I've just had a nice, boring vacation chasing paranormal entities."

Well, we would see about that. There were plenty of things that she could have left off that list.

But her not having any big news suited me at that moment because I couldn't *wait* to tell her about *Baking Warriors*. I'd managed to keep the news of the audition quiet, even though Pippa had always told me she'd kill me if I ever kept a secret from her.

She was going to practically wet herself when she heard the news. I'd been reluctant to even audition, but Pippa was convinced that I would make the perfect contestant on her second favorite television show, behind Criminal Point.

I wanted to see her face when I finally told her.

I just hoped she wasn't going to shock me before I had a chance to surprise her.

***

"Miss." An elbow dug into my side. "Flight's here."

I sat up and apologized for falling asleep on the strange guy's shoulder. "Don't worry about it," he said as I zipped up my jacket, sinking into it as I tried to hide my reddening face. I glanced at the time on the arrivals list. At least I'd managed to sneak in an extra half-hour's sleep.

Everyone pushed and jostled for position as I tried to spot Pippa in the crowd. She'd promised no crazy hairstyles but I'd seen her most recent photos and knew her present hair color was purple. In Pippa's world, though, that is not crazy. That is normal. Crazy for her would be, like...shaving an obscene word into an otherwise baldhead, or something. I hoped she hadn't done that. Especially if she was going to work at my bakery while I was away shooting the show.

There she was. The wild lavender hair made her stand out in the crowd.

But she was not alone as she walked, practically skipped, up the long hall of the arrival's lounge. I tried to push to get to her, but the crowd was too thick and I ended up with a sharp heel in my foot as a lady with a large bouffant stepped back on me.

I guess I'll wait my turn then.

"Who is that?" I whispered, looking at the handsome stranger walking far too close to Pippa. "Please tell me it's just someone she met on the plane, a new friend." They moved closer to each other and Pippa had a gross love-struck look on her face. "Oh no, don't do that!" I said as the man reached for Pippa's hand and gripped it in his before giving it a kiss.

They remained linked like that until they reached me, standing there with an expression that was frozen into a wide-eyed grin.

Pippa turned her grin towards me and started bouncing up and down. "Rach," she said, sucking in a breath of excitement. "Don't get mad at me, okay, but I have a little surprise for you." She turned back towards the mysterious stranger and started bouncing higher.

"*Who is this*?" I asked through gritted teeth, though I was still smiling. I tried not to panic.

"This," Pippa said dramatically, like she was about to announce the winner of a reality show competition, "is Marcello!" She dropped his hand and shoved hers in my face, pointing to a gigantic bauble on her ring finger.

"Rach!" she said, jumping up and down. "We got married!"

"W...what?"

She shoved the ring further into my face. Yep. It was a ring.

"When...when did this happen?"

Pippa snuggled into this so-called Marcello, who reached for my hand and kissed it. "It is wonderful to meet you," he said with an accent I couldn't quite place.

I gulped. "You too. Pippa...can I just...have a quick word with you."

"Wait here for a moment, sweetheart," Pippa said to Marcello before smothering his face with kisses. "Just a bit of girl talk."

I ushered her off to the side.

"What is it?"

"Pippa, how long have you know him?" I whispered.

"Oh, Rach, it doesn't matter how long we've known each other! It only matters how in love we are!"

"How long?"

Pippa looked sheepish. "Three weeks."

"Pippa!"

She looked up at me and pouted. "Aren't you happy for me?"

I sighed. "Yes," I said, reaching over to give her a hug. "I just can't believe my best friend got married without even telling me!" I leaned back and gave her a playful hit with my purse. "I wasn't even invited!"

Pippa shrugged as she moved back towards Marcello, like he was a magnet and she was a big piece of metal. "Don't worry, we haven't had the reception yet. I'm planning a big party in Belldale next week!" Snuggled under Marcello's arm, she turned back to me and asked, "You don't have anything big going on next week, do you?"

"Umm, actually..."

Chapter 2

Summertime had taken all of Belldale into its warm embrace. People were, in general, jollier at this time of year, the sun and heat making them lazier and less likely to stress out.

And less likely to commit murder. Belldale had been at peace for almost six months. No strange activity, no paranormal sightings, and no unexplained deaths.

It would almost have been boring if we weren't all in such cheerful moods. Summer was a good time of year for the hospitality business and everyone on our little food strip was doing very well, especially my shop, "Rachael's Boutique Bakery."

Which was why I was hesitant to leave it behind to go shoot a TV program for three months.

"I'll be fine! Of course you can leave me in charge!" Pippa squealed after I told her the news back in my apartment. "Rachael, there's no way you are missing this opportunity." She squealed again and clapped her hands.

"Okay, okay," I said, giggling a little. "Calm down though, I haven't made it through the final audition yet."

"Oh, you will though!" Pippa grabbed my hands and started jumping up and down. She was clearly still on a post-nuptial high. And I had to admit her newly rejuvenated enthusiasm for life was rubbing off on me, even though I was still skeptical about the stranger who was waiting in the next room.

"Where is he going to...fit?" I whispered, peering out the door. All I could see was the back of Marcello's head, all dark curls.

Pippa shrugged. "He's just going to have to snuggle up on the sofa with me!"

"Right..."

It wasn't the right time to have a talk about her maybe finding her own place and moving out, though I knew that moment would have to come.

I heard something breaking in the kitchen. "Oh," Pippa said, making a face. "Sorry about that. He's a little clumsy. But that's all part of his charm." She patted me on the arm. "You'll get used to it. After all, we're going to get very cozy, the three of us living here together!"

I took a deep breath and smiled at her. "Yes, we are."

There was another crashing sound, followed by a loud, "Sorry about that!"

I wondered how much sleep I was actually going to get.

***

"Honey. You look terrible. Straight into makeup. That should take care of most of it." Justin shoved me towards a makeshift tent that was brimming with men and women in black shirts holding panels of powders and bronzers and looking even less awake then I was.

"Remember, we want her looking twenty-two!"

It was a long morning. And I mean LONG. When it was finally time for me to scurry my way past the line of hopefuls that thought they actually had a chance of making it onto the show, I felt like I was going to keel over. Two hours was the amount of sleep I'd gotten the night before. And right then I was running on caffeine and Justin's barked orders.

"Now," he said, brushing my hair off my shoulder and examining my face in his hands. "Do you remember what you have to tell the judges?"

I nodded groggily. "I'm twenty...two..."

Justin nodded. "What else."

"I own my own bakery. Baking has been my passion since I was a little girl. I baked my first cake when I was only three..."

Justin let out a long sigh.

"What?" I asked, a little offended.

"It's just not very exciting, is it?" He waved his hand in the direction of the crowd that lay outside the studio. "I mean, that might pass for excitement in this place, but it just doesn't make for very compelling TV, does it, darling?" Another sigh. "Are you sure there's nothing else interesting about you, honey?" He looked upwards and clucked his tongue. "Maybe we can make something up. Did you parents die when you were very young?"

"No!" I said. "And I'm not going to pretend they did. It's gotta be bad karma or something."

"Well, we have to think of something quick." He dared a look inside the judge's room. "Something that's going to impress them."

"What about my baking?" I asked, as though that should be the obvious answer. "I thought I was supposed to impress them with my super skills in the kitchen. Isn't that kind of the point of the show?"

Justin laid a hand on my shoulder and shook his head slowly. "Oh, sweetie, you really have no idea how this TV thing works, do you?" He consulted a list on his tablet. "Maybe you're a lost cause. One of these other guys might have an interesting back story...maybe something tragic in their past that we can get them to open up about."

"Wait!" I placed a hand on top of his tablet. "I do have an interesting sort of hobby," I said reluctantly.

There was a slight glimmer of interest in Justin's eyes. "Go on."

I took a deep breath and quickly told him everything that had happened in Belldale over the past year: the three deaths, the paranormal mysteries, and my part in solving the cases.

Justin's jaw was wide open by the time I'd finished. "Now, why didn't you lead with that?" He placed a gentle hand on my shoulder and guided me to the judging room before lowering his voice. "I had no idea this town was so interesting. Huh. I've only been here a couple of days and I almost died of boredom."

"Yeah, well, it's definitely not boring all the time."

He raised an eyebrow. "I guess I just came at the wrong time of year then."

I shifted uncomfortably. "Things have been peaceful here recently. I don't want to jinx it. Besides..." I trailed off, a little reluctant to continue.

"Besides what?"

I shrugged. "All the deaths and stuff kind of gave the town a bad rap. I don't think certain members of the police department would like me bringing all that stuff up on national TV."

I could see the glimmer in Justin's eyes growing stronger. "Oh, honey," he said. "What 'certain members'? A man, I take it." He shot me a knowing look. "One that you dated, maybe?"

"No," I said quickly, wrapping my arms across my chest. "I just want to respect their wishes."

Justin nodded. "Don't worry, honey, I understand. We won't sensationalize anything." Then, into his walkie-talkie, he announced my audition number and name to the judges. "Up next we've got, Rachael. Belldale's very own number one Murder Expert!"

"Justin!"

***

There were three of them.

I tried to focus on the "nice" judge, a blonde lady named Dawn who was late middle-aged. She was known for giving the contestants constructive, rather than downright vicious, critiques. And I tried to ignore the glares of Pierre, the judge who was known for giving no holds barred criticism and occasionally reducing contestants to tears with his caustic barbs. Not that it dulled his popularity. Of the three judges, he was by far the most famous and the most beloved on social media.

Then there was Wendy. Nobody really paid much attention to her.

"Go on, dear, tell us a little about yourself," Dawn encouraged. "What is all this stuff about murders we've been hearing so much about?"

"I, erm..." I caught Justin's glare out of the corner of my eye. "Don't stammer," he had told me.

"Why don't you try one of my cakes?"

I turned around to fetch the cakes I'd prepared the day before but which the producers made to look like I'd baked that day. I knew the judges had already tasted them the day before and made up their minds, but we had to go through the motions.

"Delicious," Wendy said, pushing her long dark hair out of her face. "Wouldn't change a thing, darling!"

A nice, but fairly hollow—and, let's face it, useless—comment.

I focused on Pierre, who screwed his face up as he slowly chewed the chocolate cake I had presented him with. I wondered why he had to make such a show of it when he already knew what it tasted like and already knew what he was going to say.

He finally placed his napkin down and swallowed. Then he stared straight at me for a good ten seconds before he finally delivered his verdict.

"That was...fine," he said. Nonplussed. No expression on his face except a dead stare. "Tell me, Rachael, why you deserve to be on *Baking Warriors* over the thousands of auditionee outside?"

The nine other auditionees, I thought. But with his stare on me, I was in no state to be smart with him. Or even to defend myself.

"I...I...um, I've been baking since I was three years old," I said rather meekly. "It's...it is my passion...."

Pierre leaned back and shook his head. I saw his gesture for a producer, then heard him whisper, "Can we use any of the murder stuff?"

Justin shrugged. "If she gets through." He shot me a look over his shoulder then returned to Pierre. "Though I really don't think she will. Shall I bring in the next contestant?"

Pierre nodded. "I've had enough of this one."

"Thank you for you time," I said softly before Justin led me swiftly out of the room and told me to return to the green room. I didn't even get to hear Dawn's verdict.

I was red-faced and annoyed by the time Justin finally joined me for a debrief. He just shrugged. "It's dog eat dog, honey. You should have led with the murder stuff."

I sat down on a soggy sofa. "I'd rather not get through than use any of that stuff." I was aware that I was acting sulky but it had been a long day and I just wanted to go home. "I don't know why I'm still here. I obviously didn't get in."

Justin sighed and looked down on me in pity. "Look," he said. "Just between you and me, you've still got a shot. A good shot. Look, I do NOT say this to everyone..." He lowered his voice. "But you are going through to the next round. Just sit tight and relax. You look good on camera and the judges really liked your cakes. That's all there is to it."

I looked up at him in shock. "But Pierre didn't seem impressed at all!"

Justin waved his hand dismissively. "Oh, that's all just for TV, honey. Pierre's the executive producer. If he likes you, you'll go through. Just relax. Have something to drink." He fetched a bottle of wine from the cooler.

"No, thanks. I'm afraid if I drink I'll fall asleep."

"Come on, just a little sip! Honey, you'll have to start drinking if you get into TV."

I reluctantly accepted half a glass.

Just as Justin was plugging the cork back into the bottle a high-pitched squeal sounded from the direction of the judging room.

Justin let out a loud, exaggerated sigh that said, "I don't get paid enough for this." He threw the wine bottle back in the cooler. "Probably a rejected contestant. Or a judge who hasn't got their lunch on time. Wait here while I deal with it. I won't be a minute."

But Justin was way longer than a minute. After ten minutes had passed and Justin hadn't returned, I started to get worried.

Then I saw the ambulance.

"Are you okay?" I said, running towards a stricken-looking Justin with his headpiece in his hands. "What on earth has happened?"

Justin, white as a sheet, slowly looked over his shoulder and, with a trembling voice, simply said, "Pierre's dead, Rachael. Somebody killed him."

Chapter 3

"I'm just asking, Pippa. It's a simple question. WHY does he lose so much hair? Where does it even come from? He wasn't even in the house today."

Pippa put her hands up in a shrug that said 'I have no idea why Marcello molts like a llama, but gosh isn't he so cute for doing so?'

Which, I mean...sure. If you're in love. But I wasn't in love with the guy. I was just the girl who ran around after him with a vacuum cleaner twenty-four hours a day.

"I'm sorry, Rach. I'll vacuum more." Pippa plunked herself down and let out a deep sigh of contentment. "Isn't he just the greatest?"

Ermmm. "Yes. The greatest."

Pippa folded her legs underneath her so that I could squeeze onto the sofa next to her. "We're not taking up too much space, are we?"

Well, I was currently squeezed up onto the tiny sofa that doubled as her and Marcello's bed and I couldn't move around the apartment without banging into one of them. But I forced a grin. Pippa was happy. That was all that mattered at the moment. "No. It's fine."

"You'll let me know if it gets to be too much, won't you?"

I was just about to reassure her that I would when we both heard another smashing sound from the kitchen. Pippa started to giggle, making another 'isn't he just so cute' expression. "He has this thing," she said, laughing so hard that she could barely get the words out. "Where he tries to place an item down on the bench—like a knife, or a cup, or a plate, you know, whatever—but he totally misjudges where the end of the bench is! So it ends up on the floor!" Now totally full of mirth, Pippa threw her head back in throes of laughter.

I just stared at her. "Is that thing called bad eyesight?"

Pippa just started laughing even harder. She even slapped her knee. "No, Rachael! It's just one of his cute, little, quirky things."

Yeah, it was pretty cute and quirky that he was breaking everything I owned. I sighed myself. I had bigger things to worry about anyway.

Marcello appeared with a bowl of chips for us and placed them down on the coffee table with an apology. "I broke the jar of salsa. I'd better go finish cleaning that up." He paused. "Unless you want me to scoop the salsa up and pick the glass out, and I can bring that in for you?"

"No," I said quickly. "Thank you, that's fine."

He disappeared into the kitchen again and I just shot Pippa a look of disbelief. Even she was making a face at the suggestion of eating glass-shard-filled salsa that had been scraped off the kitchen floor.

Remind me to never offer him a job at my bakery.

He'd apparently been job-hunting that day. I shuddered at the thought of the sorry soul who'd have to employ him.

I picked up a chip and stared at it sadly. So this was what it had come to. Ever since I'd been diagnosed with a *severe* allergy to gluten, I'd basically had to switch from sweet snacks to savory. For a baker, it was almost a fate worse than death.

Pippa seemed to read my mind. About the death thing, that is, as she crammed a chip into her mouth and started to talk with a mouth full of crunchy potato. "So what are you going to do?"

I placed my chip back down and leaned back against the sofa. "Nothing, Pips. This isn't my circus. It's not my monkey."

She just stared at me. "It very well IS. Rachael, you were practically cast on that show before that guy went and died! You can't tell me you're just going to sit back and do nothing! What happens if they delay filming entirely? Or worse, redo all the auditions."

"Yes, that's the great tragedy of today, Pippa. Not the poor dead guy. The poor dead guy who was poisoned, by the way."

"You know what I mean." Pippa sat up and grabbed my arm. "You're the PERFECT person so solve this murder, Rachael!" She held up her fingers as she listed off the reasons. "One, you were there. You probably met the killer. It's got to be a fellow baker, right? Two, you can't let this opportunity slip through your fingers. Where else are you going to get a chance to become a reality TV star?" Then she got to the item she clearly considered the most important of the lot. "Three, you have plenty of experience in this area. I can't believe you're not already out there interviewing suspects."

I huddled up against the back of the sofa and muttered to myself.

"What was that?" Pippa said, leaning closer to me.

"Jackson doesn't want me interfering anymore, okay?"

Pippa opened her eyes wide. "Since when has that ever stopped you before?"

Pippa had been gone for over six months, so I didn't blame her for not understanding my change in attitude regarding sticking my nose in police business. But a lot had chanced in Belldale over the last six months. With two high profile murder investigations, the entire town had changed in character. It had become more withdrawn, somehow darker and less open.

"With *Baking Warriors* coming to town, I think Jackson—all of us, actually—hoped the town could be seen in a more positive light," I tried to explain.

"Well, that hope was short lived." Pippa threw another chip into her mouth and raised her eyebrow.

"Yes, but an amateur sleuth sticking her nose in this, one who might be about to become a minor celebrity no less, is not a good look for the police department. They are trying to revamp their image. Jackson wants them to appear more competent. To assure the town that they can keep them safe. I should just keep my distance."

Pippa gave me a long skeptical look that made me squirm. "Rach, I keep hearing a lot of 'Jackson wants' coming out of your mouth. What do YOU want? Why do you even care what he thinks anyway? Hasn't he gone and shacked up with that skinny detective with the red hair?"

Detective Emma Crawford. Yes.

"I don't care about that," I said unconvincingly.

"Sure sounds like it."

I sat and thought for a moment. Why *was* I so happy to keep my nose out of the investigation? Even though my feet *were* kind of itching to get into the fray, and I had to keep trying to stop my mind from racing— thinking over all the events of the day, trying to figure out who had access to Pierre, who was close enough to him to poison him, and who had a motive to do such a thing.

The truth was, I didn't *want* to see Jackson. So when he'd asked me—politely, mind you—to keep my nose out of cases, I hadn't really minded. I didn't mind keeping my distance from him one bit. He was happy with another woman now. And I was fine with that. Just fine. I hadn't seen him in months.

There was another smashing sound from the kitchen.

I leaned back against the sofa and closed my eyes while Pippa laughed hysterically. "I think we might owe you a new set of dishes by now."

Maybe I needed to invest in some headphones.

***

"What...the..."

The entrance to the road where my bakery stood, Pillock Avenue, was totally blocked off by vans and people racing around with boom mikes and cameras.

"What's going on?" Pippa asked from the passenger side.

"It looks like they are filming *Baking Warriors* here or something," I said, which was the only thing that made sense to me in that moment. Because that's what the swarm of people and cameras and producers wearing earpieces running around reminded me of filming on the show.

"Well, can we get through? Should we let them know that we actually work on this street?"

It was still early in the morning, 6:30 or so, and even though we had a hot day ahead of us, the fog and dew from overnight caused a smog to appear over the street. So it took me several minutes to realize that it wasn't the *Baking Warriors* film crew at all, but was, in fact, several dozen separate film crews, all with different garish logos plastered on the side of their vans.

"OH," I said, sucking in my breath. "Pippa, they're news crews."

"Oh," she said warily, leaning forward to see if there might be any space where we could fit the car through. I already knew there wasn't.

"I guess news of Pierre's death has broken," I murmured.

Pippa spun back to me. "Of course it has. Did you really think people wouldn't find out that a beloved celebrity has been killed? Did you not think that people would be incredibly interested to find out what happened to him?"

I turned the ignition off and groaned a little. "I don't know. I thought the police had ways of keeping this sort of thing quiet for a little while. Or at least controlling the media presence a little."

In the time we'd been sitting there, even more vans had pulled up to join the circus, more tents pitched, and even more vats of coffee set up.

So much for Jackson's plan to keep the town out of the spotlight.

So much for his plan to make the town feel safer.

I checked the time on the dash. We were going to be late to open.

"Let me see what I can do," Pippa said, pushing her door open. I picked up my phone and used it to quickly scroll through the day's news.

Yep. Pierre Hamilton's death was the biggest breaking story in the entire country. It was the featured story on countless local and national news websites.

This was not going to be a good look for Belldale.

I glanced up to see Pippa arguing with a reporter in a blue suit who had hair that looked too grey for his fresh looking face. I rolled down my window so I could hear what was going on. He was shaking his head at her before he threw up his hands and shouted, "I don't know what to tell you! I'm not in charge of this whole thing! Us moving our van isn't going to make much of a difference."

Pippa turned in a huff to a different reporter, a smiley looking blond woman whose smile died as soon as the news camera turned off. She scowled at Pippa and told her to get out of the way.

"Out of your way?" Pippa exclaimed. "You're the one in our way! We actually live in this town! We work on this street. And we need to get past!"

I almost jumped out of my skin when I heard a tapping on my window.

"Jackson," I gasped. It was the first time I'd laid eyes on him in what had to have been three months. During that time, I had managed to not only avoid solving crimes, I'd also managed to avoid seeing him. So I was doing well.

He looked different. Slimmer, I think it was. Or maybe his hair was longer. It seemed to sit up on his head in more of a bouffant than the last time I'd seen him. And was it my imagination or was it a little grayer than the last time I had seen him?

"Rachael?" he asked, and I jumped again as he interrupted my thoughts.

"Um, hi," I said, straightening up. I self-consciously reached up and touched my hair, wondering if the professional styling I'd received before filming yesterday was still holding up under the damp of the soggy morning. "How are you?" I asked stupidly, not really knowing what else to say.

"Well," Jackson said with a raise of his eyebrows as he shoved his hands into his pockets, his badge dangling down the front of his torso. "As you can imagine, busy."

I nodded. "We went so long without a murder too, bit of a shame." Another stupid thing to say. I was nervous. I didn't know what was escaping my mouth. I stared at the steering wheel while Jackson fidgeted back and forth on his heels.

"I heard that you were there when it happened."

"Nearby," I corrected him. "In a different room."

"Hmm."

I kept staring at the steering wheel. Another murder in Belldale happening while I was less than a hundred feet away. There had been talk for a while—from Pippa mostly, who doesn't always have her feet firmly planted in reality—that I was cursed. Silly, right?

I wasn't so sure.

"Do you need me to answer any questions?" I asked quietly.

"We'll take a statement later," Jackson replied quickly. I took note of the 'we,' not an 'I.' That meant he'd be sending some uniformed officer to ask questions, not himself.

There was that distance again.

Jackson cleared his throat. "It's good to see you again anyway, Rachael."

"Is it?" I asked.

He looked away. "Let me see if I can clear this road for you."

He stomped away towards the hoards of vans and reporters like a man on a mission. Waving his badge like a sword, he was quickly able to part the sea of cars and news crews. Pippa came sprinting back to the car, breathless from arguing with people. "I almost got punched!" she exclaimed, pulling the door shut quickly. "Rach, some of these people are VICIOUS."

I eyed them slowly as we finally managed to pull the car through the crowd. "I'm sure they are."

"Why are they all staring at us?" Pippa whispered, slumping into her seat so that she was almost on the floor of the car.

"Maybe because you were out there trying to fight them two minutes ago?"

But I wasn't so sure that was the reason. They didn't seem to be staring at Pippa.

They seemed to be staring at me.

***

My new baker-come-assistant-manager Bronson had matters well in hand by the time we finally got to the bakery. I heaved a heavy sigh of relief as I pulled the door open and was hit by the sweet smell of breads and cakes baking.

Bronson emerged from the kitchen covered in flour. "I figured you'd have issues getting here on time this morning. I rode my bike," he explained, wiping his hands on a tea towel, which he then flung over his shoulder. "Pippa!" he exclaimed as she followed in behind me. "Welcome back!"

Pippa grinned and ran up to him with her left hand outstretched.

"You're kidding me," he said, mouth agape as he took in the rock on her finger. "Who is the lucky man?"

Don't ask, I thought as I walked around to the cash register to check that we had enough change for the day. The bank was at the end of the street, and I didn't like our chances of getting through that crowd unscathed again.

Pippa continued to rattle off a list of Marcello's plethora of charms while I counted the change in the till. We didn't have enough. We had almost none in fact. And I doubted that our customers were all going to pay for five-dollar desserts with credit cards. I was about to interrupt the other two to check if either of them had any change I could use, when my phone started to flash with a call.

Justin.

I frowned and wondered whether I should answer it or not. After all, the whole reality show casting thing was all on hiatus now...wasn't it?

It would be stupid of me to think he was calling to tell me that I got on the show. Obviously that's not his priority right now, I told myself.

But what if it is about the show and my place on it, and I don't answer his call?

I pressed 'accept.'

"Rachael?" His voice sounded hurried and desperate, not that unusual for Justin, but it was missing its usual air of superiority mixed in.

"That's my name, don't wear it out." Boy, I was really saying some dumb stuff that day.

"Rachael, where are you right now?"

"At work," I said flatly. "Where else would I be?"

"You work?" He sounded momentarily flummoxed.

"Yes. As a baker! You know that!"

"Oh." Justin paused. "I thought that was just made up for the TV show. You're an actual baker?" He let out a little surprised sound. "Most of the time, the people on the show can't even bake, they just get cast because they're good for TV and then we put them through a two week intensive course to bring them up to speed. Otherwise, we just get someone else to bake the stuff for them." I could practically hear his disaffected shrug from the other end of the line. It hadn't taken him long to go from desperate sounding to dismissive.

"Justin, why are you calling me?"

He seemed to remember and the desperation returned to his voice. "You've got to leave work. You've got to come here immediately."

"I can't just leave work." I stared out the window and sighed. "Literally. I'm trapped here. But even if I wasn't, I can't just up and leave."

"Rachael, I need your help."

He always needed something from me, but usually it involved me sitting in a makeup chair for hours or memorizing an asinine script. Something told me this was a completely different matter, though. "Why, Justin?" I instinctively lowered my voice so that Pippa and Bronson couldn't hear me. "What's going on? Where are you?" I turned so that my back was to the others. Pippa is a pretty good lip reader. Luckily, she still hadn't grown tired of talking about how great Marcello was.

"I'm in my hotel room," he whispered, as though he also had someone waiting nearby on his end that he didn't want overhearing the conversation. "I'm hiding."

"What are you hiding from?" I whispered back.

"Take your pick," he whispered, exasperation entering his voice. "The press, the production crew, the police." He gulped. "Rachael, they think I did it."

Chapter 4

"Hey, where are you going?" Pippa turned, the jingle of the door giving me away before I could escape.

"I have to go get some change. For the register."

Pippa stomped over to the window. "But the press are blocking the bank." She looked me up and down. "Besides, they didn't seem to like you."

"Yeah? What was that about? Anyway, I'm sure they'll make some room. I just really need to get to the bank." I tried to push past her.

"Hold up." Pippa stared at me sternly. "I recognize that look on your face." Her eyes went wide. "You're going off to investigate."

"Shh," I said, checking to see if Bronson was overhearing us. "I am not. I'm going to the bank."

"Ohhh, shoot," Pippa said, pointing out the window. "Your boyfriend's on his way over."

"Who?" I looked to see Jackson striding towards the bakery. "Very funny, Pippa. Don't call him that." I undid my coat buttons, suddenly feeling hot and flustered. I'd blame it on the sun that was rapidly rising and melting away the dew if anyone asked.

He at least did the courtesy of knocking on the door, even though Pippa and I were both frozen there in the window like statutes.

"Detective. I wasn't expecting you."

"I did tell you one of us would be by to take a statement." Jackson glanced down at Pippa and asked if he could speak to me alone.

"Sure, I guess."

"Do you have somewhere else more important to be?" There was no hint of humor or amusement in his voice. I glanced at Pippa for help.

"No," Pippa said. "She was just heading to the bank. Isn't that right, Rach?"

"Right," I muttered. "Nothing more important than that. Why don't we go sit in my office then?"

Ever since I'd expanded the bakery by purchasing the shop next door, I'd been able to spread out a little more. The extra space meant a big kitchen, larger cool room, more space for stock, and even a little room for an office. Not that it looked like an office per se, it was really just a desk cluttered with unopened bills and unwashed coffee cups with a mini fridge shoved next to it. The whole thing was really no bigger than a cabinet, if I was honest.

"Sorry," I said, trying to shove the piles of bills to one side as I quickly hid the dirty cups. "It's a bit messy in here."

Jackson glanced up at the ceiling and nodded. "It's good to see you've expanded, though. You never had an office before. Next step will be to franchise out."

"Not quite up to that point yet," I said, sitting down. I was surprised by how casual and friendly he was suddenly being, compared to how serious he'd been in front of Pippa.

My phone flashed. A text from Justin.

Where are you???

I quickly turned the screen face down. Time to get this interview over with, quickly.

Jackson didn't seem to be in any hurry to get to the point, however. He was twiddling his thumbs and shifting in his seat, trying to get into a more comfortable position. I didn't blame him. It was plastic and from the thrift store. Still.

"I didn't see anything," I volunteered, hoping that might move things along more quickly.

Jackson frowned. "Well, that's not a very good start, unfortunately."

I supposed it wasn't, but he was confusing me. From my experience—and I had a lot of it—the cops usually do most of the questioning in these situations. But it was me that had to ask Jackson what exactly was going on.

That's when I saw it. The faintest of eye rolls and a look on his face as though he'd rather be anywhere else, asking anyone anything else other than what he was about to ask me.

Suddenly, I got it.

But I wanted to hear him say it.

"Rachael," he started to say, every syllable dripping with reluctance. "This has to stay quiet, you understand? Unofficial."

"What does?" I still needed to know what he was 'unofficially' asking me.

Jackson swallowed. "Any...involvement, of yourself. In this case."

I opened my eyes wide, acting like I was shocked by the proposition. "You want me to be involved in the case?"

"As I said. Unofficially."

I leaned back in my seat. I could barely control the satisfaction emanating from me. "Well, well, well. This is a first." I leaned forward and stared at him, a little more serious now. "Does anyone else at the station know that you are asking me this?"

Perhaps it was going to be our little secret.

"Emma does," Jackson replied. "Detective Crawford," he added, in case I was confused about who he was referring to. I wasn't. "It was actually her suggestion."

Oh.

I was feeling slightly less satisfied. "I will have to think about it."

Jackson looked surprised. Not just surprised. Disappointed. "You seemed pretty happy about it a second ago."

Even with the screen face down against the desk, I could see it flashing every couple of minutes with a new text. I had to go see Justin.

Jackson didn't need to know that I was already investigating the case. In that moment, I didn't want to give him the satisfaction of saying yes. Especially when it had been his girlfriend's suggestion. I mean, I knew it was petty, but in my opinion, he was being petty as well—even pointing out that it was Emma's suggestion. Couldn't he at least have pretended that he was on board with the scheme?

I stood up and pulled on my coat. Big mistake. The mercury was already rising. It was hot in that cramped office even in just a blouse, let alone a heavy coat. But I needed to show Jackson that I needed to leave.

"I'll have to think about it," I said.

Jackson stood up after me. "What is there to think about?"

I shrugged. "I don't know if I want to get involved in all this stuff again. Especially with my reality TV career about to start."

Jackson just stared at me. "Is this really what this is about? You care more about being famous than helping us catch a killer? You care more about your image than justice?"

I placed my hands on my hips. He wasn't right, of course—I was lying—but I didn't like his self-righteous indignation considering I was pretty sure I knew why he was there. "It's a bit rich to accuse me of caring more about image than justice when there's only one reason you're here, begging me for my help."

"I'm not begging!"

"And that reason is that you are concerned about the image of the police force. Especially with yet ANOTHER killer running around." I waited for him to dare to argue with that.

He let out a little scoff. "And you think that you running around solving this crime is GOOD for our image? If I really cared about any of that, why would I be asking you for help?"

"Secretly asking me," I pointed out. "Unofficially."

His neck seemed to tense up. "Like I said, it's not a good look."

Fine. So he was happy to ask for my help as long as no one knew about it. "And if I solve the crime?" I asked. "I suppose all the credit goes to you."

Jackson rolled his eyes just slightly again. "Solve the crime? No one is expecting you to do that. We just thought you might be able to offer a few crumbs of help, considering you were at the audition yesterday."

"You know what?" I asked, sweating in my red coat now but unwilling to take it off. "I have thought about it. And my answer is no."

Jackson's mouth dropped open as I pushed past him.

"Now, you'll have to excuse me. I've got some important business to attend to."

***

As soon as Pippa and I were back in the car, I yanked my coat off and cranked up the air conditioner. "Geez it's like a heat wave."

"It is when you're wearing a winter coat." Pippa looked me up and down. "Now, are you going to tell me where we're going?"

I glanced in my rearview mirror waiting until Jackson became the size of an ant. "We are going to go talk to Justin."

"Who is Justin again?"

"The producer of *Baking Warriors*." I still had my eyes trained on the rearview mirror. "He was the one who discovered Pierre's body."

"I knew it!" Pippa gasped, slapping her hands together. "I knew you were going to investigate!"

I turned to face her. Deadly serious. "Not a word of this to Jackson, understand? In fact, not a word of it to anyone." I leaned back in my seat. "All I'm doing is talking to Justin. I can't make any promises about what will happen after that."

But Pippa wasn't listening to me, she was already bouncing up and down in her seat with excitement. "I thought life back here in Belldale might be boring after my travel adventures. Especially now that I'm old and married."

My eyes widened.

"But investigating the death of a reality show judge?" Pippa shook her head. "Rach, this is far from boring."

"Just stay calm, Pippa," I tried to say. "I can't guarantee anything."

"Come on, Rach. You KNOW you're gonna do it."

I sighed and looked at her.

"Pippa," I said. "If I take on this case, and I do mean IF, will you help me?"

"Are you kidding me?" she exclaimed. "The bakery detectives, back together? Just try and stop me."

Chapter 5

"Wow, this place is pretty flashy," Pippa murmured as we stood in front of the Glassview Hotel. "I didn't even know Belldale had a place like this."

"I don't think production spares any expense," I said. "On the crew at least." I'd already had a sneak preview of the dormitory I'd be sleeping in if I actually got selected to go on the show. I'd be sharing a room with another contestant, and a bathroom with another four. At least during the first weeks of shooting. If I managed to remain until the end, the herd would thin out a bit and I might get my own room.

But it was nice to see that Justin was staying in luxury.

"Who is it?" he whispered from the other side of the door.

"It's me, Rachael. Who do you think it is?"

He yanked the door open. "It took you long enough." He stopped when he saw Pippa standing next to me. "Who is this?"

"This is my best friend, Pippa. She helps me when I do this sort of stuff."

Justin sighed and made a show of looking down both sides of the corridor. "People have been after me all day." He pulled us both inside the room and double-checked the door was locked before heading over to the mini bar.

"Vodka," he announced once he'd found what he was looking for. He didn't offer me or Pippa anything as he took a drink from the tiny bottle. I supposed they were expensive. "Believe me, honey, I need to drink after the twenty-four hours I've had."

"Justin, are you going to tell me what's going on? You said that you were a suspect, but you're not being held at the police station."

Justin began pacing back and forth across the carpet. "No, but I am being held prisoner in this hotel room." He stopped and stared at me. "The press are all pointing their fingers at me, Rachael." He walked over and shook me by the shoulders. "You gotta help me. I know that you're an expert at this kind of thing. You solve murder cases." He flung his arms up in the air. "Well, you gotta solve this one! You gotta help me prove that I didn't do it, otherwise my career is over."

I shot Pippa a look and settled into a chair. "And of course you want justice to be served... You want your good friend Pierre's murder to be solved."

Justin waved his hand. "Yeah, yeah."

Pippa was staring back at me. I couldn't read her mind, but I could read the look of suspicion on her face. She seemed to be saying to me, *But how do we know Justin DIDN'T do it?*

I gave her a slight shrug. *I know.*

If anything, Justin would have been at the top of my list of suspects. He was the one who found Pierre's body. Clearly, the media had leapt to the same conclusions.

And I didn't want to do that. Jump to conclusions, that is.

"Justin," I said gently. "Calm down for a moment. Take a seat."

He gulped down the rest of his vodka and took a seat at a table by the window overlooking the lake.

I stood and joined him. "Take a few deep breaths." Sitting down, I asked him, "Now, do you have any idea who MIGHT have done it."

Justin began to bite the nail of his left thumb. After a few seconds of deep thought, he nodded. "Really, it could have been anyone who was there that day."

Of course.

"But I'm pretty sure..." Justin glanced up at me. "And don't take offense to this, Rachael."

I leaned back. "I won't."

"But I'm pretty sure it was an auditionee."

I gave him a long stare. "Do you think I did it?"

Justin shook his head. "No, no. Of course not. You were in the green room, after all."

I sighed. "Who then? Do you have any names?"

"Wait here a second." He went and fetched his beloved tablet from the top of his bed. I tried not to groan at the sight of that thing.

It took him a few minutes to find the auditionee list.

"Here," he said, sliding it in front of me. "Here is a list of all the potential contestants who got up close and personal with Pierre yesterday."

I leaned over. "Why are some of the names highlighted in pink?"

Justin raised his eyebrows. "They are the people who acted the most suspicious. Rachael, I had to deal with the whole bunch of you all week, you know. Put up with everyone's tears and tantrums, assure you all you were doing all right, that your hair and makeup looked fine, and that you were definitely going to wow the judges."

Not exactly how I remembered events. Anyway.

"So, I saw everyone. Saw their best, and worst." Justin sat down and stared at me. "I know how desperate some of these people were to get on TV." He didn't break the stare. "Desperate enough to kill."

I felt a little chill go down my spine.

He pushed the tablet closer to me. "There you go, Rachael. Those names in pink. They are the people you need to be talking to."

***

Justin had narrowed the list down to two prime suspects. The first one was a woman named Renee, a struggling single mother with five kids under twelve who would have been an almost certainty to make it onto the show—unless someone else had a better backstory than her.

I was worried that person might have been me.

Justin had told me that Renee was desperate for the $100,000 prize money. She'd talked about little else during the pre-audition phase, apparently.

"Pretty good motivation," I said to Pippa as we stood in the front of Renee's house. I glanced guiltily at the front of her house. It looked like the money really *could* come in handy. The house wasn't just a little rundown. It would take more than just a fresh coat of paint to get this place looking nice. Or even livable. There were planks of wood falling off the exterior and the porch groaned as we stepped on it. I was afraid I was going to fall right through it.

I knocked on the door.

A woman, looking nothing like I was expecting, pulled the door back. "Sorry," I said. "I was looking for Renee Austin?"

"I'm Renee," she said.

"Oh." I stared at the young, perfectly dressed woman in front of me. I tried my best to hide my confusion. I certainly didn't want to be rude, but I desperately wanted to ask how the heck she was so young--or looked so young at least--with so many kids.

And how did she afford to dress so well if she was apparently so desperate to win the prize money? She wore a crisp floral dress in pink and green and her hair was pulled back with a matching headband. She looked the picture of the perfect homemaker. Not someone struggling to put food on the table.

"Can we come in?" I asked, still trying to hide my look of surprise.

"Who are you?"

That was a good question. I should have led with that. "My name is Rachael Robinson."

I saw her face change. Not that it had been soft, exactly, but now her mouth formed into a hard line. "Right. The contestant that beat me to get onto the show. I see."

I didn't know that was official yet. Had I really gotten onto the show?

Right. Not the right time to focus on that.

"What are you doing here? Come to rub my nose in it, have you?"

I shook my head and put my hands up. "No, of course not."

I've just come to accuse you of killing someone.

Probably best not to say it quite like that.

"What then?"

I cleared my throat. "I'm sure you've heard about Pierre's death," I said, trying to be delicate.

Renee raised her eyebrows. "I've heard that he was murdered, yes. On set, apparently."

"Yes. Apparently." I turned to Pippa, begging her silently for help.

"Erm," she said, turning towards Renee. "You didn't happen to see anything suspicious yesterday, did you?"

Renee lowered her eyes. "What is it to either of you two? I've already spoken to the police. Why are you at my house?"

I decided to just be honest with her. "Look. The police in this town don't always do the best job when it comes to things like this. Sometimes they need a little...help. So that's all I'm trying to do. I'm concerned—just like you are, I'm sure—about what happened to Pierre. What does it mean for our town?" I decided to try a slightly different tactic. "What does it mean for the future of the show? I'm sure you're anxious to find out whether you got on."

"What does it matter whether Pierre is alive or dead? I blew the audition."

"Hey, I thought I did too," I said, trying to be sympathetic. "But Justin assured me that I didn't. Apparently I did better than I thought I did."

Renee scoffed. "There was no 'apparently' about it. Everyone knew you were getting through. Everyone knew you were Pierre's little favorite," she said with a hiss before trying to shut the door on us.

Pippa shot me a *look*.

What is going on here?

"Renee, please, if you could just let us talk to you for a minute! Pierre didn't even seem to like me! He didn't even like my baking that much."

She shut the door with my foot caught between it and that doorframe. "Ouch!"

"I'm sure your baking wasn't the reason he liked you!"

I yanked my foot out before it got jammed again, before Renee slammed the door for good.

"What was all that about?" Pippa asked, clearly enthralled by the drama but trying to look sympathetic for my sake.

"I think my foot is broken." I tried to flex my toes and winced. "And I have no idea what all that was about. That was crazy, right?"

"Had you met her before?"

I shook my head. "This was the first time I ever laid eyes on the woman. I never even heard of her until this morning."

"Well, it seems like she knows an awful lot about you."

"Pippa," I said, slightly offended. "Whatever she was just suggesting, and I'm not even sure what that was, none of it is true. You know that, right?"

Pippa shrugged. "Hey, if you had to flirt with a judge to get onto a reality show, then I don't blame you."

"Pippa! I didn't. I only met Pierre the one time, at my audition. And I was so nervous I could hardly even speak to him. Let alone flirt."

The curtains to the front porch pulled back to reveal Renee's face scowling at us.

"Right. We should probably get off her porch."

"So who's next on the list?" I asked as I pulled out of Renee's driveway. She was still peering at us through the curtains as I rolled my car slowly backwards.

Pippa frowned and looked down at the names. "Some guy named Adam Ali."

"Adam Ali," I murmured, glad to finally be out of Renee's crossfire. "Man, that name sounds familiar. I really hope it's not who I think it is."

It was. Adam Ali was a thirty-five year old man, claiming to be twenty-five, who was convinced that he had been robbed of a life in show business. He had ginger hair that had been highlighted blonde, pale skin, and blue eyes that were far too bright.

It had been *years* since our last meeting.

I knew him because he owned a wedding cake business. When I'd first opened my boutique bakery, he'd tried everything possible to get me shut down, including getting other shop owners and residents to sign a petition that alleged that my bakery sold goods containing illegal substances and that I was a hazard to the family-friendly neighborhood.

Eventually, when I'd informed him that I didn't even *make* wedding cakes and never intended to, he backed off.

Still, I knew just how competitive, and underhanded, Adam could be. No wonder Justin had him pegged as a suspect. I could only imagine the lengths he would go to in order to ensure his place on TV.

"Pippa, Adam isn't going to just open up and talk to us. He probably isn't even going to let us in his shop." I turned off the ignition and thought. "We're going to have to come up with a good reason for going in there."

Pippa held up her left hand. "Duh?" she said, pointing to it.

"Oh, Pippa, you're a genius! Your reception!" I threw my head back. "Oh, I'm almost glad you actually got married now!"

"What?"

"Huh? Nothing," I said quickly, taking my seatbelt off. "I mean, of course I'm glad you got married. As long as you're happy, I'm happy."

"Right."

"Come on, let's go inside!"

Adam's face bloomed into a large grin as soon as he saw Pippa and the ring on her finger. "Don't worry, there's a wedding band as well, as you can see, but we haven't had the reception yet!"

I lingered back out of sight and almost got trapped in a large display of taffeta decorations falling from the sky.

I tripped over a display and almost sent a very expensive four-tier cake flying.

"You!" Adam said, his mouth dropping open. He raced over and straightened the display, shooing me away. "Have you come here to sabotage my store?"

"No, I wouldn't stoop to that level," I said, gripping my purse straps as I tried to steady myself on my feet. "I'm here with my friend Pippa."

"Oh, you two are friends?" His disappointment was palpable.

Pippa nodded. "Yes, best friends. Rachael would have been my maid of honor as well, if me and Marcello hadn't eloped."

Adam shot me a skeptical look before placing his hand on his hip. "So are you two actually here to buy a wedding cake?"

Pippa nodded. "Yes, of course!" A look of shock spread across her face when she flipped over a price tag and saw the price.

"They aren't cheap, honey, but they are the best." Adam turned to me pointedly and added, "I am the best baker in Belldale, after all."

I tried not to bite. I really did. "Is that so? Then why did I get cast on *Baking Warriors*, and you didn't then, Adam?"

Adam's mouth dropped open. "You auditioned for *Baking Warriors*?"

Huh? "Oh, come on, Adam, don't pretend you don't know I was there. Or that I was the judges' favorite."

Adam pouted a little and crossed his arms. "I *didn't* know you were there, actually. The least you could have done was stay away and give me my moment! After you opened up the only other rival boutique cake shop in town and took away all my customers!"

I rolled my eyes. "I don't even do wedding cakes. My store has nothing to do with weddings at all."

I could tell immediately from his reaction that I'd said the wrong thing. "Oh really, Rachael Robinson? Is that so?"

I was less sure now. "Yes?"

Adam clicked his tongue in his cheek. "What is all this I've been hearing about you holding wedding receptions then? Do you not cater those? With cakes?"

I looked at Pippa for help, but all she offered was a shrug with a 'you're on your own here' look.

I swallowed. "Well, yes, but that's only a recent thing. And I just hold the receptions. It's not just wedding receptions we do, it's birthdays, bar mitzvahs, and other celebrations," I said, stumbling over my words as I tried to paint the situation in a more positive light. "I think a lot of the brides and grooms bring *your* cakes in to my store actually. They must know yours are the best." I had no idea if that was true. Nor did I have any idea if Adam was buying any of this. I doubted he was.

"Well," Adam said, with a little flick of his bangs. "Mine are the best." Okay, maybe he was. I had to remember, flattery was the way to this man's heart.

"Adam," I said, pouncing on the fact that his guard was down a little. "I suppose you heard about what happened to Pierre yesterday?"

"Yes, sweetheart, I was there." He stared at me. "I heard the screams." He turned his attention back to one of his cake displays, fixing a ribbon tied around a thick slab of fondant. "Though I've been avoiding all social media today. I can't bear to read about any of it." He placed his hand up to his heart. "It's such a tragedy, isn't it?"

"Yes, it is." I tried to read Adam's tone while he was talking, but it was impossible to tell if he was sincere or not.

"Adam, did you see anything yesterday? Hear anything? Besides the screams."

"Who are you? The police? No. All I heard was the screams of that PA that found him."

"Producer," I corrected him. "Justin is a producer, not a PA."

"Well, whatever. I didn't see anything before or after that. I was more focused on myself." Big shock. "And my own audition, than on anything anyone else was doing."

I thought about this. "Did you think your audition went well?"

Adam glared at me. "I know I gave the best audition of anyone there. I'm sure I would have gone through to the next round as well, but I'm not sure we'll ever know now, will we?" Adam flicked his bangs again, sadly. "Who knows if the show will even film now? It's a tragedy. I was made for TV, Rachael. I just can't believe all of this is happening."

Adam looked over at Pippa. "So are you going to purchase one of those or not?"

Pippa backed away awkwardly. "I'm going to have to think about it, but I'm honesty really very interested."

She kept backing away until she was right at the door. I bid farewell to Adam and quickly followed her out.

"YOU'RE going to bake my wedding cake, right?" Pippa whispered to me as we ran past the shop front.

"Pippa, I've never made a wedding cake before!" I said, opening the car door. "But yes. I will." I shot one last look back at Adam's shop. "I wouldn't trust anything that had been made by Adam."

It was midday and the sun was glaring down. Even with the air conditioning on full blast, we were sticking to the seats. But with the windows down and my foot on the accelerator, our trip through Belldale with our hair flowing in the wind was fairly pleasant.

"You were right, he really doesn't like you," Pippa said. "He DEFINITELY still holds a grudge." Pippa mused over this for a second. "Do you think he could have killed Pierre to get back at you? Because you got through and he didn't?"

I sighed a little, pulling my sunglasses on. "He said he didn't even know I was there. And he seemed pretty convinced that HE was the one who got through."

"And do you believe him?"

I thought about that for a moment. "I'm not sure."

Chapter 6

"Pleaasssseee," Pippa begged, stretching out every vowel so that it sounded like the word had five syllables. She clasped her hands together. "I promise that he won't let you down."

My face was frozen in a look of shock and horror like I had been covered in lava at Pompeii and made to stand that way for all time.

Pippa waved her hand in front of my face. "Rach? Are you still alive in there?"

I was finally able to move my face. "Pippa, tell me this is one of your little jokes. You are pranking me, right?"

"I'm not, Rach! Marcello needs a job. Like, really needs one. I promise you he will be a model employee."

"Pippa, he breaks everything. He thinks that you can fish the glass out of salsa and still serve it! He drops hair everywhere!"

"I know he's not perfect..." Understatement. "But he can be trained. He'll be different at work than he is at home. You'll be there to keep an eye on him. And if he does totally mess up, you can fire him, and I promise there will be no hard feelings." Pippa grabbed me by the arms. "Please, just give him a chance, Rachael."

I couldn't believe I was about to agree to this. "Fine," I said with a heavy sigh. "I'll give him a chance. But this is on a trial basis only, okay?"

Pippa nodded and jumped up and down. I had to double check she understood what I mean. "Trial. Basis."

"Yes, Rach! Thank you!" She ran out of the kitchen and came back with Marcello, who was grinning ear to ear. He reached out for my hand and kissed it. "Thank you so much, Miss Rachael. I promise that I will be your humble servant at work. You will not regret this decision."

I was already regretting it, though. And I knew I would only regret it more when the next day came.

***

I hadn't taken my eyes off him from the moment he'd walked in the store.

"You know, you can trust him a little," Pippa whispered to me as she tied her apron behind her back. "It's not like he's going to burn the place down."

"Pippa, if he works here, it's on my terms. And that means never taking my eyes off him for one moment."

Pippa held her hands up. "Okay, okay, you got it, boss. Now, what do you want Marcello to do first?"

Hmm. Definitely nothing involving food, which was difficult in a bakery. Drinks maybe? I wondered just how badly he could screw up a cup of coffee.

"Does he know how to use a cappuccino machine?"

"I'm sure he can learn. He is Italian, after all!"

But as soon as the milk hit the frother and Marcello had managed to cover himself, me, and Pippa in hot milk before dropping the entire jug on the ground, I knew that he couldn't learn. At least, not until we were closed to customers and I had the time to teach him. And I'd had a few glasses of wine first.

"I'll get a mop."

While Marcello was in the cleaning closet—I figured there was only so much trouble he could get up to in there—I took a minute to check my phone.

370

I had a new message from Justin. **What happened yesterday with Renee and Adam???**

I'd been putting off messaging him. I wasn't yet sure what to make of either of them, they both could have done it, and I wanted to dig for some more information on both without Justin's opinions of them clouding my own good judgment.

I decided not to reply. Just as I was about to put my phone back in my pocket, a call from a private number flashed up on the screen.

I hovered over the 'reject' option before finally tapping it. I never answer calls from private numbers as a matter of principle. If it's someone I know, or it it's important, they can leave a message.

They did, but unfortunately not a text message. A voice message. I sighed and glanced towards the mop cupboard, wondering what was taking Marcello so long. *I really should go check on him.*

But with everything that was going on, I was worried the message could be important. Maybe it was Jackson. Maybe something had been discovered about Pierre.

I listened to the message while keeping one eye out for Marcello at the back of the shop.

"Hello...Rachael?" It was the kindly voice of an older woman, one that I thought I recognized but couldn't quite place. "I'm not sure this is the right number, I received it from Justin. Anyway," the voice continued briskly, if a little unsurely. "This is Dawn Ashfield calling, from *Baking Warriors*. I'm still in town. Production is in a bit of limbo right now, as you can imagine. But we have some good news for you. Give me a call back when you have a chance, dear," she said, before leaving her number.

Dawn Ashfield just called me? Well. Now I wished I had broken my stance on picking up calls from private numbers. I was just about to punch her number back in when I heard a squealing noise coming from the direction of the kitchen.

Or maybe the mop closet.

"What is that smell?" I muttered. Then I saw it. Gray smoke rising from the top of the door of the kitchen.

Pippa burst through the swinging doors coughing and spluttering. "Rach! Quick! Call the fire department!"

I sighed and began pressing the numbers. I didn't even have to ask how it had happened.

I wan't even surprised.

***

"To be fair to Marcello," Pippa said. "He didn't know that you weren't supposed to mix those two kinds of cleaning fluids...next to an open flame."

I surveyed the damage to the kitchen while we both hunched in together on the bottom part of a bench. Luckily a lot of it was superficial. And luckily we had more than one oven because one of them was doused in fire extinguishing foam.

I was more concerned with the loss of profits from the entire morning we'd had to close the shop.

"I'm sorry. I never should have asked if he could work here. But even I never thought he'd do this," she said, throwing her hands up at the blackened room.

"I thought he would do it," I said flatly. I wasn't even mad. I had been expecting something like this to happen. My only surprise was that it wasn't even worse.

"So I suppose he is fired then?"

I turned slowly towards Pippa. "Yes, Pippa. I think it's safe to say that the trial period was not a success."

Pippa sighed and stood up. "I'll help you clean up then. We can't stay shut all day."

"Umm," I muttered, distracted by my phone ringing again. I'd totally forgotten all about the phone call from Dawn. I still didn't know what this important news was she had to tell me. I glanced at Pippa, who started to scrub down a stovetop.

"Hey, you know what? You should go home and make sure Marcello is okay."

Pippa turned around in surprise. "Really?"

"Yeah, it's fine. I think we should just close for the day."

"Only if you're sure."

I was sure. Sure that I wanted to call Dawn Ashfield back and find out what the heck was going on. I was sure that if Dawn was calling me herself that the news must be important.

That meant I must be important.

Maybe filming is going ahead in secret. You know, they'd have to be a bit sensitive about it following Pierre's death...and I've been cast...and they just need to know when I'm available and how discreet I can be.

Man, I was starting to sound like Justin. Or Adam. It's just that the reality TV bug had bitten me hard. I needed to know what was happening with the show.

Pippa took her apron off. "So are you coming home with me?"

"Er, no. Are you all right to walk?" I asked her. "It's a bit cooler today so you should be fine. I've got some banking I need to take care of."

"Banking? Come on, Rachael, that's your go-to lie."

"It's not a lie this time. Promise."

As soon as Pippa was out the door, I punched Dawn's number into my phone.

"Hello, dear," she said, like she was a little surprised I'd actually called back. "I hope you're coping okay after everything that's happened."

"I'm sorry for your loss," I said. "I know that you and Pierre were very close."

"It's a tough time," she said. "Listen, Rachael, I've got something very important to tell you."

"Is it about the show?" I asked, a little too eagerly.

"It is," she replied. "Are you available to meet up sometime?"

"Yes, of course I am!" Way too eager again. "I am free right now actually."

She chuckled a little. "Right now might be a little too soon for me, dear. How about tomorrow?"

"Oh," I said, trying not to sound disappointed. "Yes, tomorrow is fine." I supposed there wasn't much point to closing down the bakery for the day now.

"Meet me down at the studio at 11:00 AM. I'll see you tomorrow."

***

"What should I wear?" I called out, running into the living room with a dress in each hand, only to come face to face with Pippa and Marcello engaging in a giant make-out session.

"Oh," I said, braking on my heels. "Sorry. I'll give you some space."

"No, Rach! It's fine," Pippa said, waving me back. "After all, this is your apartment."

Marcello was looking red-faced and sheepish. "Hello, Rachael." He straightened up, though Pippa was still half-draped over him. "I just want to assure you that I will pay you back for all the damage at the bakery. Just as soon as I get another job."

I tried not to open my eyes too wide at the mention of Marcello finding *another* job. Who would be crazy enough to hire him? I had to wonder what kind of job Marcello would even be suited for. Some place where he didn't have to make anything, touch anything, or take on any responsibilities. My mind was coming up blank.

"It's okay, Marcello. I've got insurance." But I had to wonder if insurance would cover an employee who wasn't even officially employed yet. I hadn't put Marcello on the books for his 'trial' period. Anyway, I had bigger things to worry about. Like what to wear for my meeting with Dawn Ashfield in the morning.

"Does it even matter?" Pippa asked. Pippa was the kind of girl who could be 'girly' in certain ways—take marrying a perfect stranger and gushing about his every eccentricity like a love sick puppy, for instance—but who was completely ungirly at other times. Take clothes, for instance. She wasn't the kind of girl to gush over outfits. She didn't even like shopping. So I wasn't surprised when I held up the dresses to ask "Blue or purple?" and her eyes glazed over.

"It *does* matter. I need to impress Dawn. Pippa, I think this is a sort of secret audition. Or maybe we're even going to start filming. After all, Justin told me I was practically a shoe-in to make the cut. And Dawn has influence on the show, you know. Without Pierre around, she probably makes the final decision. I'm kinda nervous."

"Well, I think either dress is fine." Pippa frowned. "But don't get your hopes up too high. She could want to see you about anything."

Just then my phone started to ring. "That's probably... Oh! It's Justin." At first I was a little disappointed, but then I realized something. "Pips, if Justin is calling me then that DEFINITELY means that filming is back on!"

Pippa went back to kissing Marcello while I took the phone call. "Justin?" I said excitedly. "I think I know what this phone call is about."

"You do?" he asked, cutting me off.

"Yes," I said, holding up the blue dress in front of the full-length mirror in the hall. "It's about the show, right?" I lowered my voice in a cheeky, conspiratorial manner. "It's about filming, isn't it?"

"Yes, it is," Justin said, surprised. "Oh, so you already know that filming is being put on hold indefinitely."

I dropped the dress. "Excuse me?"

"I'm having to call all the auditionees," Justin said with a sigh, showing just how over it all he was. "Tell them all that the show is technically 'on hiatus' until this whole Pierre business is sorted out. Basically, if the show ever comes back--and I mean IF--then we'll have to hold all the auditions again."

I was stunned into silence. "But, Justin, I thought you said Pierre liked me, that I was going through to the next round."

"Pierre did like you," Justin said, just a little too pointedly, I thought. "But Pierre is dead, Rachael. He won't have much sway over who gets on the show from beyond the grave."

I moved into my bedroom and slumped down on my bed. "I just thought... Never mind."

Justin must have heard my glumness. "Hey, it's okay. You can audition again. You were great."

"So you said."

Justin clucked his tongue and lowered his voice. "I don't suppose you had a chance to speak to Adam and Renee, did you?"

"I did, actually. Still forming my conclusions there."

"Ha." I could hear Justin's heavy sigh down the end of the line. "Honey, I just got off the phone with Adam myself, and let me tell you, he is ECSTATIC over the news."

"Ecstatic? Why is that?"

"Well, honey, he knew he didn't get through. He blew his audition, and not just in the 'kind of' blew it way that you did. I mean, his cake was *inedible.* Maybe we could have pushed him through if he had any kind of personality to speak of on the day, but he totally froze up, and not even in an entertaining way. Pierre hated him. We'd already sent him home that day WELL before Pierre's body was found."

Hang on. But Adam said he'd heard the screams when Pierre had been found.

And that wasn't the only thing he'd told me.

"But Adam told me that he'd gone through to the next round. Or at least that he was pretty sure he had."

"Nope," Justin replied. "We'd told him thanks but no thanks. Try again next year. So, you can imagine that this is all very good news to him. If we rehold auditions then Adam gets another shot." Justin sighed. "Not that I think he has what it takes, but hey, I'm just the genius producer of the whole thing. Rachael? Are you still there?"

"Er, yes," I said, standing up. I'd been lost in my own thoughts. "I have to go, Justin. Thanks for calling."

"Hey, Rachael," he whispered again. "You ARE still working on trying to clear my name, right?"

"I am Justin. That's why I've got to go. I think I better make another visit to Adam Ali."

Chapter 7

"Dawn?" I asked tentatively, as I stuck my neck into the greenroom like a nervous gander. No one there.

Hmm.

Maybe I should just leave. After all, there was no way that Dawn wanted to confide in me about my top secret casting on *Baking Warriors*. I cringed now, remembering that I'd been so sure of her intentions, so sure that I'd made it on TV. What made me cringe even harder was how much I'd wanted it to be true.

My heart started to thud a little. *What if it's bad news she wants to tell me?* Maybe she wanted to tell me that my audition was so abhorrent that I should never bother embarrassing myself by trying again.

I should just leave. I need to talk to Adam.

"Hello, dear!"

I stifled a scream as I managed to control myself from jumping out of my skin. Dawn was standing behind me with a big, warm grin on her face that immediately put me at ease. She was probably only old enough to be my mother, but she had that 'grandmotherly' vibe about her that made you want to spend the afternoon with her baking cookies. Or just being taken care of by her.

For a few seconds I missed my own grandmother. I was ashamed to find that I could feel tears beginning to prick my eyes and I quickly turned away.

"Oh, heavens, are you okay, dear?" Dawn placed a hand on my arm and stroked it gently. That, unfortunately, only made the tears fiercer.

"I'm fine," I said quickly, putting a bright smile on my face. "Just had a silly moment there."

Dawn smiled sympathetically. "I suppose you've heard that filming has been delayed indefinitely. But don't worry, dear, you'll be able to audition again when the time comes. I'm sure you'll be on the top of the producer's lists. Is that what's got you so upset?"

I shook my head quickly. "No. Geesh, I hope I wouldn't cry just because a TV show was being delayed. I hope I'm not quite that desperate to be famous." Was I though? I wondered if the disappointment of the news Justin had given me was actually mixing together with my sudden grief and making me feel more emotional than I would have otherwise.

I didn't want Dawn to think me that shallow. "I'm just missing my grandma today." I glanced around the studio where the *Baking Warriors* logos and branding still stood, all pink and white lettering with puffs of flour and sugar surrounding the font. "She was the one who taught me to bake." I bowed my head. "I thought that being on the show might make her proud. Well, if she can still be proud of me, wherever she is now." I took a deep breath. "She passed away a few years ago, just before I opened my bakery. She never got to see that either."

"Oh, I'm sorry, dear. Come on, why don't we go grab a coffee and we can talk about it." She smiled that warm smile at me and I teared up again, but nodded, grateful for the opportunity.

The venue Dawn had chosen didn't exactly thrill me.

But as we walked through the automatic doors of Bakermatic, I smiled anyway and offered a polite nod to the manager, Simona, as I slid into the booth across from Dawn.

"I love this place," Dawn said, glancing around the store. "So bright and yellow. Like happiness."

The place hadn't exactly caused me a great deal of happiness. For a while there, the low prices and underhanded practices of Bakermatic had threatened to put my boutique bakery out of business. But we had reached a sort of truce these days. Meaning, basically, that we just stayed out of each other hair, and Simona didn't send staff down the road to hand out fliers in the front of my store.

"I'll order," I said. "What would you like?"

Dawn said she'd have a cappuccino and a brownie. I had to bite my tongue to stop from pointing out that none of the cakes were baked on the premises and that they arrived in plastic, filled with preservatives. Whatever Dawn Ashfield wanted, Dawn Ashfield got, as far as I was concerned.

It was a little awkward when I finally got to the counter to order from Simona, but not for the reason I'd originally thought it would be.

Simona wasn't quite looking at me as I ordered the cappuccino, brownie, and a vanilla latte for myself. I thought we were over the whole mortal enemies thing so I was a little surprised.

"How's business been?" I asked, as casually and as friendly as I could.

Simona just nodded as she punched the orders into a tablet screen. "Sugar?" she asked as her long black ponytail swung forward, covering her face and almost obscuring her words.

"Er..." I hadn't asked Dawn. "Just a couple of packets on the side."

Simona finally looked at me. Then her gaze drifted out the window to where the tents filled with press still stood to form a makeshift campsite. "So, is what they are saying true, Rachael?"

I shrugged, unsure. "That depends on what they are saying." I thought about Justin still holed up in his hotel room. "I know they are trying to pin it on one of the producers, but I was there and I don't think he did it." I wasn't really sure I ought to be speculating like that. I also wasn't sure why I was in such a rush to trip over myself to defend Justin.

Simona made a face as though she had no idea what I was talking about. "No," she said, lowering her voice into a whisper. "I'm talking about the rumors about you and Pierre."

I felt my face redden. The creep of the blush must have been slow at first but after a few seconds, my cheeks burned like a furnace and I was certain I must be red as a tomato. "That's...that's in the press?" I whispered. I glanced over my shoulder in dismay to look at Dawn.

Did she know?

Oh, this was so humiliating.

"I'm sorry, Rachael. I assumed you knew."

I shook my head. "I haven't looked at any of the news," I mumbled, grabbing my sugar packets and taking them back to the table. I'd been avoiding all the press coverage so that it didn't influence my investigation. Now their glowering glares and sniggers the other morning made so much more sense.

I slunk into the plastic booth, wishing that the yellow seat would swallow me up.

"You okay, dear?"

Simona delivered the coffees to the table and I muttered another thanks. My hand was trembling as I ripped the sugar packet open and dumped the contents into my latte.

I had to ask. "Dawn," I started to whisper, before we were approached by a young woman in her early twenties with a short mahogany colored bob and a purple pea coat.

"Sorry," she said, her voice gushing. "But, you're Dawn Ashfield, aren't you?"

I paused, stirring my coffee and looking at Dawn, waiting anxiously for her response. Would she be annoyed at being interrupted like this?

It was clear this sort of thing must happen to her all the time. She graciously posed for a photo while the girl, practically bouncing up and down with excitement, aimed her smart phone at the two of them, her arm around Dawn. "Thank you so much!" she squealed, before running off.

"I suppose you get that quite a lot," I said, taking a sip of my latte before scanning the room. I hadn't noticed it when we'd first walked in, but now I saw that half the people in the shop were casting furtive glances in Dawn's direction and whispering to each other to check amongst themselves if it was really her, wondering if they had the nerve to come over and ask for a photo like that one brave girl had.

Dawn waved her hand and picked up her cappuccino. "Oh, it's all just part of the job. I've been at this a long time, dear. It's become second nature over the decades. I've come to expect the constant interruptions. Water off a duck's back now."

I nodded but I was trying not to frown. I knew that Dawn had been baking for a long time. She was one of those faces that occasionally turned up on morning TV shows when I was little. She had also published dozens of cookbooks over the years, but it wasn't until she'd been cast as a judge on *Baking Warriors* five years earlier that she'd actually gotten truly famous.

Anyway. I supposed she knew better than I did when it came to her own experience.

"You were asking me something, right before that young lady came over?"

I was suddenly too embarrassed to ask if Dawn knew anything about the rumors about me and Pierre. I was sure that if she did know about them—and surely she did—then she would be discreet about it.

I cleared my throat. "I was just wondering, Dawn. Not that I'm not thrilled to be having coffee with you, but why did you want to meet up with me? Does it have something to do with the show?"

Dawn chuckled a little. "You are anxious to be on the show, aren't you, dear?" She reached over and placed a hand on mine and it felt warm and leathery. "But take if from me, dear, fame isn't all it's cracked up to be." She took a sip of coffee and ended with a heavy sigh. "Take it from Pierre."

"Right." She still hadn't answered my question though. "I'm sorry about Pierre, by the way. I know the two of you were close friends." They were always in magazine features together, raving about how they couldn't live without the friendship and support of the other while they were filming. "It must be tough for you right now."

Dawn stared down into her coffee cup. "Yes," she whispered. "To be honest, though, it still hasn't quite hit me. Maybe once we're all out of this town. Nothing really feels real at the moment while we are all in limbo." She lifted her eyes and I caught sight of tears sitting in the bottom of them. "By the way, dear, I don't believe any of those salacious rumors about you and Pierre. I was there. I know you only met him the one time. But, you know, people do talk."

I could feel my face redden.

"Don't worry, sweetheart. They've gotta have something to fill the magazines and websites with. It's only because you did so well at the audition. People were jealous, I guess." She settled back in her seat. "If Pierre hadn't been killed, then you likely would have been the one to go through to the next round. And you didn't even use that sad backstory about your grandma!" She must have caught sight of my face because she looked immediately stricken and hurried to apologize. "You must forgive me. Years of working in reality TV have rubbed off on me. I'm starting to sound like a producer. All this talk about backstory, like the events aren't real things that have traumatized people. Please, you must tell me a little about your grandmother."

I nodded and told her about how she started to teach me how to bake when I was just three years old. "My mother had me when she was very young. She was single and had to work full time to support me, so we moved back in with my grandma. Nana was the person who looked after me full time from when I was just a few months old, right up until I started school." I recounted some of my best memories to Dawn, of the way Nana had taught me about the science of baking, as she called it. She baked every thing with precise measurements, always used a pair of finely tuned scales to make sure there was the exact right amount of flour, sugar, butter, etc., in a dish, never ever eyeballed it, and knew that you couldn't just double the ingredients in a recipe and expect it to taste the same. "Recipes are there for a reason," she would always say.

"Even though it could occasionally be frustrating, I learned a lot from her strictness, and everything she taught me has stuck with me." I grew quiet for a moment. "She passed away only a few months before the store opened. I always wish I'd brought the date forward, but I was my grandma's granddaughter. I waited until everything was perfect before I went forward."

"You must really miss her," Dawn said gently.

"I do."

"I hope all this death business hasn't gone and stirred all that up." Dawn paused. "But I guess you're used to grisly murders now, aren't you?" She shivered a little. "The kind of thing I avoid. I can't even watch a scary movie or read a crime novel. What has drawn you to try and solve these cases, dear? It's a rather peculiar hobby, if you ask me."

I was a teeny bit taken aback. "I wouldn't say I've ever gone looking for these things, or pursued them. They just seem to find me. Wherever there's a murder, there I am." I made a face, though I tried to cover it up with a little laugh. "That's probably more morbid than if I had gone looking for them, isn't it?"

Dawn shrugged a little. "For some people, tragedy just seems to follow them."

I wasn't sure that was it. I had no idea why these sorts of things seemed to follow me around. "I do know that I seem to have a knack for solving these cases, though."

Dawn's eyebrow shot up a little. "Don't tell me your investigating Pierre's death?"

I wasn't quite sure how candid I should be. After all, it was all on a very hush-hush basis. Unofficial, as Jackson would say. "I wouldn't say investigating. I'm just keeping my eyes and ears open."

Dawn looked impressed. "Well, I hope you do manage to turn something up. The sooner we are out of this town and away from the press scrutiny the better. I'm as desperate as anyone to know what happened to Pierre and I can't say I've got all that much faith in your local police department. Please tell me you will look into it, Rachael."

I wondered how Jackson would feel to know that it wasn't just the locals who had lost confidence in the

Belldale police department. Even the out-of-towners were skeptical.

"I can't promise anything, Dawn. But I will try my best." I placed my empty latte glass down. "You never told me why you wanted to meet with me."

Dawn rested her face in her hands and gave me a warm smile. "I just wanted to check in with you, Rachael. Have a coffee. Chat. And we've done that." She grabbed her purse and extended her smile even wider. "You remind me an awful lot of myself when I was your age. And I wanted to offer to mentor you at any time. If you're interested, that is."

My eyes grew wide. "Interested? I'm more than interested. Dawn, I'm sort of taken aback right now. Are you really willing to do that?"

She chuckled again. "Of course, my dear. But right now, I really need to be getting back to my hotel. Justin wants to see me for something, and you know how persuasive he is!"

I followed her out of the shop. "Oh, I know it."

***

The apartment looked like a bomb had gone off. For a second I had to wonder if that was what had actually happened. It wasn't just a matter of mess—though as I stepped over the piles of clothes and books on the floor, I almost tripped and sprained my ankle—but there was also debris lying on the floor. Broken bits of wood, some glass, trinkets lying everywhere.

"Did we have an earthquake?" I asked as Pippa appeared in the hallway. Maybe I'd been so wrapped up in my meeting with Dawn that I hadn't even felt it. Maybe it had been confined to our apartment.

"Sorry, Rach," Pippa said, making an awkward face. "We weren't expecting you back so soon." She spun around and looked at an overturned bookshelf that no longer had any shelves in tact. That explained the debris all over the floor. "Marcello was moving some of his bags and he wasn't watching where he was going."

There was a surprise. "Did he also have a bull trailing behind him?" I asked in disbelief before following her into the living room. "Hang on," I said, staring at the piles of bags and luggage. "He was moving bags INTO the house?"

"Yes?" Pippa said unsurely. "I know they are taking up a bit of space."

"Pippa, I assumed he'd be moving his bags OUT of here, by now."

Pippa's face fell. "You don't want us here anymore?"

I sighed. "It's not that I don't want you here. You know I always said you could live here as long as you want or need, Pippa. But that was when you were single. This is a one-bedroom apartment! We can't have three people living here! Especially when one of them is..." I bit my tongue to keep from saying something I would later regret. "...Marcello."

"I see," Pippa said, crossing her arms and refusing to look at me. "You don't like Marcello. Well, don't worry, Rachael. We will be out of your hair as soon as we can! We won't put you out any longer. "

"It's not like that, Pippa. And it's not that I don't like Marcello as a person," I said, exasperated. It was true. I did like him. It was just that... "I just like not having my stuff ruined every day."

Pippa's face dropped and her indignation drained away a little. "I know he can be a hassle to live with," she said quietly. "Honestly, I appreciate you putting up with us as long as you have." She caught sight of the mess in the hallway. "I'll help you clean that up."

"Don't worry just now," I said, grabbing her arm. "It can wait 'til later. Let's just have a quiet night in. Eat some snacks, watch some Criminal Point. Marcello is at his new job washing dishes tonight, right?" Pippa nodded. "So, what do you say?"

"I say, sounds great," Pippa said with a forced smile, before wrapping her arms around my neck. "Thanks, Rach. And I promise, we'll find our own place as soon as possible. If not sooner."

***

"So, stop keeping me in suspense. What did Dawn have to say for herself? Are you getting cast on *Baking Warriors* or not?" Pippa sat back on the sofa, curling her knees up underneath her with wide eyes, waiting for my answer.

I stuck my chopsticks in the carton of gluten-free satay rice noodles and shook my head as I stared up at her from my position on the floor. "You were right, I shouldn't have gotten my hopes up. Filming is delayed indefinitely. I will have to re-audition if I ever want a chance of getting on the show." I took another mouthful of noodles. "I'm not even sure I still want to, to be honest."

Pippa leaned forward. "But, Rach, you've got to," she whispered. "Otherwise, whoever killed Pierre is going to get just what they wanted. You can't let them actually receive their bizarre sense of justice."

I shrugged. "Or, I could just find the person who did it."

Pippa shrugged as well. "I guess. I still want to see you on TV though. You've got to do it for me if you won't do it for yourself." She munched down on her own cashew and vegetable stir fry noodles. "So what were you summoned to the studio for then?"

"Huh? Oh. Dawn Ashfield just wanted to talk to me to see if I wanted her to mentor me. It was kind of a surprise."

Pippa raised an eyebrow, impressed. "See! Now you've GOT to re-audition. It would be crazy not to. You could do worse than Dawn Ashfield for a mentor. Cripes, you'll probably win the whole thing if Dawn takes you under her wing."

"That's the truth." I dug around for some more noodles before stuffing them into my mouth. "I guess I'll have to think about it, weigh all the options." I thought about my nana again for a second.

Pippa murmured thoughtfully for a second. "Huh. It really seems that having the auditions done over would benefit a couple of people, doesn't it?"

I nodded and reached for my glass of white wine, taking a sip. "It certainly benefits the people that missed out behind me."

"Say, Renee and Adam?"

I nodded again. I still hadn't had the chance to talk to Adam. I explained what I'd learned about him to Pippa.

"So he DID know you were there that day?" Pippa's mouth dropped open a little. "I knew it."

"Seems like it." I placed my noodles down. I was stuffed. Savory dishes had a way of filling me up far quicker than sweet foods ever had.

"So, are we going to talk to Adam again?" Pippa asked. She picked up her phone. "He's been bugging me actually, sending me texts and emails to follow up, asking if I am going to buy one of his cakes."

"And are you?" I struggled not to laugh.

She sighed and leaned back on the sofa. "No!" she said with a laugh as. "They're overpriced and not half as good as yours. But I suppose I could pretend I'm still interested if it helps us investigate. Can you stomach going into his shop again? Dealing with all that taffeta and ego?"

I leaned back on my wrists on the floor. "I guess I'm going to have to."

***

But it didn't come to that. At 7:00 AM the following morning, it was Pippa and I who found Adam Ali at OUR place of work, not the other way around.

Pippa jumped in fright as she stood up from placing a cake in the bottom display shelf to find Adam with his beak pressed up against the glass. His eyes seemed particularly small and beady that morning as he scanned the contents of our store through the window before stalking towards the door and pulling it open with a quick yank.

"I thought you said you didn't supply wedding cakes here!" he said, pointing to the cake that Pippa had just placed in the display cabinet.

I watched the scene quietly from the register as I counted the change. Pippa was better at talking her way out of trouble in situations like this than I was.

"That's not a wedding cake," she replied.

"Well, it's white."

"That's because it's white chocolate," Pippa said quickly. "Other cakes besides wedding cakes can be white, you know."

Adam narrowed his eyes and bowed down to get a better look at the cake. "That looks like fondant to me," he said.

"It's not. It's white chocolate. Regular old icing. It's just extra smooth. We have a special spatula that we use." Pippa looked over at me for help.

"Adam," I said, and he finally turned his attention to me. "Can we help you with anything this morning?" I was thinking that he could certainly help us with something, but I didn't want to make him any crosser than he already was before I started to interrogate him.

He finally managed to pry his nose away from the display stand. He pointed to Pippa before saying, "I was trying to track down this one. To see if she had any actual intention of purchasing one of my prestigious wedding cakes. But now I can see she has no intention to. Why would she buy from me when the shop she works in supplies wedding cakes?" He finished pointedly, glaring at me with his icy blue eyes.

Seeing as he was already irritated and had no plans of backing down or playing nice, I decided I may as well come right out and ask him.

"Why did you lie about knowing I was at the audition?"

With his red hair and pale skin, it didn't take much of a blush for Adam to turn bright red. "I didn't lie," he said feebly, reaching out to tap his fingers on one of my counter tops. "I had no idea you were there, darling. Why would you say otherwise?"

I straightened up and exchanged a look with Pippa. "Justin told me. He told me that not only did you know I was there, you knew that I did better than you. That I was going through and you weren't." I hesitated, wondering if I ought to really stick the boot in. "Justin told me that you bombed your audition, actually."

Adam performed the motion of flicking his hair over his shoulder even though his hair was nowhere near long enough to actually do that.

"Justin doesn't know what he is talking about," Adam mumbled, not taking his eyes away from the cake display. I thought I could detect a note of bitterness in his voice that wasn't there due to any shame or embarrassment over screwing up his audition. I exchanged a look with Pippa, who seemed to pounce on the tone in his voice.

"Did you get along with Justin while you were preparing to interview?"

Adam lifted his head high in the air and pouted. "As well as anyone could get along with that guy. With his ridiculous expectations and his air of self importance."

Pippa and I were still looking at each other. Whatever Adam's problem was with Justin, it was personal, not professional.

I cleared my throat and ventured a guess. "Adam, did you perhaps get along a little too well with Justin?"

Adam was still pouting but he threw me an indignant look. "Whatever it was that happened between us, it was all one way, let me tell you. I turned Justin down and he responded by blowing my audition for me."

"Adam, I'm sure Justin wouldn't do that."

"He did. He tampered with my audition piece. I just know it. Left the cake out of the fridge or something so it tasted bad. I've never seen a person spit out one of my creations in my life, and suddenly all the judges are spitting my cake out, saying it was one of the worst things they have ever tasted." Adam shook his head. "No. It was Justin screwing with it. It just had to have been. I'm telling you, he wanted to take revenge on me for rejecting him. That was it." Adam finally looked me directly in the eyes. "Well, now I will have my chance again. A total do-over. With any luck, Justin won't be working at the show by the time the new auditions roll around."

"Adam," I said slowly. Accusingly. "Why you think that Justin won't be around? What did you do?"

He didn't answer me.

"Are you the one that leaked the rumors to the press that Justin was the one who did it?"

Adam's attention was fixed back firmly on the cake display. "Maybe."

"Adam!"

"Well, I had to get revenge on him somehow! He ruined my one big chance to make it."

404

I threw my head back in frustration. I had Justin holed up in a hotel room, constantly texting me asking whether I had found the killer yet so that he was off the hook, and the entire rumor was down to a lover's spat.

Adam kept trying to defend himself. "If Justin is kicked off the show then I will get a fair chance. It's only fair. He deserves it if he's going to tamper with the outcome of the show!"

I rolled me eyes a little. "That's a producer's job, Adam. To tamper with the outcome of a show." I stopped and stared at him.

I had to ask it.

But Pippa jumped in ahead of me.

"So it looks like Pierre's murder worked out pretty well for you," Pippa started to say slowly, inching her way towards a squirming Adam.

"Well, maybe, but only accidentally." Adam straightened up and cleared his throat. "What are you trying to suggest?"

"Did you kill Pierre so that you could take revenge on Justin? Or Pierre, for that matter. For spitting your cake out."

"No!" Adam squealed. "I might have been angry about losing my chance, but I would never do something like that. That's insane."

He held his hand up to his neck to mimic a pearl-clutching motion. Pippa and I looked at each other. I knew we were both thinking the same thing. *How can we trust a word this guy is saying?*

Adam looked at me. "Anyway, I'm not the only person making up rumors and selling them to the press," he said pointedly.

"What are you talking about, Adam?"

He raised an eyebrow. "Don't you want to know how the rumor about you and Pierre got leaked to the press?"

I sighed. I did want to know, but I didn't really want to give Adam the satisfaction that he was clearly deriving from being the holder of this information.

Pippa nodded at me. A signal to me to drop my pride.

"Fine, Adam. Tell me who told the press about that."

He shrugged. "I don't know her too well. Just met her at the audition. Some single mother with five kids. When you got through ahead of her, she kind of lost it.

Said she was sure that you must have used more than just your baking skills to impress Pierre. And when Pierre died, she told me she was going straight to the press." He shrugged. "Said she thought it would make you look guilty."

Chapter 8

"Are you ready?" Pippa asked me as I took a deep breath.

"Yes. It's time I finally faced up to this."

Pippa stepped back and looked over my shoulder as I finally brought up the news headlines that had been running constantly since Pierre's death.

"And I've got an actual real life paper here for you as well, if you need it," Pippa said.

I could feel the waft of air on the back of my neck as she waved the newspaper behind me. "That's super helpful."

"Ohhh." I could hear Pippa whispering behind me. I could hear the wince in her voice. "It's pretty bad."

The gossip sites were plastered with garish photos of Pierre and me, badly photoshopped into them with headlines like "*Baking Warriors* Love Scandal - Contestant Cheats Her Way In."

"This is insane, Pippa. We never even had a photo taken together. We never even met except for that one time at my disastrous audition."

When Pippa didn't say anything, I swung around in my chair to find her making a confused face that she quickly tried to straighten before I saw it. "What?"

"Well, I thought you said your audition went really well. Isn't that why you were going through to the next round?"

"Well," I said, a little unsure. "I *thought* my audition went badly. Pierre didn't seem to like my cake, but Justin assured me that he did really like me."

"Oh."

"Pippa! It's not like that!"

She glanced over my shoulder back at the gossip sites. "No, I'm sure it's not."

"It's not, Pippa!" But I had to cross my arms over my chest as I thought about it all. "Justin just said that Pierre had to pretend not to like my cake for TV. It's all fake, you know. Just like these news stories," I said pointedly.

Pippa nodded firmly. "I know. Sorry, Rach. It's just that they can be pretty convincing."

I spun back around to face the computer. "Yeah, well, Renee did a pretty good job of spinning a good tale for them. She's mixed enough true details from the audition process in with the lies so that it seems more convincing." I dropped my face into my hands.

This was all so embarrassing. I was only glad that my nana wasn't around to see my public humiliation. Even the thought of her reading these gossip articles made me want the earth to swallow me.

"So, what are you thinking?" Pippa asked. She settled down, perched up on the desk next to me.

"If Renee killed Pierre, it makes sense that she would try to frame someone else as a suspect. It's a pretty good plan. Maybe not the most original, but a solid plan nonetheless."

Pippa clucked her tongue a few times, in deep concentration. "To be fair, though, or maybe her plan just backfired, but people don't really seem to be blaming you for his death if you actually read the articles. They are more focused on the scandal of it. Of the fact that you cheated your way through."

"Hmm," I murmured. She was right. Not that I'd cheated my way through, but that no one was really pointing the finger at me. They thought I had a crush on Pierre, not that I was trying to kill him. "Either way though, it takes the attention off the actual crime. That could have been a smart move on her part. She was desperate to get on the show, Pippa. Just like Adam was. She might have been just as upset as Adam was when she missed out. Pierre's death benefits her as much as it did Adam."

I slumped back on the sofa. "Just about the only person his death doesn't benefit is me."

"Exactly. Maybe Renee didn't fully think that angle though before she leaked the story to the press. Her plan failed."

I sat up. "But why would she even do it in the first place? Was she really that angry at me for making it to the next round over her? Unless she did kill Pierre, I can't see why she would do such a thing."

Pippa checked the time. "It's late. Almost 9:00. Do you think we should go over there tonight?"

"She has young children, Pippa. They might be sleeping. Besides, if she was really a dangerous menace to society, surely the Belldale Police would be on to her by now."

We each looked at each other before we burst out laughing. "Well, maybe not." Pippa reached over for her tea and took a big slurp. "Speaking of the police, have you heard from Jackson lately?"

I shook my head and pursed my lips. "Nope. Ever since I turned him down—I mean as an investigator, Pippa, don't let your imagination run wild—he seems to be avoiding me."

"Sulking?"

I sighed. "I don't know. I can't presume to know what goes on in his head."

"And he's still living with that skinny detective, right?"

"As far as I know." I was eager to change the subject. "Speaking of living with partners. Have you and Marcello had any luck finding a place to live yet?" I asked hopefully.

"Ooh!" Pippa jumped up and pushed me off the seat so that she could get to the computer. She quickly brought up a real estate site and excitedly showed me the listing for a two-bedroom apartment at a rock bottom price.

I leaned forward. "That's half what I pay and it's double the space."

"Yep." Pippa nodded as she flicked through the photos. "There's a proper bath as well. And there's a big yard, if we want to get a dog. The landlord allows pets, apparently."

"Pippa, what's the catch?" I suddenly caught the address of the property. "Pippa, this is over the other side of the highway! It's in downtown Belldale," I said, really trying to hide the look of horror on my face. I don't like to be a snob, but Belldale is definitely a town of two halves. I'd only been to this area once before in my life, when Pippa had dragged me to a meeting of her paranormal club.

"I know," she said cheerfully. "The area is about to blow up big time."

"It is?"

She nodded. "So we should grab this place now before rent prices go up."

I sat in silence for a moment. There was another reason I wasn't that keen on Pippa's new zip code. Well, technically, that side of town shared the same zip code, but it may as well have been on a different continent as far as I was concerned. "But, Pippa, it's so far away."

"Don't worry," she replied. "I'll still make it to work on time every day."

"It's not that, Pips. It's that you won't be able to just pop over for a coffee or a chat whenever you want." I stared at the empty sofa. It suddenly hit me that Pippa wouldn't be living on my couch anymore.

It suddenly hit me that she was *married.*

And it didn't seem to be one of her crazy schemes, or something she got sick of and gave up on after a few weeks.

She really loved Marcello. She was serious about him.

And she was really going to move in with him.

"Rach? You okay?" Pippa said with concerned, leaning back to look at me.

"Yeah," I said quickly, trying to hide the sniffling sound in my voice. "It's just been kind of an emotional day for me, that's all."

I stood up. "Let me know if you need me for a reference," I said with a big smile. "For when you apply."

Pippa made an apologetic face. "We kind of already did apply. Fingers crossed, we'll hear by tomorrow."

"Oh." I sucked in a deep breath. "That's great, Pips," I said before I gave her a big hug. "I'll cross all my fingers. And toes as well."

***

I heard Pippa make a sort of inhuman cry that I couldn't tell if it was a squeal of joy or disappointment.

I ran into the front of the bakery from the kitchen, my hands still covered with flour and held up daintily with my elbows bent, as I ran over to Pippa, who ended the call on her cell phone.

"Well?" I asked, assuming it had been her real estate agent on the phone. In the split second before she answered, I wasn't sure whether I wanted her to get the apartment or not.

We can all squeeze in together. It hasn't been THAT chaotic. We can make it work!

Hang on. What about Marcello? It HAS been that chaotic. It's been very chaotic.

Pippa grinned at me. "You're going to be happy!"

Was I?

"We got the apartment!" She started jumping up and down and raced over to hug me. I joined her in jumping up and down but tried to keep my floury hands away from her. We must have looked a strange sight to the people walking past.

"I am happy," I said. "Happy for you. I have to admit, Pippa, that when I first met Marcello..."

"Yes?"

"Well, I wondered if you had really thought it through. You have to admit the marriage was a bit of a rush, and Marcello is a bit eccentric to live with."

"And now?" she asked expectantly.

"Well, now I think that Marcello is a complete and utter disaster. But, Pippa, he's your complete and utter disaster. And that's all that matters."

"Thanks, Rach."

"Well, I guess we may as well start packing when we get home." I accidentally clapped my hands together sending a puff of flour bursting into the air. "I'll help you, don't worry."

"We'll have three pairs of hands then," Pippa said.

"Won't Marcello be at his dishwashing job?"

She made a face. "He kind of already got fired from that. He broke twenty-five plates on his first night."

"Of course he did."

***

"Umm," I said cautiously, as I watched Marcello pick up a knife to slice through the packing tape. "I'm just a little concerned," I whispered to Pippa. "First, I thought we were putting stuff into boxes, not taking stuff out. Second, should Marcello really be holding a knife?"

"We need to open some of the boxes we've already packed. Marcello says he accidentally packed the keys for the new apartment and we can't find them anywhere."

"Right. And the other point I brought up?"

"He'll be fine, Rach. Marcello isn't a child. He's a fully-grown man. He can be trusted with a knife."

"Okay. You're right. Of course." I slowly turned my attention to the box I myself was packing. Marcello's bags had only arrived a few days earlier, but he'd somehow managed to unpack every last one of them so they all needed to be re-packed. Then there was Pippa's stuff. "I think we're going to be here all night," I murmured. "Especially if you want to move into the new apartment in the morning."

Suddenly I heard a scream followed by what I could only assume were expletives in Italian. I spun around to see blood spurting out of Marcello's hand as he lifted it up in the air.

"Oh, sweetheart!" Pippa said, racing over to him. "Oh my gosh, the knife has gone right through."

"Oh my," I exclaimed, taking a step back as my head began to grow foggy. I could feel it happening, could feel the strength draining from my legs. If I didn't sit down, I was going to faint.

I almost made it to the sofa before I collapsed. My legs were against the sofa while I was laying flat on my back.

"Rach!" I heard Pippa scream. She ran over to me and tapped me on the cheek.

I was groggy, but conscious. "I'm fine," I said, swatting her hand away. "Just give me a second. Go focus on Marcello."

She ran back over to a still-bleeding Marcello. "Here, use this shirt to stop the blood." I had my eyes open a peek and could just make out the image of Pippa wrapping a white shirt around Marcello's index finger.

"Oh shoot! This isn't my shirt! Sorry, Rachael!"

I closed my eyes again and waved my hand. That was the least of my worries right then. I reached up to my forehead and tried to take a few deep breaths. I didn't like being so hopeless while someone clearly needed my help.

I wobbled onto my feet and made my way over to where Marcello was hopelessly flailing about. "I think you should tie that shirt a little tighter around the wound."

Pippa turned to me.

"I'm so sorry, Rachael! I've got to get Marcello to the emergency room."

I waved my hand, still a little uneasy on my feet. "No, it's fine. Of course you do." I ushered them out of the room, Marcello clutching my white shirt around his finger. The blood slowly seeping into it was turning the whole thing various shades of red and pink like an extra bloody sunset.

I swallowed. *Just accept that it's a write off, Rachael. It's not worth getting upset over. At least it wasn't anything more serious. At least Marcello only stabbed himself.*

"I'll keep packing while you're gone," I assured them as I followed them out to the car.

"Rach, you don't have to do that."

"Trust me, if I know the Belldale Hospital Emergency Room, you won't be getting out of there for six or seven hours."

I caught Marcello wince. "Well, maybe five if you're really lucky," I tried unsuccessfully to reassure him.

I closed the driver's side door for Pippa and she sped off into the night.

"I guess it's just you and me now," I said to my glass of wine as I took several gulps, hoping it would calm my nerves a little after the sight of all that blood. I thought back to my earlier conversation with Dawn, thinking how funny it was that she thought I would purposely pursue crime solving when I would faint at the first sign of blood.

With my disposition returning to normal, I sighed a little as I looked around at all the carnage strewn across the floor. "How did he manage to make this much mess when his bags only arrived a few days ago?"

I stopped myself. I knew perfectly well how he had managed to do it. He was Marcello.

Trouble followed him.

I supposed I could relate to that, so maybe I should be a little more understanding of his trials and tribulations. Pippa sure seemed to have infinite patience for him. But they were newlyweds. What was going to happen when the sheen wore off and Pippa was stuck living with a walking disaster?

I opened a box and started filling it with the odds and ends that were littering the floor. Books, postcards, old notepads, and photos.

I was still a little shaky, so when I scooped up the first handful of books and photographs, they slid out onto the floor. I slumped down on the sofa and placed my head between my knees for a second.

Come on, Rachael. Pull it together. You've got a long night of packing ahead of you.

I lifted my head and forced myself to keep going. But as I scooped the pile up again, another photo slid out and fluttered to the floor before it landed face down. Once I'd stuffed the rest of the items into a box, I reached down and picked up the photo, turning it over absentmindedly, expecting, I suppose, to find a photo of

Marcello as a child in Italy or maybe a more recent photo, perhaps one taken at his and Pippa's shotgun wedding.

But that's not what I found.

Staring back at me was a smiling Marcello with his arm wrapped around Pierre Hamilton.

What the?

No. It can't be.

I turned the photo over again. As though the back of it might give me some clue as to whether it was real or not. To be honest, it had been some time since I'd held a real photo in my hands. But as far as I could tell, it wasn't doctored in any way.

How on earth did Marcello know Pierre Hamilton?

And why had he arrived in Belldale the day before Pierre was killed?

Suddenly the weariness returned to my legs, and this time it wasn't caused by the blood stains in the carpet.

Chapter 9

My head was still spinning the following morning when Marcello and Pippa finally returned home from the emergency room at 5:00 AM. Even when I closed my eyes, the dizziness remained, my bed becoming a life raft that I tried to cling onto. Trying to sleep was fruitless.

Pippa poked her head in my room to whisper that Marcello was all stitched up and ready to survive another day. "Well, maybe," she whispered.

I was lying with my back to her, facing the wall. I pretended to be asleep, trying not to breath or make a single movement.

"Well, goodnight then," Pippa said before tiptoeing away. She flicked the hall light off and I finally breathed a little.

This was not how I wanted our last night living together to go. And I wasn't just talking about Marcello's accident.

I didn't want to be lying in the dark, wondering if I was living with a killer. Wondering if it was even safe to close my eyes.

But how could I possibly bring this up with Pippa? She was smitten with the guy. She'd only take my accusations as more proof that I didn't like him, or that I thought she'd rushed into the marriage.

I had to remember my nana's adherence to methodology. She would never get two steps of herself. Or go off recipe.

I had to apply that to the case.

Take a deep breath, Rachael.

Think of the facts.

All I had was a photograph. That didn't prove anything.

But it did prove that Marcello knew Pierre. And, from the looks of it, they were close.

Why then has Marcello not shown any grief or sorrow, or even any interest in Pierre's death? The thought sent ice up my spine.

And his marriage to Pippa. It had all happened so suddenly. What were the odds of Marcello turning up in town the day before the murder?

I sat up in bed.

Maybe I should call Jackson.

I had my finger hovering over his name in my phone, just about to press the call button.

I stopped myself. *And tell him what? That I found a picture of two men in my living room?*

He'd probably think I was insane. And I wasn't sure he'd be wrong.

I needed to get some sleep. Maybe things would look clearer in the morning.

***

"Holy..." I started to say as I looked at the time on my phone. 11:00 AM? I hadn't slept that late since I was a teenager. I threw off my blankets and ran into the living room where Pippa and Marcello were still fast asleep on the sofa. I glanced at the boxes of Marcello's items. They were missing something. I reached into my gown and almost cut my fingers on the sharp edges of the photo that seemed to burn a hole there.

"Pippa," I said, shaking her awake and trying to ignore Marcello for a moment while I roused her.

"Huh?" she asked sleepily, rubbing her eyes. "What's going on?"

"It's 11:00 AM! That's what! Who is running the bakery?"

Pippa waved her arm at me and closed her eyes again. "It's cool, it's cool. Branson is there. Don't worry, Rach. I figured we could all use a morning off after last night."

"Aren't you planning on moving this morning?" I said in an urgent whisper.

"I don't think we'll be able to. We might have to stay for another few days, if that's okay."

I sighed. "Fine," I mumbled.

None of this noise seemed to have woken Marcello. He was in a deep sleep that I suspected might have been aided by painkillers the way he was drooling on a cushion. I glanced down at his finger. There seemed to be over a dozen stitches there.

"They saved the finger then?"

Pippa's eyes were still wired shut as she snuggled into the back of him. "Yep," she said. "But they say it's gonna be numb for a while, which might make it hard for him to find work in a cafe or restaurant."

That wouldn't be the only thing holding him back.

Well, now that I had the morning free, I figured it was time to pay a visit to Renee. But as I pulled my jeans and t-shirt on, I felt my energy draining towards that line of inquiry.

The person I really wanted to be investigating was Marcello.

I glanced out the window and was surprised to find that it was gray. From the look of the dark clouds forming in the distance, it was clear that we were in for a summer storm.

I crept out the front door and grabbed an umbrella on my way. I didn't want to wake Pippa. Not before I had decided what to do.

***

The rain had already started by the time I pulled into Renee's driveway, making everything humid and sticky. I'd only been out of the house for fifteen minutes and I already felt as though I needed a shower. And I didn't even want to think about the state of my hair. I just hoped I didn't bump into any handsome men out this way.

"Renee?" I called out through the screen door after I'd knocked and no one had appeared. I could hear the sound of kids running and playing inside, knocking over toys and trampling on each other. I assumed Renee was home and hadn't left five kids to fend for themselves.

But clearly she didn't want to speak to me.

I was just about to leave when I saw a silhouette behind the screen, jolting me a little. My nerves were clearly still shot after the events of the night before.

"Hi there," Renee said quietly. I wondered if she was going to pull the door back, invite me in. The rain was coming down heavy now and I was wearing a rather thin t-shirt.

"I wouldn't be able to come inside, by any chance, would I?"

Renee pulled the door open slowly. She was still wearing that nice floral dress she'd been wearing a few days earlier. It suited her with her new short bob hair cut. "I didn't think you'd want to come inside here," she said softly.

I glanced around the old house. "It's not that bad in here." From the look on her face, I'd clearly misunderstood what she meant. "Sorry, I didn't mean anything."

"I mean, I didn't think you'd want to talk to me after..." Renee stopped talking. "Well, I assume you know what I did?"

I nodded. "I do. That's why I want to talk to you, Renee."

She pulled the door back all the way and sighed gently. "Come in then. I suppose I do owe you an explanation."

Renee pulled some cookies out of a plastic packet and arranged them awkwardly on a plate while I waited for her a few feet away at the dining room table.

"Sorry, this is all I've got," she said, a bit ashamed. "Usually I bake my own fresh, of course. I suppose cookies from a packet don't hold much appeal to you."

I smiled at her. "Usually they would be fine, don't worry. I mean, it's not the packet that's the issue for me. I'm afraid I have been diagnosed with an allergy to gluten."

Renee looked stunned. "But how do you get by with the bakery?"

"I've introduced a lot of gluten-free items," I said, gratefully accepting the tea she placed in front of me. "So I can at least taste test some of what we are serving."

Renee was quiet for a moment. "When I found out that you had got through the audition ahead of me..." Her voice trailed off and she had to clear her throat before wrapping her own hands around her mug of tea for moral support.

"It's okay," I said. "I'm not here to accuse you. Or judge you. I just want to find out what happened."

"I just saw red," Renee explained, staring down into the depths of her teacup. "I wanted to get through more than anything. You know how much the prize money is, right?"

"Of course." I bit my tongue when I thought about how unlikely it was that any of us there on that day were going to win, though. Even if we'd gotten through—and that was a low chance in itself—then we had to beat twenty-three other bakers, all of them more ruthless than the next, to get right to the end.

Renee waved a hand around her house. "You can see how much that money would have meant to me, and my kids." I could hear them watching TV in the next room, the box temporarily sedating them.

I nodded, feeling guilty now. Maybe I'd never deserved to be cast over Renee. I thought back to Justin and all his quotes and sound bites about what made good TV, but what about the people who really needed the experience? What about the people it could be a matter of life and death for? Was good TV more important than any of that?

"And when Justin let slip that Pierre hadn't actually liked your cake," Renee said, finally looking up at me to cast me a suspicious look. "Well, I just looked at you, young and pretty, and my mind started putting two and two together...even though the answer probably didn't add up."

"I only met him that day," I said quietly.

"I know," Renee said.

"So why did you tell the story to the press then? Were you really that mad at me?"

Renee shook her head. "It was nothing personal, Rachael. The press descended as soon as Pierre was killed, you probably know that. They wanted anything, any little tidbit or gossip from the contestants, and they were willing to pay us for our stories." Renee gulped. "They were offering money. And the juicier the story, the more money they handed out. Even if it had nothing to do with Pierre's actual death."

I sucked in a small breath. Suddenly Renee's outfit and fancy haircut, the ones that didn't quite match the rest of her surroundings, all made sense. "How much did they pay you?"

Renee took a sip of her tea. "Enough." She looked at me. "Let's just say I don't need to win a reality TV show competition anymore." She offered me a weak smile. "I'm sorry, Rachael. But I'm sure you would have done the same thing."

I wasn't sure I would have, but I didn't have five kids under twelve. Under the same circumstances, I probably would have done anything to provide for them. I just nodded. "It's okay. I can handle the rumors, and the gossip. But Renee, I just have to know what happened to Pierre. Did you see anything that day?"

Renee shook her head. "Nothing. I was alone, crying in the green room when it happened."

"And can anyone confirm that?"

She shot me a look. "No. I was alone. But I spoke to Dawn Ashfield soon afterwards. She comforted me. Ask her, she can tell you just how upset I was about the whole thing."

***

So much for not running into any handsome men out this way.

I groaned when I saw the police car pull into the driveway, leaving enough room for my car to get out, but not leaving me enough time to scramble into it to check that my hair looked okay.

"Jackson. I'm surprised to see you here."

He gave me a wry look. "I'm not surprised to see you," he said rather pointedly. But his tone was a little jocular. He cleared his throat. "I hear that you've been poking your nose around?" He raised an eyebrow as he waited for my response.

"And how did you hear about that, exactly?"

"Well, from everyone I interview. Seems you're always there half an hour before I am."

Now it was my turn to raise an eyebrow. "Oh. So I'm there before you, am I?"

He cleared his throat again. "Anyway. I thought you didn't want to help out?"

I didn't say anything.

"Right. You just didn't want to help me out. I see how it is."

I sighed. "YOU didn't want me to help you out, remember?"

"I seem to remember asking for your help."

"No," I said, cutting him off. "You made a point of letting me know that it was Detective Crawford's decision to ask me, not yours."

Jackson's face fell a little. "That's why you refused? Rachael, why do you care if it was Emma's decision or mine?"

I squirmed a little. I didn't really have a good answer for that without revealing the rather shameful truth— that I had been jealous. That I *was* jealous.

"I don't care. I didn't care. I just didn't feel like you really wanted me to help out. That you only asked reluctantly."

"And that matters why? Isn't the only important thing that the case gets solved?"

He was right. It should have been the only important thing. Maybe I'd been foolish, letting my pride get in the way. It was all starting to feel pretty petty now.

"I only started to investigate because my friend— well, he's sort of my friend—Justin was getting the blame, and he wanted me to find out who was really responsible," I explained, lamely. "Honestly, I had no intention of looking into it at all until then."

"Oh, we know all about Justin, don't you worry about that," Jackson replied. His tone was very heated. "We're keeping a very close eye on him."

"Wait, you guys don't think he did it, do you?"

Jackson was quiet for a moment. "You know I can't really share that information with you. But if you've got any information for us that might be useful, I suggest you share it."

"Oh," I said, indignant. "So this is a one way street, is it? I have to tell you everything I know but you can't share anything with me?"

"Yes, Rachael," he replied. "That's how police business works. I wouldn't like to think you were keeping any valuable information from us. Are you?"

I thought about that photo of Marcello with Pierre.

It's not time yet. You don't know anything for sure.

Pippa would kill me.

I shook my head weakly. "No. Only what you already know, I'm sure. I've just talked to Renee and I'm sure you got the same information out of her that I did."

"Well, maybe you ought to come down to the station so we can compare notes and confirm that. After I've interviewed her myself, of course."

"Fine," I said with a sigh. Didn't look like I really had much choice in the matter anyway.

***

The old familiar smell of the Belldale Police Station hit me before I was chaperoned to the interview room. The smell was a stale one, tinged with a shot of melting-plastic and cigarettes, even though it was obviously illegal to smoke inside. Someone had been burning some kind of vanilla oil to try and inject some sweetness into the air.

"I'm sure Renee didn't do it," I said, even before I'd sat down in the old familiar seat of the interview room. "I can tell you that right away. You don't need to look at my notes." Mostly because I didn't have any and I was worried he might actually want to see physical proof of my hunches.

I wondered if I kept at this investigation game, whether I would have to start taking notes like a real detective. But that would be sort of like committing to it. And I still wasn't sure I was quite there yet.

Jackson shifted uncomfortably as he settled across from me, in a far more comfortable, padded seat. "What makes you say that? How can you be so sure that Renee is innocent?" I analyzed his tone. It didn't sound like he didn't believe me, necessarily, just that he was eager to know what evidence I had.

I shrugged. "She only wanted to go on the TV show for the money. She has that now. So she has no reason to want Pierre dead."

"You mean the money she got from the press?"

I slunk back in my seat. Jackson knew about the rumors. Of course he did.

He continued, "But she wouldn't have known she had that when she committed the murder. Hypothetically, of course."

Good point.

I quickly ran through what Renee had told me, before filling him in on everything I knew about Adam Ali and Justin as well.

Jackson nodded slowly. "Those are our three main suspects then?"

"Do you mean they are the cop's three suspects when you say *our*? Or do you just use it to refer to me?"

He still wasn't giving much away. If he'd just accidentally let something important slip in a moment of weakness then he wasn't going to admit to it.

I sighed. "Yes. Those are the three suspects."

Jackson leaned back and the front two legs of his chair raised off the floor a little. He examined me closely.

"And you're sure you don't know anything else that you're not telling us? There's no secret suspect up your sleeve?"

I shook my head. "Why would you even ask that? I've told you everything I know. I've told you about everyone I suspect might have killed Pierre."

"Because if you are keeping something from us, Rachael, that would be a very serious matter."

I bit down hard on my tongue. It was about to spill out: *Marcello did it!*

But I just shook my head. "Looks like I'm not that much more competent than you are right now."

Jackson leaned forward suddenly in his chair, bringing the top two legs down with a thud. "I think we're done here."

Chapter 10

At least Marcello couldn't cause any trouble while he was asleep. It was my preferred state for him.

But Pippa awoke as I approached the sofa. It was already 10:00 AM of the newly appointed 'moving day' and I knew she'd appreciate the suggestion I was about to put forth.

"How about I move the boxes for you guys? Go on ahead and you can catch up with me later. I know that Marcello can't do much with his finger all stitched up like that," I said, swinging a look towards Marcello's index finger that still looked liked a swollen sausage that had been badly stitched up. "And you ought to stay here to look after him, don't you think?" I added, trying to sound sympathetic.

Pippa nodded a little hesitantly. "Only if you're sure though, Rach."

"Couldn't be more sure."

With the boxes loaded in the back of my car and the keys to Pippa's new apartment firmly in the pocket of my jeans, I was all set...for the chance to snoop through all of Marcello's stuff.

Sure, I felt a little bit guilty for lying to Pippa, but it was all going to be worth it when I found proof, undeniable proof, that Marcello had known Pierre Hamilton and had been there the day he was killed.

It took even longer than I'd feared to get to Pippa's new place in downtown Belldale. Looked like she was soon to be no closer than a twenty-five minute drive away from me. Right now, she was a twenty-five second walk away from me.

That was if she still wanted to go ahead with the moving plans.

I had an inkling that once I found what I had a hunch I'd find, her plans might change somewhat.

When I finally pulled into her new place, I barely had time to even appreciate how nice the apartment was.

If this was located anywhere else, say on the other side of the highway, I'd live here, I thought, as I hurried in with the boxes. I wanted to be inside, out of the way of preying eyes, before I unleashed the carnage.

Using the same knife that Marcello had used to slice through his finger, I began to gut the boxes, one by one.

I had no idea how long it would be before Pippa, and maybe even Marcello himself, joined me.

Items spilled out as I sliced the boxes open. I got down to my knees and sifted through them, looking for something, anything, that would confirm the unthinkable: that Marcello had killed Pierre.

It was a mad scramble at first and I realized I was getting nowhere the way I was chucking things over my shoulder and frantically sifting through books, photos, receipts, and random accessories.

I took a deep breath and thought about what my nana would have told me. "Take your time, Rachael. Be methodical. Don't leave anything to chance."

I started over and began to sort the items into piles, taking the time to check over each one carefully.

"There has to be something here."

Time passed without me realizing it as I flicked through Marcello's journals and diaries and passport. Most of the writing was in Italian and anything I couldn't read, I secretively placed in my purse to take with me—either to show to someone who spoke Italian, or to translate it later myself with the help of Professor Google.

I was just about to pack everything up and send Pippa a text when something came fluttering out of one of Marcello's leather backed journals.

A bus ticket.

Innocuous enough at first, I turned it over and read the details.

I froze. It was a ticket for a concession pass to Hillsville Park. The place that played host to the *Baking Warriors* audition and the makeshift studio on audition day.

My heart almost stopped beating. I even reached up and thumped my chest to try and get it working again. With my hands shaking now, I checked the dates.

Then double-checked them.

July 22nd. The day of the auditions. The day that Pierre Hamilton had died.

I was so shocked that I didn't hear the footsteps enter the empty apartment behind me. I probably wouldn't have heard an earthquake in that moment.

I probably wouldn't have heard *Marcello* in that moment.

But it wasn't him that entered the apartment. It was Pippa. And it was too late for me to hide the wreckage.

I spun around as I saw the shadow behind me.

"Rachael?" Pippa's voice said. "What the heck are you doing?"

***

I scrambled to my feet, trying to hide the evidence of what I was doing by kicking the exposed items underneath an overturned cardboard box. I shoved the ticked into my coat pocket.

I gulped. "Pippa, it's not what it looks like." Even though it kind of was exactly what it looked like.

"Why are you snooping through Marcello's stuff?" At first Pippa's face was nothing but confusion, but all color and expression drained from it as the realization dawned upon her.

"What? Rachael, please tell me there's another reason why you are going through Marcello's things." Her voice was a breathy whisper now. "Please tell me that, I don't know, that you're secretly obsessed with him or something! Or secretly in love with him. Anything would be better... Anything but...but..." She couldn't even finish her sentence.

"Pippa, I didn't want to tell you until I was certain..."

Pippa shook her head and backed away from me, tripping over a box as she went. She barely even noticed as she straightened herself up.

"Marcello knew Pierre, Pippa."

"No, he didn't," she whispered furiously. "Don't be stupid."

"He did. He was at the studio that day, Pippa."

But she didn't want to listen to me. "Big deal, what does that prove? So what, he was at the studio." But her eyes were wild and her voice shook.

Pippa crossed her arms over her chest like a petulant child. "You're only saying all of this because you don't like Marcello. You think I made a mistake by marrying him."

"Pippa, I have proof," I said, turning over the box to find the bus ticket. "Here, look at this," I said, waving it in her face. But she turned away and stuck her nose up like I had poked a dish of sour milk underneath her nose.

Pippa was still backing away from me while my arm was outstretched, the ticket still dangling from it.

"I can't believe this, Rachael. I thought you liked Marcello!" She stamped her foot on the floor this time, becoming more and more like a four year old by the second. "Did you only volunteer to help move his stuff so that you could come up with this crazy theory?"

I dropped the arm holding the bus ticket. Time to try a different tactic.

"When did you meet Marcello, Pippa?" I asked gently.

"What does that matter?" Pippa asked, but some of the insolence was gone from her voice and she looked up at me plaintively.

"Pippa, when you met him, did you tell him where you were from? Who you lived with? Anything like that?"

Pippa shook her head tearfully. "I guess so," she said, as tears dropped to the ground. "I told him I was from Belldale, of course, and he was so excited to get married and move here. Or at least, I thought he wanted to move here." She sucked in a sharp breath. "Maybe he just wanted to come here to..."

I hugged Pippa tight to me. "It's okay. You'll be safe now. You don't have to worry. I'll call Jackson." I just hoped it wasn't too late.

"It can't be true, Rach." Pippa's lip started to tremble. She slumped down onto the floor and looked around the empty apartment before bursting into tears, her whole body shaking while a horrible noise that sounded like a dying animal escaped from her lungs.

"Pippa, it's okay," I said, hurrying towards her, but she pushed me away. It wasn't so much a case of shooting the messenger as it was of shoving the messenger onto the floor.

"Pippa, please."

"I thought he loved me," she sobbed, burying her head in her knees as she rocked back and forth. "But all this time he was only using me."

"Pippa, please." I knelt down besides her and tried to place my arm round her shoulders.

"I should have known that someone as handsome as him would never be interested in someone like me," she wailed.

"Pippa, that's not true. Of course they would be. It's just Marcello specifically that wasn't."

Her wailing only grew louder. Okay, that was a stupid thing to say.

"I'm calling him right now!" Pippa lifted her head and searched frantically for her phone.

"Pippa, wait, I'm not sure that's such a good idea."

But she climbed to her feet and pushed me away. She already had Marcello on the other end of the line before I could stop her.

"I know what you did, Marcello! I know that you killed Pierre!" she shrieked. "How could I ever have been so stupid as to marry you? I never want to see you again!" She shouted, before adding, "And I don't suppose I will, now that you are going to be in prison for the rest of your life!"

She hung up and threw the phone across the room. "Pippa, I don't think that was a very good idea."

The phone was already smashed into a hundred pieces. Along with all the other wreckage, it fit right in.

Pippa looked at the mess and burst into tears. "Oh, it looks like Marcello has been here!" She sobbed in a weird mixture of sorrow and affection. I raced over and gave her a hug.

"We have to go though, Pippa. And I need to call Jackson right away."

***

The police car was already waiting out the front of my apartment as I quickly pulled into the driveway, my brakes letting out an ear-piercing screech as I pulled to a stop.

I raced up the driveway towards Jackson, who was exiting the front door, suspiciously empty handed.

Jackson just glared at me. "He's gone, Rachael. Marcello is gone."

Chapter 11

Two Months Later.

The stale smell of burnt plastic and cigarette smoke hit me.

I had something I needed to do that morning. Before my life—possibly? hopefully?—changed that afternoon.

"Is Detective Whitaker here?"

He led me into the interview room.

"You look awfully dressed up," Jackson said when he entered. "Off on a hot date?"

I'd gotten a brand new haircut and added a burgundy tint to my brunette hair. And I'd splurged on a new outfit.

"Not exactly." I shifted uncomfortably. "Jackson, I just wanted to make things right with us again."

He glanced around to make sure the door was securely shut. "You're just lucky you aren't in any more trouble than you already are."

"So you won't accept my apology then?"

"You shouldn't have kept that information from us, Rachael. Now Marcello's on the run and we might never have a chance to catch him. An apology hardly cuts it."

I was frustrated. "You mean someone else might catch him? A cop from a different jurisdiction or different state, making you look bad?" I asked. "That's what this is really all about, isn't it? I came to you as soon as I had proof. You're just being stubborn. Refusing to take my calls for two months straight. This is personal, not professional."

Jackson just shook his head and looked away. But I knew I was right.

"I have to go," I said quietly. "It's an important day."

***

Pippa had barely moved from her spot on the sofa in two months.

"It's okay, Rach. I won't stay here forever." Her hand draped over one side of the sofa as she reached for a packet of supermarket cookies that were lying on the floor. They'd been left open over night and as she listlessly bit into one, there was no crunch. "I prefer them this way," she said in her usual zombie-like voice before she continued to munch on it with her eyes glossed over.

I was hoping that Pippa wouldn't stay there forever, but far more for her sake than for mine. This depression had gone on long enough and it was threatening to suck her under and never let go of her.

"Well, wish me luck," I said lamely as I waved my car keys in the air.

"Huh?" Pippa turned her glassy eyes towards me, confused.

"It's the do-over of the auditions today. Remember?"

"Oh." Pippa brightened just a little and put down her cookie. "Break a leg, Rachael."

***

Justin had obviously had a mini-makeover of his own sometime during the past two months. His dark hair was now long and floppy and his new bangs sported a stripe of bright blue.

"Rachael!" he exclaimed brightly before racing over to give me a hug inside the Hillsville Park studios. It was a bit eerie being back there. Justin seemed genuinely pleased to see me and I had to admit I felt a bit of warmth towards him as well. Maybe absence really did make the heart grow fonder.

"Can you believe all this?" he said, breaking the embrace. "I still can't believe it myself. Is that guy still on the run? Have you heard anything?" Justin asked, bringing a hand up to his chest.

I shook my head. "I'm kind of on the outs with the police department."

Justin let out a loud, dramatic sigh. "I'm just glad I'M off the hook for the whole thing. And I guess I've got you to thank for that."

"I guess so. Have you seen Adam since it all happened?"

Justin rolled his eyes. "Only once. This morning. He's being a total nightmare, as per usual. Don't know what I ever saw in that guy." He flicked his bangs out of his face dramatically in a way that reminded me of Adam.

"He's here then?" I asked. "And Renee?"

"Both of them are back for another round of torture," Justin said, looking down at his trusty tablet. "Speaking of, Renee is up first. I've got to go track her down."

It surprised me that Renee had turned up to audition again. She'd said that the blood money from the gossip sites had been almost as much the prize money from the show.

I supposed she could always do with *more* money. Who couldn't? Still, something about it didn't sit right with me.

I was still mulling it over when I heard a familiar voice.

"Rachael!" Dawn said warmly as she practically skipped over to me. I was so happy to see her. "Oh, I'm so glad to see you made it back." She gave me a comforting hug that helped to soothe my nerves as I took in a breath of her lavender perfume. "Do you have five minutes? Come join me in my dressing room for a coffee?"

"I think I might have to go with herbal tea," I said, worried that the coffee wouldn't be great for my already shot nerves.

"Herbal tea it is then."

I started to follow her into her room when I heard heavy footsteps running after me.

"Rachael, where do you think you're going." Justin started to admonish me, but his tone softened when he saw I was with a guest of honor. "Oh, hello, Dawn," he said with an awkward little curtsy. "I just need to have a quick word with Rachael," he said with a sickly sweet smile. "You don't mind, do you?"

Dawn shot me a look before giving Justin her blessing. "I'll wait for you in my dressing room," Dawn said.

"I'll be calling for you in fifteen, Rachael," Justin said sternly. "Make sure you're ready. The new judge Colin Evans is an even harder taskmaster than Pierre was, if you can believe it, and he WON'T wait for you. Got it?" He clucked his tongue. "I've got your gluten-free cheesecake all ready for them to taste." He stopped and scrolled through his tablet. "It was chocolate, right?"

"Peanut butter," I corrected him.

"Right. It will be ready. Just make sure you are. Right, Rachael? You got it?"

I nodded firmly. "Got it."

***

"Oh shoot," Dawn said just as she'd poured the hot water into my teacup. "I've got to be ready to start filming in five minutes or Justin is going to skin me alive." She chuckled. "Why don't you wait here and finish your tea?" Dawn patted my knee while I settled into her comfy suede sofa. "You deserve a rest after everything you've been through."

I gratefully accepted the offer as she tottered off, but it was hard to relax knowing that the clock was counting down and Justin was waiting.

I decided not to cut it too fine. Ten minutes before my call time, I picked up my coat and walked to the door.

"Just where do you think you are going?"

Renee pushed me back into the room and locked the door before I could comprehend what was happening.

"Renee!" I shouted. "Are you kidding me?" I kicked against the door, figuring it was a joke and expecting that she would be back to let me out in a few seconds.

But she didn't return. "Renee?" I called again, more frantically this time.

"Let me out!" I screamed, banging on the wall. "You can't keep me locked in here!"

I was starting to panic.

Oh, this cannot be happening.

Renee really does have it out for me.

Then, a shock of ice ran down my spine.

What if I'd been wrong about Marcello?

I could hear my name being called over the loudspeaker. I looked down at my phone desperately. No reception. I banged on the door again. Geez, those doors were thick.

"JUSTIN!" I screamed. My phone might not have had any reception, but it was still capable of keeping the time. And letting me know that three minutes of my allowed audition time had already dripped away. If I didn't get out of there, like, immediately, I was going to miss my already tiny window.

Window.

I glanced over at the far side of the dressing room. It was tiny. But that wasn't the only problem. The one small window was at least seven feet off the ground.

The sofa wouldn't budge the first time I yanked at it. I stood up and took a deep breath, trying to figure out how to go about it logically. I ran around to the other side and pushed, rather than pull, putting all my weight behind me as I pushed off with my knees, lunging towards the grey monolith.

I winced, looking down at the expensive suede, which I was sure was not meant to be climbed on. But this was an emergency.

Right before I was about to pull myself up towards the window, I glanced back at the spot where the sofa had been.

Sitting there, right in the middle of the floor, was a brown-colored cheesecake. It had been hidden under the lounge chair.

"What the heck," I said, jumping off the sofa and running over to the cake sitting on the floor. I leaned over and sniffed it. The smell was unmistakable. It was definitely peanut butter.

I looked at the crumbly crust. It was unmistakably gluten-free.

It was definitely my cake.

I just sat there on my knees, staring at it for a minute in complete confusion.

Why does Dawn have my cheesecake in her room?

And what cake were the judges going to taste?

My heart skipped a beat when I remembered what Justin had said. "It's chocolate, isn't it?"

The realization hit me.

They're not eating my cake! They're eating a tampered cake.

I stood up and quickly began to pace. On that day, my first audition, Dawn had never eaten my cake. And Wendy had only pretended to, having eaten the 'real' cake before the auction even took place.

Only Pierre had eaten the cake.

It wasn't Marcello who had killed Pierre. Or Adam. Or Renee. Or even Justin.

It was Dawn.

And now she was going to kill someone else.

The loudspeaker crackled and the next name was called out.

I'd missed my chance.

I just hoped I still had time to save a life.

Chapter 12

I banged and banged on the door and finally it opened, causing me to stumble forward face first as I almost ended up on the ground.

"I'm sorry," Renee said politely as she smoothed down her dress. "It was nothing personal, Rachael. I just couldn't have you doing your audition. They are only going to cast one woman from Belldale and it HAS to be me."

So she was as cutthroat as ever.

"It doesn't matter," I gasped, pushing past her. "I just need to get to the audition room. Do you know if anyone has eaten my cake?"

I was sprinting breathlessly towards the audition room while Renee chased over me. "No," she called out. "You never auditioned, so why would they?"

Good point. I paused just for a second to catch my breath. "You might have inadvertently saved a life by locking me in that room, Renee." I reached out and placed my hands on her shoulders for support, while she shot me a horrified look.

"What are you talking about?"

"We have to go! Who knows what other cakes she has poisoned. Come on, let's go!"

***

I burst into the room.

"Put that cake down! It could kill you!"

"Rachael, what the heck are you doing?"

I turned to see Adam's stricken face. So, it was his audition. "Erm." I swallowed. "Sorry, Adam. It's nothing personal."

I turned my attention back to the three-story wedding cake sitting on the judge's table. "BUT DO NOT EAT THAT CAKE."

"Oh, Rachael!" Adam said, pushing me out of the way. "Do you always have to ruin everything for me?"

"I'm sorry, Adam," I said, bringing down the only weapon I had, my purse, to smash the wedding cake.

Adam shrieked. "How could you?"

I stood back and looked at the wreckage, and at Dawn's crumpled face behind it. Her ashen expression told me everything I needed to know.

"I'm sorry, Adam," I whispered. "I had to do it. Even if it wasn't poisoned, that cake was a travesty."

***

"Please," I pleaded with Jackson. "I know you're not talking to me, but just let me have one minute to speak to Dawn before you take her away. Haven't I at least earned that?"

He sighed reluctantly before he pulled Dawn around to face me, her hands still handcuffed behind her. Jackson turned his face away in a futile effort to give us some privacy.

"Just tell me, Dawn. Why did you do it?" I tried to keep the shaking out of my voice. Tried to hide the hurt over my surrogate nana betraying me like that.

"I was about to be replaced on the program." Dawn turned her head towards the studio and let out a bitter laugh. "I wasn't making good TV, as they say," she

463

murmured, her voice suddenly sounding like it was coming from so far away.

"But what did Pierre have to do with it?"

"Pierre Hamilton was the executive producer. It was all his decision." Dawn turned back to face me. "Do you know how long I waited, sidelined to pathetic morning shows for decades, overlooked and underappreciated, just waiting for my one shot at fame? After years of scratching and clawing my way into a primetime position, I wasn't going to let anyone take that away from me. Certainly not Pierre Hamilton," she spat. "And not this new guy either. Colin Evans wasn't going to take my job away from me either."

"No. You did that to yourself. Did you have to use my cake to do it, though?"

Dawn offered me an apologetic smile. "I'm sorry, my dear. It was nothing personal."

I took a step back and nodded at Jackson. "You can take her away," I whispered.

In the end, the producers selected two contestants from Belldale to appear on the next season of *Baking Warriors*.

And I wasn't either of them.

**

The flight was late, but I had a feeling Pippa would have waited a million years for that plane to land.

"Marcello!" Pippa screamed, running so fast that her legs were nothing but a blur underneath her. "I can't believe it!" she gasped, flinging herself into his arms.

I hurried after her, keen to see the happy reunion. Eager to see that Marcello was in one piece. I mean, it was Marcello. Maybe the best we could hope for with him was several pieces.

"But why did you run away, sweetheart? When you knew you didn't do it?" Tears were flowing down Pippa's face.

"I couldn't live like that, with you thinking that I did it, that I was guilty," Marcello said. "I knew how it would have looked as well, with my reputation for accidents. I knew everyone must think I could do such a stupid thing. All I would have to do would be walk past a cake and accidentally poison it." Marcello pulled away from Pippa for a second and looked at me.

"I was such a big fan of the show and Pierre. I met him years ago and got that photo." He stopped to collect himself. "I went along to the audition thinking I might get on the show. Of course I didn't, but I didn't want to tell Pippa where I had been that day because I'd told her I was out looking for a job." He turned back to Pippa. "I'm so sorry, my darling."

"No, Marcello, don't say that. I'm so sorry, baby," Pippa said as Marcello wrapped her hands in his. "I should never have doubted you."

Marcello kissed her hands and told her it was all right, that none of that mattered anymore. "Just as long as we're back together now."

I watched them for a moment and I could see that they were genuinely happy and in love. And even though Marcello could break just about anything, I knew their relationship was one thing he would make sure he'd keep together.

"Come on, you two," I said, laughing. "We've got a wedding reception to organize."

Epilogue

Three months later

"You look beautiful, Pippa," I said as she carefully examined her dress in the door of the silver fridge, which was serving as a mirror. We were standing in the kitchen of the bakery, about to make our big appearance in the reception area.

"It's not too 'wedding-y,' is it?" She turned to me, concerned. "It's not too 'bridal'?"

"Um." I looked at the bright purple dress that perfectly matched her hair. "No, I don't think it's too bridal. I don't think I've ever seen a bride wearing anything like that." I walked over and gave her a kiss on the cheek. "I do think it's just perfect for you, though."

We laughed, and danced, and made sure we ate every bite of wedding cake under Adam's watchful eye. He was recently back from shooting the show but had signed a strict confidentiality contract, so he couldn't tell us how far he'd gotten.

From the way he'd hounded Pippa into letting him cater the reception, I had a suspicion he'd been eliminated in the first round.

"I still can't believe I paid for this," Pippa said, shaking her head as she nibbled at the thick almond icing. "Rach, you really need to expand into the wedding cake market."

"Shh!" I said, and we both giggled.

"Well, should we call an early end to this wedding reception?" Pippa asked me with a wink after a few more spins around the dance floor.

"What? Why?"

Pippa pointed at the clock. "It's almost 7:30."

"And?"

She gave me a 'you've got to be kidding me look.' "Don't you know what it's the premiere of tonight?"

I threw my head back with a little groan. "No, Pippa. I don't want to see it."

"Come on," she said, linking her arm through mine. "Let's find a TV."

***

I didn't manage to pull my face out of my hands for even a second during my 'audition' scene, which was part of a tribute to Pierre that aired at the start of the program. But the sound of my voice and my stuttering over my words was more than enough to make me want to die.

"I can't believe they kept that in there," I groaned.

"They must have thought it made good TV."

Pippa, Marcello, and I were all squeezed onto the couch together, huddled round the TV set. They kept telling me they were going to get their own place soon, but there was no rush.

All during the episode, I kept reliving my on-screen debut in my head, meaning I barely paid attention to what was actually happening on the screen. It was all a bur of icing sugar and chocolate and tears and Adam flailing about dramatically, posing for the camera every time it came near him.

I was wrong. Adam DID make it through the first episode.

"Tune in next week when disaster strikes one unlucky contestant," the voice over said ominously.

"Is it sabotage?" The camera zoomed in on a slow motion shot of Renee, who was found surreptitiously tampering with what appeared to be Adam's cake mix.

"The most evil contestant we've ever seen on *Baking Warriors*," the booming voice shouted as the special effects turned Renee's eyes red.

I rolled my eyes. She was only adding an extra teaspoon of sugar to Adam's mixture.

"I'm glad I got out when I did, though," I stated. "I just wouldn't have made good TV."

Thank You!

Thanks for reading the *Bakery Detectives Cozy Mystery Boxed Set (Books 1 - 3)*. I hope you enjoyed reading the stories as much as I enjoyed writing them. If you did, it would be awesome if you left a review for me on Amazon and/or Goodreads.

If you would like to know about future cozy mysteries by me and the other authors at Fairfield Publishing, make sure to sign up for our Cozy Mystery Newsletter. We will send you two FREE books just for signing up. All the details are on the next page.

At the end of the book, I have included a preview of book 4 in the Bakery Detectives series, *Rest, Relaxation and Murder*. It is available on Amazon at:

FairfieldPublishing.com/rest-relaxation-murder

As a special surprise, I'm also including a preview of the first cozy mystery from my friend Miles Lancaster, *Murder in the Mountains*. I really hope you like it!

FairfieldPublishing.com/murder-in-mountains

FAIRFIELD COZY MYSTERY NEWSLETTER

Make sure you sign up for the Fairfield Cozy Mystery Newsletter so you can keep up with our latest releases. When you sign up, **we will send you TWO FREE BOOKS!**

FairfieldPublishing.com/cozy-newsletter/

Now, turn the page and check out the previews.

Preview: Rest, Relaxation and Murder

There was a loose timeline to the game. We were supposed to have a round of drinks, then go around, introduce ourselves as our 'characters' and then wait until appetizers were served before we did the first round of questions and alibis.

We were all sitting there, tapping our fingers against the table, waiting for the food to arrive, and the game to start.

"I'm so hungry I am going to eat my character card," Pippa whispered as she leaned over to me. "We haven't eaten since that fast food restaurant we went through at 6am."

"I know," I said with a sigh. "Everyone else would have had their catered meal on the bus at least," I said, looking at them all with envy. My character card was starting to look pretty tasty as well.

Robert looked across the table and winked at me again. "Taking a while, isn't it?"

I coughed nervously and looked at my watch. "You know what? I'm going to check on what's going on."

Pippa looked startled, as did the other guests as I

stood up. "Well, someone has to," I muttered as I threw my napkin off my lap and stomped towards the kitchen.

I should have knocked, but I was so used to entering commercial kitchens unannounced that I didn't stop to think. Besides, I was lightheaded with hunger by that point. So I just barged through the doors.

I stopped when the yelling fully hit me.

"Well, I don't know how to do it!" one young chef, a woman with bright red hair sticking out from under her white cap, yelled.

"You're the sous chef!" a young man in a dirty apron–probably a kitchen hand–yelled back.

The woman threw her hands in the air. "What does that matter! Ann never lets me actually cook anything." She banged her hand down on a bench. "They are all her recipes. Gosh, even if they weren't, Ann was supposed to do all the prep. We've got nothing, Aaron!"

"Well, figure something out!"

They both stopped yelling when they realized I was standing there and turned to stare at me.

"Oh, hello," I said meekly. "I was just...erm." I looked around at the empty benches. "I'm a guest at the retreat and it's just... We are getting quite hungry out there. Is everything alright?"

The woman sighed and waved her hand over the benches. "Well, we may as well come clean," she said dejectedly. "We've got nothing to serve tonight. You're going to have to make do with sandwiches." She wouldn't look me in the eye.

I frowned. Something was clearly not right. And it wasn't just that we were going to be stuck eating sandwiches for dinner.

"What's going on?" I asked, looking between the two of them.

The kitchen hand, Aaron, looked away from me as well. "Nothing," he muttered.

"It sounded to me like—forgive me if I'm wrong— your head chef never turned up?"

The woman turned away and began to wipe a bench that wasn't dirty. "It's no big deal," she said. "Ann does this sometimes."

"Vikki," Aaron said. "Come on. She wouldn't just disappear like this. Not on the first day of the retreat. Not without telling a soul. That's not like Ann."

Vikki spun around, her face red and her eyes wild. "It's exactly like Ann. She's flaky. Unpredictable."

Aaron shook his head. "Not about her work. Come on, Vikki. We've got to come clean." He stopped and looked at me, almost like he'd forgotten I was there.

"Come clean about what?" I asked slowly.

"Nothing," Vikki said.

Aaron starting scrubbing at another clean bench. "Just that we've got no food," he finally said, throwing off his apron. "I'll take the bullet," he said, storming out of the door. "I'll tell the guests."

That left me alone with Vikki, who was still averting her eyes.

"Ann is missing?" I asked her. "For how long?"

She screwed her face up. "What does it matter to you?"

"Have you told the police?"

Vikki shrugged. "She'll turn up. One way or another."

I held her gaze for a long time. "Right," I said, turning around to follow Aaron out of the room. I returned to the dining table to find my fellow guest groaning at the idea of sandwiches replacing a warm five-course meal.

Aaron held his hands up. "Hey, I'm sorry," he said. "Don't shoot the messenger."

I stared after him. Was he just the messenger, though? I watched his back all the way to the kitchen before he disappeared behind the swinging doors.

Pippa looked up at me aghast. "Come on," I said, "let's go." I pulled her up by the arm. "We can just eat chips from the mini bar for dinner."

"Hey," Pippa cried as I pulled her out of the dining room. "The game's still going on!"

"Forget about the game," I said as I pulled her around the corner into the corridor. "There's more than a game going on, Pippa," I whispered.

"What are you talking about?" Pippa whispered back.

I looked over my shoulder towards the kitchen. "Something's not right, Pippa. The head chef, some woman named Ann, is missing." I shook my head. "And I don't think there's an innocent explanation for it, Pippa. Something is going on. Something is very wrong. And those two in the kitchen know what it is." I stared back at Pippa. "And it's up to us to investigate."

Thanks for reading a sample of my book, *Rest, Relaxation and Murder*. I really hope you liked it. You can read the rest at:

FairfieldPublishing.com/rest-relaxation-murder

Make sure you turn to the next page for the preview of *Murder in the Mountains*.

Stacey Alabaster

FairfieldPublishing.com/rest-relaxation-murder

Preview: Murder in the Mountains

Screams were not a normal part of the workday at Aspen Breeze. When Jennifer heard the anguished cry of the maid, she ran around the desk and sprinted out the door. Clint, not through with his breakfast, followed at her heels. The door to the room had been left open. The maid stood on the thick burgundy carpet in front of the unmade bed and pointed at the hot tub.

Water remained in the tub, but it wasn't swirling. The occupant, a red-haired, slightly chubby man whose name Jennifer had forgotten, was face down. His blue running shorts had changed to a darker blue due to dampness. Reddish colorations marred his throat. Another dark spot of blood mixed with hair around his right temple. Pale red splotches marred the water.

For a moment, she felt like the ground had opened and she had fallen into blackness. Legs weakened. Knees buckled. She shook her head and a few incoherent syllables came from her mouth. Clint's arm grasped her around her waist.

"Step back. It's okay," he said.

It was a silly thing to say, he later thought. Clearly, it was not okay, but in times of stress people will often say and do stupid things.

He eased her backward, and then sat her down on the edge of the bed. He walked back and took a second look at the hot tub. He had seen dead bodies when he covered the police beat. It wasn't a routine occurrence, but he had stood in the rain twice and on an asphalt pavement once as EMTs covered a dead man and lifted him into an ambulance.

By the time he turned around, Jennifer was back on her feet and the color had returned to her cheeks.

She patted her maid on the shoulder. "Okay, it's all right. We have to call the police. You can go, Maria. Go to the office and lay down."

"Yes, ma'am."

She glanced at Clint and saw he had his cell phone out.

"...at the Aspen Breeze Lodge," he was saying. "There's a dead body in Unit Nine. It doesn't look like it was a natural death." He nodded then slipped the cell phone in his pocket. "They said the chief was out on a call but should be here within fifteen minutes."

"Good." Jennifer put her hands on her hips. Her gaze stared toward the hot tub. A firm, determined tone came back in her voice.

"Clint, those marks on his throat. The red on his forehead. This wasn't an accident, was it?"

"We can't really say for sure. He might have tripped and hit...." The words withered in the face of her laser stare. "I doubt it. I...I really can't say for sure but...I doubt it."

They looked at one another for a few seconds. Light yellow flames rose up from the artificial fireplace and the crackling of wood sounded from the flames. Jennifer sighed. She realized there was nothing to do except wait for the police.

The silence was interrupted by a tall, thin man, unshaven as yet, who rushed in.

"Bill, what are you doing with the door open? It's still cold...." He stopped as if hit by a stun gun. Eyes widened. He stumbled but caught himself before he fell to the carpeted floor. "Oh, no! What happened?"

Jennifer shifted into her professional tone as manager. "We don't know yet, sir. I assume you knew this man."

He nodded weakly. "Yeah, Bill's been a friend of mine for years."

"I remember you from when you checked in yesterday, but I'm sorry I can't remember your name."

"Dale Ramsey."

Ramsey had a thin, pale face that flashed even paler. There was a chair close to him and he collapsed in it. He had an aquiline nose and chin but curly brown hair. His hand went to his heart.

"Sorry you had to learn about your friend's death this way, Mr. Ramsey," Jennifer said. "I regret to say I've forgotten his name too."

"Bill Hamilton."

Jennifer turned back to Clint. "Do you think we should move the body? Put it on the rug and cover it with a blanket?"

Clint shook his head. "I think the police would prefer it stay right where it is, at least for now."

Jennifer nodded. A steel gaze came in her eyes. She looked at Ramsey, who almost flinched. Then he shook slightly as if dealing with the aftermath of a panic attack.

"Mr. Ramsey, I am the owner of this Lodge and obviously I am very upset someone used it as a place for murder. So I trust you won't mind if I ask you a few questions - just to aid the police, of course."

Ramsey swallowed, or tried to. It looked like a rock had lodged in his throat. "Of course not. I...I do will anything I can to help," he said.

"Six single individuals checked into my lodge last night. That's a little unusual. I was commenting on that to Clint just last night. Now it turns out that you knew the deceased. Do you know the other four people who checked in?"

"Yes...I...yes."

There was a pause and Jennifer noted the look of sadness in his eyes.

"I realize you are upset, Mr. Ramsey, so just relax and take your time."

"We are all members of the Centennial Historical Society. All of us are history buffs," he finally answered.

"Why did you all check in here?"

Ramsey shifted in his chair. "This may sound unbelievable."

"Let's try it and see," Jennifer said.

"About a hundred and twenty-five years ago there was a Wells Fargo gold shipment in these parts. An outlaw gang headed by a man nicknamed The Falcon stole it. He got the name because he liked heights and the Rocky Mountains and had actually trained a falcon at one time. Rumor is, the gang got about a hundred thousand worth in gold, coins and bars. What's known is the gang drifted apart and a few members got shot, but the gold was never found. We believe it's buried very close by, up in the Rocky Mountain National Forest."

Jennifer nodded. The entrance to the forest was less than five miles from Aspen Breeze. All drivers had to do was turn left when they left the lodge and they would hit the entrance in about ten minutes.

"The Rocky Mountain National Forest is a huge area, thousands of miles there of virtually unexplored wilderness. You better have a specific location or you'll spend your lifetime looking and never find anything," she said.

'We have researched this gang for years. We think we know approximately where the gold was buried. It's more than just recovering the gold. This would be a historical find of enormous significance. We were going up there today to try to find the site."

"Maybe someone didn't want to share," Clint said.

Ramsey shook his head. "I doubt it. I've known these people for years. I don't think anyone would kill Bill. Besides, whoever it was would have to kill all of us too if he wanted to keep the gold to himself. Bill was in the high tech field, lower management, but he also liked the wilderness. He knew this forest better than any of us. We were counting on him to help find the site of the gold. He had searched the forest a number of times during the past five years.

I came out with him a few times. He thought he knew where the outlaws had hid their stash. He shared his opinions with us, but he was the one with the most expertise. Eddie, Eddie Tercelli, one of our group, is the second most knowledgeable about the location. He was out a few times too with Bill searching. But it would be tough for him to find the place on his own."

A blue light waved and flickered in the room. They heard a car door open and then slam shut. They looked up as the officer walked in. He wore a fine, crisp blue uniform with a bright silver badge. He had a slight paunch over his belt, but it didn't make him look old or slow. The intense gray eyes under the rim of the black police cap took in everything. His revolver was clearly visible on his right hip.

"Chief Sandish," Clint said, nodding.

Thanks for reading a sample of my first book, *Murder in the Mountains*. I really hope you liked it. It is available on Amazon at:

FairfieldPublishing.com/murder-in-mountains

Or you can get it for free by signing up for our newsletter.

FairfieldPublishing.com/cozy-newsletter/

Miles Lancaster

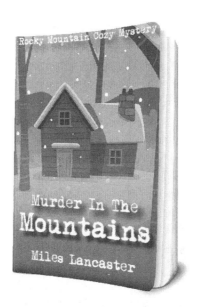

FairfieldPublishing.com/murder-in-mountains